DESOLATION
POWERS LEGACY BOOK I
STARR Z. DAVIES

CHARACTER ASSASSIN BOOKS

BOOKS BY STARR Z. DAVIES

<u>Divica Stormborn Chronicles</u>
Stormvalor
Stormveil
Stormcrown
<u>Divica War of Two Crowns</u>
Volume 1: Darkness Falls
<u>Powers Series</u>
Ordinary
Unique
(extra)ordinary
Superior
<u>Powers Origins</u>
Miller: Origin
Enid: Origin
Celeste: Origin
<u>Powers Legacy</u>
Powers Legacy: The Prequel
Desolation
Infiltration
Insurrection
Invasion
<u>Fractured Empire Saga</u>
Daughter of the Yellow Dragon
Lords of the Black Banner
Mother of the Blue Wolf
Empress of the Jade Realm
Prosperous Eternity
<u>Stand-Alone Stories</u>
Stones: A Steampunk Short Story

For everyone.
Because we all feel a little inadequate, just like Paige.

Author Note

Powers Legacy sprang to life because of Paige. While Gavin plays a critical role, this is her story and her struggle. She came to me as I finished writing my historical fiction series and began whispering in my ear. She still hasn't stopped.

For years, I have cultivated a reputation for fast-paced books with real characters—many of whom end up dead. It's how I was given the nickname Character Assassin. Paige's story is not like anything I've written before. While there certainly are a fair share of very real characters with dark backstories, the books are also slower and more deliberate. The focus is, primarily, on Paige as she explores the world and learns about herself. While there is some action, the Powers Legacy books won't be the endless rollercoaster of battles that the original Powers Series was.

Be aware that there is alcoholism and discussions of abuse in these books. Zephyr has a very dark past that he constantly tries to hide from while pretending he isn't hiding from anything at all. He covers his demons and his pain with alcohol. I included this aspect into the story because, sadly, it is a very real problem in our world that most of us choose to ignore. Zephyr's family is no exception to this rule. If hearing about child abuse is hard for you, I recommend reconsidering this book. While I did my best to avoid showing it directly, the mentions of it and the memories of it do come to the surface from the very beginning. I, by no means try to glorify this dark topic, but it is something that exists in a very real way and affects those involved in ways we can never truly see. I hope it helps us all better understand that not all scars are on the surface. Some people hide their pain well.

After reading a review of *Ordinary* and *Unique* that called out Miller's sexuality as if it were something that needed a warning, I figured I should mention that there are non-hetero couples in this series. I am a strong champion for the LGBTQ+ community, and to me their relationships are just as commonplace and real as any "traditional" couple. If same-sex couples makes you uncomfortable, this may not be a series for you. The relationships are just as real between M/M or F/F characters are just as real as they are between M/F throughout this series. My hope is that no one even cares and it doesn't make any of my readers uncomfortable. Love is love.

You might notice Gavin thinks and acts just a little differently from others. Genius often comes with its own limitations. Gavin is brilliant (so brilliant I had a hard time writing his character!), but he also has undiagnosed dyssemia (or NVLD)—more commonly called "socially inept"; a term I dislike *immensely*. Dyssemia is far more common in our world than we realize, and I loathe calling it an illness or to say that he suffers from it. It simply changes the way he percieves people in social situations, and makes it difficult for him to read social cues as well as the average person. Dyssemia made him the target of bullies growing up, and still leaves his co-workers baffled in his wake. Gavin has learned to adapt in social situations in ways that others may not understand. He realizes this is a shortcoming within himself, but can't (and doesn't see the need to) fix it. As I wrote this story and saw these clues come to light, I began researching. My hope is that I bring this to light and help others understand a little better. Gavin accepts that he is not broken—even if he admits it is a shortcoming within himself. I hope you can understand him a little better as you read.

If you are returning as a reader because you loved Ugene's story, I hope you enjoy learning about his children—my broken and beautiful children—and how they shape the world just like their dad.

Cast of Characters

Elpis

Paige Powers — Somatic Muscle Memory; Psionic Precognition/Dreaming (and more to come...)

Gavin Powers — Psionic Perfect Memory & Psychic Navigation; Naturalist Matter Manipulation, Mutation, Environment Creation, Electromancy (and more to come...)

Easton Sinclaire — Somatic Strongarm; Kingdom recruit

Harper — FlexVision; returned to Elpis

Doctor Adams — Healing Hands; returned to Elpis

Olivia — Tracker; died in the Battle of Old St. Louis

Ugene Powers — Powerless; Paige/Gavin's dad; current Minister of Elpis

Enid Powers — Environmental Creation; Paige/Gavin's mom

Aron — Visual Linking; data analyst & Gavin's co-worker

Tudor — Parabolic Hearing; Department of Security Specialist; Paige's ex

Higbee — Natural Mutation; Gavin's boss

Bianca Pond — Super Somatic; Department of Security Colonel; Paige/Gavin's adopted Aunt

Director Levi — Levitation; Director of Department of Security

Alex Miller — Electromancy; Paige/Gavin's adopted uncle

Councilwoman Howser — Telekinetic; councilor of Elpis

Director Perlberg — Psychometry; Director of Department of Science & Technology

Captain Wilson — Department of Security Captain

Mat, Carlos, Nate, Sam, Benny, Elly, First Sergent Camden — Specialist training team with Easton/Paige/Tudor

THE HAVEN

Drake — Silencer

Emil — Lie Detector

April — Wind Dancer

Dani — Transmutation Conversion

THE KINGDOM

Alric Strong the Third — former king; deceased

Alric Strong the Fourth — former Crown Prince; deceased

Queen Elena Strong — Lie Detector; mother of Alric the Fourth, Bronwyn, Cypress, and Dominic

Lady Emry — Blood Cleansing; former king's consort; Zephyr's mother

Lord Baron Strong — Elemental Control; Admiral of Tides; brother of Alric the Third

Bronwyn Strong — Telepathy; princess; second-born child

King Cypress Strong — Item Tracing; third-born child; King of the Kingdom of Tides

Dominic Strong — Influencer; forth-born child; Keeper of Tides

Zephyr Strong — Power Negation; only child of Lady Emry; Captain of Tides

Lord Vincent Greene — Operator; oversees horse breeding and sales

Nat — Energy Absorption; friend to Zephyr and his First Mate

Finrik — Operator; mainland recruit

Ian — Aurology; mainland recruit

Tributes

Alice — Environment Manipulation; mainlander

Holly — Futuresight; mainlander; left behind her one true love

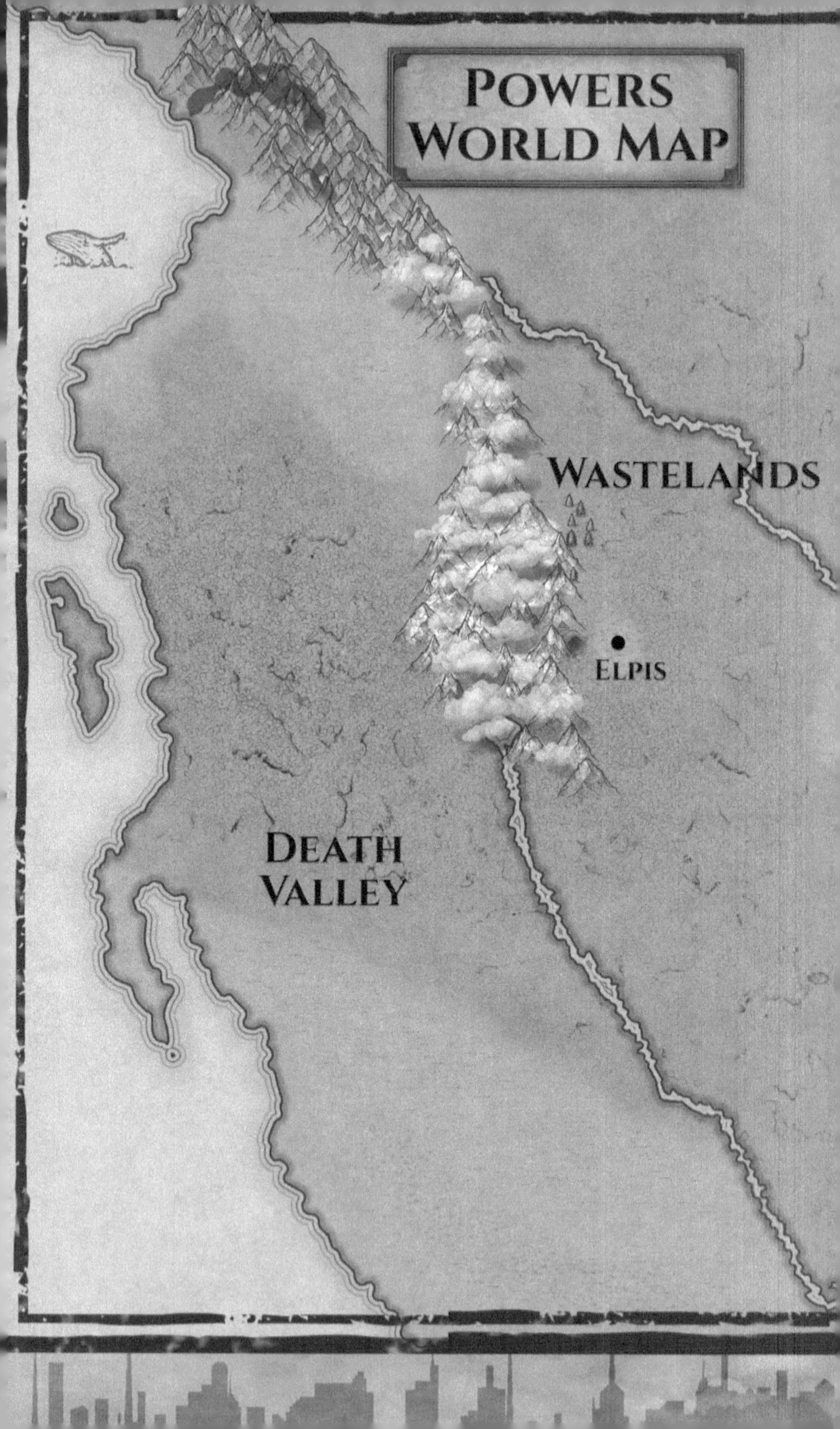

POWERS WORLD MAP
WASTELANDS
ELPIS
DEATH VALLEY

BARREN NORTH
THE CAPITAL
THE HAVEN
THE KINGDOM
OLD ST. LOUIS
RADIATION ALLEY

Elpis History
A Textbook Excerpt

Revised Edition

Over a century ago, human evolution took another leap into the future. How gradually it happened, we cannot be certain. When, exactly, it happened, we also cannot pinpoint. But we do know that humanity changed forever. A select few developed mutated strands of DNA that gave superhuman abilities. These people came to be known as Superiors. Afraid of the Powers of Superiors, ordinary humans (now known to have been called Inferiors) attempted rounding up these superpowered individuals. Some died. Some became experiments. A few fought back.

How long the war between Inferiors and Superiors lasted is undocumented. What we do know is that the war ended in a complete collapse of civilization. One Superior, known to us as Atmos, had Atmokinesis Power on a massive scale. He triggered an apocalypse that sent a chain reaction around the world. Nuclear power plants everywhere suffered meltdowns. They saturated the earth or exploded, creating full-scale nuclear destruction of cities, towns, and life as it was known everywhere. Only a handful of those with Powers survived the collapse.

Elpis rose from the ashes, the last bastion of hope for humanity. The Founders established a safe haven for Superiors; a city that would offer protection from the desolation of the outside world. People slowly trickled in; eventually, they stopped coming. We now know that the Founders created a barrier of Powers—using a dangerous Power stone—to block out the disease and evil of the world beyond our borders. Whether those outside the barrier remain is yet undetermined.

To build a strong foundation for Elpis, the Founders divided Superiors into Four Branches of Powers.

Divinic

Using Heavenly, Cosmic, or Healing Powers, these individuals can perform a variety of seemingly divine acts. Divinics typically perform one of the following: reading the stars to predict the future, detect threats to themselves, track locations, read auras, read the future/history of a person/object, heal with a touch, communicate with the dead.

A Divinic usually works in social work, religious leadership, or medicine. They are the backbone of Elpis health and safety.

Naturalist

Using the power of nature itself, these individuals can perform a variety of natural mutations. Naturalists typically perform one of the following: natural/energy transmutation, hemetological blood cloning/replication/separation, naturalkinesis of gas/liquid/solid/plasma, naturalcreation of environments/matter/objects, matter manipulation/mutation, DNA/form mimicry.

A Naturalist usually works in factories creating goods necessary for the entire structure of Elpis, or in a greenhouse creating food, cleansing water, or adapting raw materials. They are the backbone of Elpis commercial goods and food production.

Psionic

Using powers of the mind, these individuals can perform one of the following mental tasks: telepathy, telekinesis, mental influence, clairvoyance, and psychometry.

A Psionic usually works in construction, media, reception/guest relations, as a detective/PI, or as a mental health professional. They are the backbone of Elpis social and mental health and safety.

Somatic

Using the power of their own body, these individuals can perform one or two acts requiring physical prowess. These include one of the following: strongarm (super strength), muscle memory, or one of the enhanced senses of touch/taste/sound/smell/sight.

A Somatic usually works in construction, restaurants, the Department of Security, or as an athlete. They are the backbone of Elpis security and expansion.

Founding Historical Importance of Powers

Until recently, an individual's entire life was determined by not only the Branch of Power they fell into, but the strength of that Power. The scale of strength had been determined by a Directorate-created test later to be perfected and named the "Cass Scale". The stronger one's Power ranked on the Cass Scale, the better their job prospects and social standing would be. Higher ranks resulted in: better pay, better housing, more social connections, potential leadership roles, lower taxes. The Founders believed that the amount an individual could contribute to society—based on the strength of their Power—should directly corrolate to their taxation. The more you contributed, the less you paid. The less you contributed, the more you paid back in. They believed it balanced the scales of society.

The Fall of the Directorate

In 133 EF (Elpis Foundation), the Directorate instituted a series of Propositions which oppressed those with little or no Power. These Propositions forced the people into mandatory retesting (resulting in several hundred deaths), forced experimentation in conjunction with Paragon Diagnostics Power-related testing (resulting in hundreds more deaths), and even subjected some lower-class citizens to experimental drug injections. The injections either enhanced Powers, or killed. Efficacy for these injections was horrifically low.

One Paragon Diagnistics test subject, Ugene Powers—a Powerless citizen—escaped the locked facility with dozens of his fellow test subjects. He joined forces with an underground rebel faction, the Protectorate, and exposed the Directorate and Paragon Diagnistics to the entire population of Elpis. The Powerless young man stood his ground and showed Elpis that it is not the strength of a Power that determines one's capacity to contribute, but the limits of one's own inner strength, intelligence, and ambition. Ugene

Powers led the revolution that ended with the collapse of Paragon Tower, as well as the entire corrupt Directorate. The revolution resulted in thousands of deaths we honor each year on Liberation Day.

From the ashes of Liberation Day, a new social structure was born. One that no longer favors the strength of one's Power. Everyone is treated equally.

Elpis has reached a golden era.

1

PAIGE

I RACE DOWN THE mountain, leaping over boulders and fallen aspen trees, catching my balance when I slip in the snow. My team follows, struggling to keep up with my Somatic muscle enhancements. A bitter breeze chases us like a great wave, eager to swallow our breath. Despite the thermal layers and thickly lined boots, the chill seeps into my bones while sweat rolls down my spine.

This was supposed to be a standard operation. Go up the western mountain. Find information about a specific quartz that Elpis needs. Return to headquarters to report our findings.

But when we reached the quartz pocket and recorded our findings, we were ambushed. An unknown militia lived in the mountain. Of course it would be part of this test. Prepare for anything. Including unexpected attacks from unknown people. That's what our instructors have drilled into our brains to prepare for the world outside of Elpis—because we don't really know what's out there.

None of us expected anyone to be in the mountains—though we should have. Where did they even come from?

Mistake number one.

A quick survey of the surrounding scene tells me we are in serious trouble. While our snowy camo blends with the surroundings, our enemies are virtually invisible. They must be out there somewhere.

A bitter wind pushes straight through my lungs. I hunker down close to one of the aspen trees and wait, eyeing the mountainous landscape around me. Tudor joins me, with his body so close to mine I would be able to feel his heat were it not for this blasted, bitter cold wind.

A fresh layer of snow coats the ground beneath the aspen trees. Snow. Something we don't see much of in Elpis. I would marvel at the cold white fluffy blanket, but my focus must remain on the mission.

To my right, crouched beside the adjacent tree, our team leader, Easton, scans the path behind us.

Bullets zip through the air, striking trees, boulders, snow. Ten of us were sent on this mission. The ambush claimed two of our teammates. I can hardly see the rest of the team hiding among the trees.

But it isn't our visibility I'm worried about. It's the endless barrage of bullets our attackers have that worries me most. We need a plan. A damn good one too. I sure hope Easton is preparing something.

The gunfire stops. Silence swallows the mountainside. Only the sound of my hammering heart and Tudor's even breathing breaks the quiet.

These mountain men blend into their surroundings. They know how to use the trees, rocks, and snow to their advantage. It makes spotting and firing at them near impossible.

Bianca—our training officer who also happens to be my adopted aunt—placed Easton in charge of this mission because of his recent test scores. I've seen them. While his scores are respectable, they aren't any better than my own. I should be leading. Tudor agrees, but he won't say it in front of anyone else. Then they would know about the blossoming relationship between us—something we both agree is better left unknown. It's against the rules.

Tudor glances at me, and I can see the same uneasiness in his dark eyes that I feel. Why did they stop firing at us?

"Paige!" Easton calls.

Mistake number two. I wince as his call carries on the breeze. Way to announce our location. And he's supposed to be our leader. *Amateur.*

Gritting my teeth and dipping my head against the bitter wind, I rush toward him in a crouch and drop to a knee in the snow at his side. Tudor follows on my heels.

"Sir?" I say, aware of the sharpness in my tone. I don't care for Easton. Not that it's a secret.

He scowls. "There's a ridge fifty yards to our southeast. Take Tudor with you and scout to see if we can find cover or slip away through it." He points down the steep slope toward a rocky outcrop. "Tudor, reach out for signs of others."

My gaze locks on the ridge. If there is nowhere up there to hide, Tudor and I will be sitting ducks out in the open, begging for a bullet. But twenty yards to the right of that ridge is a gap between two rock formations. It looks like a path leading straight down the mountain—which is where we need to go. We need to get the intel on the quartz deposit back to headquarters.

"What about there?" I ask, motioning toward the gap. "It's better protected and could lead us right where we need to go."

"I gave you an order, Powers," Easton snaps. "I don't care who your dad is. You don't outrank me out here in the field. Nepotism will only get you so far."

Nepotism! I earned my place on this team just like anyone else. Just like Easton. My father, the current minister of the city and legendary Hero of Elpis, had nothing to do with my placement in the Department of Security. Being selected to train as a Specialist is no small matter. It's one of the most coveted positions in the military. I worked for it, trained for it, just as hard as anyone else.

Besides, if Dad had his way, I would sit behind a desk like my brother, wasting my Somatic Muscle Memory skills. He certainly wouldn't encourage me to try taking charge of a military operation. He already expressed his dissatisfaction with my career choice.

All my life, Dad has been overprotective. When I was thirteen and my brother Gavin was fourteen, Dad sat the two of us down and told us we had the potential to be different. Special. Our DNA has the capacity to carry not just one Power, but many. Perhaps all. After everything Dad did as a teenager—engaging in fights against Superpowered individuals without a Power of his own, launching a rebellion against the old government and a group of extremists—it feels hypocritical for him to try smothering us with his overprotective blanket.

I may not have developed extra Powers like my brother, but I'll be damned if anyone—my father or Easton—will hold me back from using what I have.

Easton has some nerve. I know exactly where I want to put his notion of nepotism.

I clench my teeth so hard it makes my jaw hurt. Does Easton want us to fail? Or maybe just me.

The anger burning in Tudor's eyes reflects my own. I'm not sure if he is angry with Easton's leadership, or the nepotism comment.

"They are close, *Sir*," Tudor says, glancing at the trail we left through the trees and shrubs, winding up the mountain at our backs. His tension seeps into me, and I follow his gaze but see nothing. Tudor's Power is Parabolic hearing, which allows him to focus on a particular area to filter out sounds. If he says our pursuers are close, he isn't just guessing. He knows it. "We should make a stand and take them out before we continue back to the city. Otherwise, we risk leading them right to our borders."

Easton practically growls his response. "I gave you orders. And when we get back, I will report the two of you for questioning my commands. Go. Now. We will cover you down the slope." His broad shoulders seem to grow as he radiates anger. Perhaps they do grow. Maybe he is flexing his Enhanced Strength like a gorilla would thump its chest to show dominance. The idea is laughable.

Easton gives orders to the rest of the team through the comms to use fire-suppression to cover the two of us while we make a break for the ridge. Part of me wonders if he chose me for this task hoping I would take a bullet. It's not really a secret that his love for me is in equal measure to my love for him.

Tudor and I wait for them to get into position. We move in unison, rising into a crouching run, me leading the way with him taking up the rear right on my heels.

No sooner than three steps out in the open, the gunfire resumes. Bullets strike around the two of us as we dart behind trees and boulders for cover. A bullet strikes a tree just as we duck behind it. The other six members of the team return fire.

"Tudor, Paige, move!" Easton calls into the comm.

We ignore his command. I wait for Tudor to signal, trusting his hearing to choose the best moment to break cover. He gives a small indication and I dart out first, staying low. The gunfire grows more intense.

Mat's panicked voice cuts through the comm. "Nate's dow—" His words cut off with a grunt.

Tudor curses under his breath.

I glance back, expecting to see the rest of the team entrenched in their hiding places, firing at the attackers. Instead, the remaining four members of the team run, with Easton leading the charge. Mistake number three.

The rest of the team isn't running toward us. Easton leads them right to the gap I had pointed out. *Jerk.*

Distracted, I slip on the snow, but Muscle Memory kicks in. My body instinctively adjusts. Tudor's hand clamps down on my arm and yanks me against him behind a massive boulder. Bullets strike the ground where I had been a moment ago. The two of us stand close as we listen, keeping our breathing steady.

"Anything?" I whisper.

Tudor's eyes glaze over as he focuses on his Power. The only sounds are the gunfire and our careful breathing. "We won't make it to the ridge," he whispers back. "They're closing in."

"How many?"

A pause. "Eight on the slope. Three on our tail. We lost Benny…" Another pause. "And that was Carlos, and Sam." Anger contorts his face.

I curse under my breath, then scan our surroundings. Only Tudor, Easton, and I. And Easton left the two of us for the gap. We need to make a stand and finish off the attackers, find a way out, or a place to lie low where they won't find us. Once they pass us by, we can backtrack and find a different route down the mountain. Then our tracks will be lost among all the others.

Adding a Telekinetic to our team would go a long way in situations like this. Most Specialists in training are Somatic, with the Power to enhance the body. We could do with more variety on our teams. A Psionic Telekinetic whose ability is to move objects with his or her mind, or a person with Divinic Precognition who could see the immediate future. Maybe then we wouldn't be in this mess, losing our entire team.

Don't focus on what we don't have, Paige. Focus on what we do have. Not that it's much. It's only the two of us now. Well, and Easton for whatever he's worth.

"Which way are they coming from?" I ask.

Tudor sets to work with his Power once more, before motioning to the gap I noticed before. "We should be able to get there if we make a quick break for it. Only about twenty yards. Wait until I give a signal."

I nod. Tudor and I always work well together, a natural connection between us that has only recently started extending off the field as well. If the higher-ups found out about our budding relationship, they would reassign us apart from each other. Relationships between Specialists in the same unit are forbidden. It compromises our instincts in the field. Not that we are Specialists yet.

He brushes his fingers over my cheek. I lean into the touch, even if it is a glove on my skin and not his hand. We are under pressure, surrounded, and I definitely shouldn't be thinking about how his touch makes my heart skip.

The moment passes quickly. Tudor adjusts the grip on his gun, preparing to move. I follow his lead. "Easton, we are headed your way. Don't shoot us."

With his free hand, Tudor raises three fingers, then lowers one. I understand. Only two of those closing in on our location remain.

Tudor drops to a knee and raises his gun.

I bend my finger around the trigger. The Muscle Memory flexes in my legs, ready to move. *Breathe in. Out. In. Out.*

Tudor fires. I break into a sprint for the gap. Only ten more yards. I can do this. Just as they trained me to do, I keep my body low and use as much of my surroundings to cover my escape as possible. The sound of Tudor's boots crushing the snow is all the confirmation I need to know he follows.

A gunshot.

Five yards.

My heartbeat remains steady. I've grown accustomed to my adrenaline. My body has figured out how to balance it all out.

Another shot.

One yard.

Tudor curses and shoves me through the gap. "Run, Paige!"

I stumble a few steps, alarmed by his reaction, but quickly correct my balance. Gunshots echo off the stone walls of the narrow pass. I glance back.

No one is behind me.

Tudor is gone.

No! They didn't get him.

"Tudor," I hiss into my comm.

Silence.

"Paige, keep moving," Easton snaps through the comms.

I can't fail. *I can't fail.*

The gunshots cease. Eerie silence swallows the narrow stone gap. I hold my gun ready and peer back the way I came, shuffling carefully backward deeper into the pass. Is Tudor dead? Terror grips me. He can't be dead. He just can't.

Tears burn in my eyes in the cold mountain pass. I blink furiously. If anyone else is out there, I don't want to call out and make them aware of my presence. But I can't leave Tudor behind. Dad never would have. He would gather everyone and escape.

I take a moment to steady my breathing. Easton materializes at my side, yanking me back deeper into the pass with his superior Enhanced Strength. I resist, but he's stronger.

"It's just us," Easton says harshly. "And we need to complete the mission."

"We don't know what happened to him," I snap.

A bullet sends pebbles raining down on the two of us from the rocky walls above. Easton releases his grip on my arm and raises his gun.

I spin around, weapon ready.

Tudor bursts around the bend in the pass, running faster than I've ever seen him run before. "Go. They're coming!"

Easton sprints down the mountain pass, catching his balance carefully with each quick step. I wait for Tudor to catch up, firing at the men hot on Tudor's heels. One takes a bullet to the shoulder and spins.

There are too many of them. For every one that falls, another appears. We don't have enough bullets for all of them.

Tudor stumbles as a bullet strikes his calf. I lower my weapon and crouch to haul him up. "Let's go," I say.

But his weight is too much. The attackers are closing in.

Farther down the pass, Easton pauses, eyeing the men chasing us. Then he looks up at the snowy mountains above. My heart sinks. He is about to make a sacrifice play for the sake of the mission. Again.

"We need to get this back to the city," Easton says as he raises his gun and flips the switch on the side to concussive fire.

"Easton, no!" I scream.

But it's too late. He fires a concussive shot at the mountains above.

A whump cracks across the sky above. Then the mountain trembles. Snow rushes toward the pass, thundering down the mountain straight for us. The attackers cease firing and attempt fleeing, abandoning their chase.

Tudor and I have no chance to escape the avalanche. The first bits of snow burst over the top of the pass and I hold my breath, praying it will pass us by. Easton disappears down the pass to safety.

I will die here. I failed. My team. Bianca. Dad. Elpis.

Snow falls into the pass.

"Pai—"

Tudor's voice cuts out as the heavy weight of sudden snow crushes the two of us.

I am not my father's daughter. I am nothing.

2

GAVIN

I SLIDE A FINGER across the data hovering over my desk. The screen changes to a tracking map of the United States. Or what was once the United States, anyway. Now it's a broken, desolate wasteland. As I examine the map, I can't help but wonder just how much of a wasteland it really is. Dad always says there must be something else out there. We can't possibly be the only city left in the country—or the world. But ever since the Council of Representatives let down the barrier surrounding the city, we have heard nothing, found nothing.

Still, the search continues. Limited as it may be.

I love my job in the Department of Science and Technology. It allows me to put all my best skills to use. Matter Manipulation and Mutation, Perfect Memory, analytical analysis. I've always been smarter than everyone else. It isn't me bragging. It's a provable fact.

I finished school a year earlier than my classmates. School had nothing more to teach me. Once I started outsmarting my teachers, they had enough. The principal arranged administration of an exit exam. I have no doubt he was eager to get rid of me. I scored near perfectly. I'm pretty sure the principal didn't appreciate my insisting on seeing my incorrect answers, only to prove that I was right, and the test was wrong. Having Perfect Memory is both a blessing and a curse sometimes.

For a year now, I have worked on the same floor in the Department of Science and Technology, examining radiation data as well as reviewing old maps and working with a team to update those maps to the best of our ability based on the data our drones have returned. According to old maps, Elpis is built on the ruins of the city of Colorado Springs. I had fun using data from the drones to calculate our location to the nearest possible coordinates.

Everything we do here is in the name of learning how livable our world is, and if there truly is anything else out there. Rumor has it the council is organizing a series of missions to venture out into the unknown remains of the world.

If we successfully venture into the world beyond Elpis, we can not only gather needed resources and update our understanding of the known world, but possibly even find other life. That is the key to rebuilding the broken world.

The rumor of these upcoming missions to find new resources and seek other societies isn't just speculation. My sister, Paige is training for them. I've also overheard Mom and Dad speaking in private about it. Elpis may not know, but I do. Change is on the horizon. I just hope to be part of it.

After a couple months on the tenth floor of the DS&T building, I presented a case to the floor supervisor. I had been tinkering in my free time with the schematics for our drones and boosted their range. If we really need to find out what's out there, we need to venture farther. The drones could only travel about fifty miles from city limits before we lost signal. Not nearly far enough to collect the data required—radiation levels, images of the changed landscape, signs of life, among other valuable information. Using my Matter Mutation Power, I increased our range to five hundred miles. Still not as far as I wanted, but it was far enough for us to reach green grassland.

And if there's grassland, there could be other life. That's what I spend my days seeking.

I slide a finger along the map to the easternmost edge of the five-hundred-mile range. Readings from the radiation monitors appear. The millisieverts are not so high there that it would be a danger. Perhaps the world is ready for us to return. Dad will be thrilled to hear it.

A hand waves in my face. I startle back and slide out the earbuds. Listening to white noise helps me focus in the usually busy, noisy office.

"Gavin, the day is done," Aron says, standing beside my desk. "Let's go get a drink."

My gaze sweeps the lines of desks all around the floor. Everyone has already shut down their holoscreens and left for the day. "Is it that late already?"

Aron chuckles, perching on the edge of my desk. "I don't understand how someone with Perfect Memory can lose track of time like you. I guess it's true what they say."

I flinch. "What who says?"

"People. In general. They say that all genius has its weakness. Yours must be time."

"I'm not a genius," I mutter, turning my attention back to my screen. I am, but bragging has gotten me into trouble.

"Tell that to our Trivia Night record," Aron says, smirking crookedly at me.

I do my best to ignore the way he smiles at me. After a month on this floor, no one had really spoken to me. After two months, Aron invited me out for a drink after work to get to know each other. By the end of the month, he invited me to join his trivia night team.

The others on the trivia team didn't seem to care for me at first, but after we won three trivia nights in a row by a landslide, their tunes quickly changed. It's the closest I have come to friends since Liam. After I misjudged his feelings toward me near the end of eighth grade, that was it for our friendship. It's a memory that still haunts me. I won't take the same chance with Aron, no matter how much his smile makes me ache.

Aron straightens and presses a hand down on my shoulder. I glance at his hand. It doesn't mean anything.

"Let's go, Gavin."

My fingers twitch. I want to reach up, touch his hand. Of their own accord, they start moving toward his.

Aron tenses.

I jerk back.

"What is that?" he asks.

His reaction has my heart all the way in my throat.

"What?" I manage to croak.

His hand slips off my shoulder as he stabs a finger at my monitor.

My gaze slides along his arm—sleeves rolled up to expose his shapely his forearms—and along his hand. Then I spot what he noticed on my holoscreen. I frown and lean closer.

A ring pulses lightly against the very edge of the drone's range.

My fingers fly over the smooth keyboard. A drone doubles back toward the signal. Aron and I both wait, a deep, agreeable silence between us. Without thinking, I tap the screen to record the image of the pulsing ring.

"What if that can kill the drone?" Aron whispers, as if anyone else is around to hear anything.

I lick my lips, eyes glued to the screen. "It couldn't." I say the words with confidence, but I don't know what that ring means.

And I don't like not knowing.

"I like that look on you," Aron says.

The words bring that hammering of my heart back as I glance up at him. And again, he is smirking at me.

"What look?"

"For once, Gavin Powers doesn't have an answer, and you look...resentful." Aron drops to a knee beside my chair and turns his attention back to the drone feed.

"Resentful?" The insinuation is insulting. "You think *that's* a good look for me?"

"You don't like not knowing something."

I resist the urge to roll my eyes. "That's obvious. Anyone would know that."

"It's how the rest of us live every day."

"How exhausting."

The conversation cuts short as the drone reaches the limit. I type a few commands on the keyboard swiftly. A wavelength appears on the screen.

"A radio wave?" Aron breaths. "Can we hear it?"

"These drones weren't designed to record sound." An oversight I will have to bring up to our superiors. "It can pick up the changes in the wave pattern around it, but not the actual sound." A few more quick commands, and the drone records the wave pattern.

"We could try putting the wave into a pattern simulator to decode the message," Aron says.

I shake my head. "It would only discern highs and lows. Pitches. Not words. The question we should ask is, where is that signal coming from and why?" I type in a few commands on the keyboard, drawing several potential radius trajectories to pinpoint the location based on the angle and spread of the ring's edge.

"The Great Lakes," Aron replies, pointing at the massive lakes. "Dolphin or whale sound? Wouldn't that be something?"

I watch the irregular movements of the wave pattern. "Not likely. First, neither could live in the lake. That's freshwater and they are saltwater mammals. Second, from what I learned from pre-collapse texts, their sounds have regular patterns. This one is all over the place."

The drone stops recording. I slide all the information into a file and drag it toward the transfer star on the desktop where my tablet awaits. Perhaps with some time alone tonight, I can try to figure out what this signal means. If I share it with Dad, we could work together. Just thinking about a project to share with him makes me smile.

Aron grabs my wrist and pulls it in the opposite direction sharply. The file slides along the surface with my finger, away from the transfer star.

"What are you doing?" he snaps.

"Transferring the files. Then I can work on it at home."

"No. You can't do that. You will be out of a job before you leave this building if they think you are stealing information. I don't care who your dad is." His fingers remain wrapped around my wrist as his dark eyes plead with me. "Don't do it, Gavin."

I snort. "You're overreacting. File transfer is permissible if you are working on a project from home, as long as the file remains encrypted, and the information isn't shared anywhere else. If I transfer it off my tablet to anyone else or any other devices, then I can be fired. But I don't plan on doing that."

Aron's grip tightens, and he leans closer. "No. We take it to Higbee and let the supervisors deal with it."

"But—"

"That's their job, Gavin. Not yours."

I can't stand the idea of handing our discovery over to anyone else. And there is no way I will sleep tonight if I don't get some time to dissect it, to find answers.

"Higbee, then drinks," Aron insists, pulling me to my feet.

I rise, unable to understand how he can be so eager to hand this off. Aron always struck me as the curious type. Doesn't he want to know?

Aron slides himself between me and the desk, his back facing me. Suddenly, his hands fly over the keyboard. He's sending it to Higbee for me!

I lunge forward, reaching for his arm as he slides the file into the message. "Aron wait!"

But it's too late. Before I can finish my protest, the message is sent, along with the file. My shoulders sag. Anger pulses through me. I slap a hand on the desk, closing the files and logging out. Then I snatch my messenger bag off the back of my chair.

"Are you mad at me?" Aron asks, jogging to match my strides.

I stomp toward Higbee's office in the far corner of the floor. If he is there, maybe I can plead with him to let me stay on the project.

"Don't *ever* touch my desk again, Aron," I snap. "I don't touch your work, even when you do it wrong."

"Don't be a jerk. I was trying to save your job."

"I don't need your help. I won't lose my job. I'm perfect at it. They can't afford to sack me."

Aron snorted. "Wow. Arrogance much?"

"Do you have any idea what this could mean?" I ask as we round the last row of desks and approach Higbee's office. Our supervisor sits at his desk behind his glass wall. "Dad always said we can't possibly be alone in the world. This could mean he's right."

"He said that?" Aron pauses a moment in alarm, then jogs a step to catch back up. "Are you planning on giving this information to him? He might oversee the city, but even he has to go through the proper channels."

Aron jumps in front of me, blocking me from Higbee's door. "Just what do you think you can do if you go in there? Convince him to let you take this to the Minister? He will analyze the data, send it to his director, and they will decide how to proceed. We've seen nothing like this before. I can guarantee they will fast-track this data."

I wave my hands for him to move. "What if that signal is our only chance to prove Dad's right, but we must act now? Going through the proper channels could mean we lose precious time. If that's a person, we need to send a team out there to expand our range and investigate." I'm not sure where all of this is coming from. But something of it smacks of danger if we drag our feet.

Then it strikes me. I do know where this is coming from. Five years ago, Dad uncovered the truth about the founding of Elpis. About the dangers of the world beyond our borders. And it went much farther than radiation. According to the journal cube my dad found, the outside world was dangerous. The founders locked us in the city like Pandora's Box.

And Dad opened the box five years ago. Five years of silence. Five years of nothing. Until now. According to the journal cube, people used to live beyond our borders. Dangerous people. We could all be in trouble.

I need answers. *Now.*

Aron crosses his arms, fighting off a smirk. "Who are you and what did you do with Gavin Powers?"

"What?"

"Rebel. The apple doesn't fall far from the tree, does it?" That smirk on his face makes some of the anger burning in me dwindle. Does he have any idea how I feel about him? Would he even care?

"What's going on, gentlemen?" Higbee asks from his doorway.

Aron steps aside as he turns to face our supervisor.

"A message, sir," I say before Aron can steer us away.

Aron groans.

"Message? From whom?"

"That's a great question," I reply.

Higbee frowns, looking from Aron to me and back again.

"It's from the Great Lakes," I say.

Higbee's brows climb his forehead. "*Where?*"

I push past Aron and into Higbee's office. "We sent you the information."

"So much for drinks," Aron mutters as he follows us into the office.

3

PAIGE

"**S**IMULATION COMPLETE," EPI SAYS in her smooth, robotic AI voice.

I immediately shuck off my sim-suit and stride across the simulation room where the ten team members are all gathered. Easton unzips his sim-suit casually, as if he didn't just kill Tudor and I inside the simulation. Anger burns white-hot in my veins. The arrogant, self-centered jerk is about to get a lethal dose of my wrath.

"What the hell, Easton?" I snap.

Tudor practically trips over himself in his haste to get out of his suit and throw himself in my path. He knows better than to touch me though, and only holds his hands in front of him in supplication. "I get it, Paige, but take a breath."

The rest of the team watches, slowly stepping out of their own sim-suits as they observe another Paige-Easton throwdown.

"He killed us, Tudor! Why are you defending him?"

The lights on the simulation floor wink out. Easton saunters toward me, stopping behind Tudor and crossing his arms over his chest defensively. "The mission comes before anything else."

I step closer.

Tudor places his hands on my shoulders and leans close. "Calm down."

I ignore him, unable to control the molten-hot rage making my limbs tremble. I clench my hands into fists at my sides. "My Dad knew a guy who said things like that. Guess who was right in the end?"

"Playing the daddy card already, Powers?" Easton sneers behind Tudor's shoulder. "If I hadn't done what I did, we *all* would have died, and the entire mission would have been a failure."

I shove Tudor away from me as he tries grabbing my arms to steer me away from Easton. This isn't over. I won't be steered away.

All eyes are locked on the two of us, waiting for the fists to fly. Again.

"Paige..." Tudor's low voice gives warning.

I glare at him. "You're taking his side?"

"He did what he had to do for the mission."

Easton's smug smirk grows. I want to punch it off his face.

"He could have given us a few more seconds to join him instead of bringing an avalanche down on our heads." I poke Easton in the chest as I edge closer. "You know I'm right, but you don't want to admit it. If I didn't know better, I would think you *wanted* me to die on that mountain."

Easton swats my hand away and shakes his head. "Get over yourself, Powers. Just because your daddy is the Hero of Elpis doesn't mean you are too. If you ask me, you don't belong here." He turns and strolls toward the door.

The words are more effective than any of his punches. They root me in place and render me speechless. Does he really think I see myself that way? Do the others? I covertly scan the other faces in the room, but none of them are giving me more than an uncomfortable cursory glance as they follow Easton toward the door.

They do. They all think I'm here because Dad got me this job. They all think I see myself as entitled, better than they are. I don't. I worked hard to earn a place on this team. Sure, I probably had an edge because Bianca, the Department of Security Colonel, has been training me to fight since I was a kid. When my Muscle Memory ability manifested at eleven, Aunt Bianca recognized it immediately. One night, when she and her husband Levi came for dinner, Gavin had accidentally knocked the bowl of biscuits from the table, and I caught it almost instinctively.

The fact that Aunt B oversees the Specialist Training Program probably doesn't help my case. Over twenty years ago, Aunt Bianca had died helping test subjects escape the cruel experiments at Paragon Diagnostics. Somehow, her brother Forrest resurrected her. But to his own ends. He wiped her memories, planted new ones, enhanced her Somatic Strength, turning her into a Super Strongarm. Then he used her against my dad. No one in Elpis is anywhere near as strong as her. Aunt B can outrun, outfight, and outmuscle anyone.

Powers are normal in Elpis. Everyone has some sort of Power to varying degrees from one of the Four Branches of Powers. People like Mom are Naturalists with the ability to somehow create or mutate organic matter in the natural world. Gram is Psionic—mind-related powers like Telepathy, Telekinesis, or Psychometry. Mom and Dad's friend Rosie is a Divinic with healing abilities. Most Divinics have some sort of mystical or celestial Power like Rosie's Healing Hands or the ability to see the future. Divinic is the rarest Power Branch.

Aunt B and I are Somatic. While she has both Strongarm and Muscle Memory abilities, mine are limited to just the latter, allowing me to teach my muscles movements almost perfectly. I spent years honing my fighting skills under Bianca's tutelage.

It's because of our collective Powers that our ancestors were able to survive and create this city as the rest of the world suffered from intense radiation.

Tudor hands me a bottle of water. Everyone else has left the room.

"You let him get to you too easily," Tudor says.

My shoulders sag as I accept the bottle and take a swig of water. "They all agree with him, don't they?"

"Does it really matter what others think?"

I snort and start toward the door. The fact that he won't give me a direct answer tells me all I need to know.

***

AFTER SHOWERING AND CHANGING, the team sits together in the debriefing room to go over the events from the training simulation. Our training officer, Camden, breaks everything down in a brutal play-by-play, using a holoscreen to show all of us what he saw. It's like watching a movie. But one where everyone dies at the end. Except Easton.

I chew the inside of my cheek to keep from smiling as Camden dresses Easton down for not using everyone's Powers more effectively to reduce the casualties. He points out every mistake Easton made in his decision-making right in front of all of us, as well as ways to improve on it in the future. It's a brutal hot seat all of us have been in at one time or another, but I relish hearing Camden tell Easton everything he did wrong.

Unfortunately, Easton takes it all in stride, nodding in affable agreement and offering his own insight where appropriate. Having Camden call him out doesn't even ruffle Easton's feathers in the least. Not like it did to me when I led a mission. As much as I loathe Easton, I admire his ability to take criticism from his superiors.

Camden doesn't only focus on Easton. He takes the time to pick apart every little mistake all ten of us made during the simulation. Carlos' failure to use his Somatic Tracking to smell trouble before we fell into it. Sam veering left when the team when right. Each of us are stripped bare under Camden's feedback.

"Paige," Camden says, drawing me up straighter in my seat.

I square my shoulders.

"Your hesitation in the pass is partly to blame for your own death in the simulation," he says.

"Sir," I say, nodding in agreement. What else can I do? "I'm aware that my hesitation resulted in Tudor getting shot, which slowed us both down. In the future, I will go back immediately."

Camden nods in appreciation.

I catch a glimpse of Easton down the row smirking. I would ask why he hates me so much, but I already know the answer. It's because of who my dad is. I can't escape his legend anywhere. People expect me to follow in his footsteps, live up to the legend.

But how can I live up to the legacy of someone who brought down a corrupt government and helped create a new government that focuses on social equality? There is nothing to stand up against. The new regime thrives on transparency. Elpis has reached a Golden Age because of the work my father did.

There is nothing for me to save.

There is nothing for me to liberate.

All I can do is work to protect the people of this city.

The team goes through the usual wrap-up of the day before Camden dismisses us. Everyone stands and begins gathering their belongings.

"Some of us are going for drinks, if you want to join," Tudor says.

"Some?" I ask, glancing at Easton.

Tudor grimaces. "It might do you some good to unwind with us, Paige."

This isn't the first time the team has gone for drinks. Nor is it the first invitation. I've never gone because I feel out of place. Today, I know I am. I have no desire to sit around and have drinks with these people, allowing them to make jokes at the expense of others and find new ways to bond. No doubt when I'm not around, I am the focus of some of their conversation. What do they say about me behind my back?

I follow the team toward the door, listening to the two of them chatter about some personal crap in their lives. Nothing I really care about. They don't want me in their personal business.

"I'm not really in the mood for drinks," I mutter, glancing at the rest of the team as they pull away down the hall. "Besides, I'm sure they would rather I not be there so they can say whatever they want behind my back."

Clearly, Tudor doesn't like the response. He scowls and shakes his head. "Maybe if you actually showed them you have a fun side, they might change their minds."

"Do I have one?" I ask.

He opens his mouth, but thinks against it and doesn't respond. Again, I deflate.

"I think I'll pass," I say.

I would rather sit at home and listen to Gavin talk all night.

4

GAVIN

HIGBEE SINKS BACK IN his chair, jaw slack, staring at the holoscreen projecting the data Aron and I sent to him. Aron sits casually in a chair across the desk, somehow managing to appear bored, as if his interest in any of this turns off when the clock strikes five to leave. It disgusts me a little. How can he be so blasé about this?

"We need to share this with the Minister of Elpis," I say, not daring to invoke the "Dad" clause in my statement. I learned a long time ago that it's best if people don't immediately connect me to him.

Higbee shakes his head slowly, as if in some internal argument with himself. Suddenly, he leans forward and snatches his cell phone off the edge of the desk. A moment later, a line rings. Did he just call my dad?

An unfamiliar voice picks up, a woman I don't know. Higbee gives her very brief—and not altogether accurate—account of what we discovered. I bite my tongue to keep from correcting his mistakes.

"Sit tight," she says with an authority I can't help but admire. I never speak with that much authority. "We will be there shortly."

I can't hold my tongue any longer. "I'm telling you, Da—the Minister will want to know about this as soon as possible," I insist, nearly saying "Dad" instead of Minister.

"Not yet," Higbee says sharply. "We have to be sure of what we are on to here before we interrupt the Minister and council after hours."

"He won't mind—"

"I said we wait," Higbee snaps. "Just as we were told to do."

Aron pats the chair beside him, but I turn and start pacing the window outside. Every few steps, I pause, staring east as if I would be able to see the signal.

Within an hour, the office is crammed with people all pouring over the data. They have effectively pushed me to the outer ring of the conversation. I can hardly even hear what they are saying—why is Enhanced Hearing not among my list of Powers?—nor can I see what they're looking at on the holoscreen. Every now and then, I glimpse statistical comparisons I've never seen before. Data that has me practically frothing at the mouth to read. But they won't let me close.

Irritated, I covertly pull my phone from my pocket and send a text to Dad.

Something is going on. Make sure the barrier is activated.

Five years ago, Dad discovered a protective barrier forty miles outside the city. It forms a ring around Elpis and the surrounding landscape, including the Greenhouse seven miles outside of city limits where Mom works. The barrier is highly dangerous and instantly disintegrates anything that touches it. The truth about the barrier's creation was less than pleasing to the members of the council, but the fact that Dad found a way to raise and lower the barrier at their will gave the city a fighting chance at finding the resources we needed when the Greenhouse suffered massive crop failure.

Now, Uncle Levi oversees the Department of Security, advising the council on when and if the barrier needs to be raised again. Aunt Bianca oversees the training of Specialists in the DoS, people who go out on resource missions beyond the Elpis borders. Or at least that's the plan.

Paige signed up for the Specialist training—which has Dad more than a little angry. But when Paige decides something, only Aunt Bianca can ever talk her into changing her mind. In the case of this job, Aunt B took Paige's side. The ensuing argument between Aunt B and Dad had been the most epic argument I had ever witnessed. Dad had refused to talk to Aunt B for weeks afterward.

I watch my phone anxiously for a response. If something is out there, he needs to be sure the barrier is up until these geniuses figure out what is going on.

My phone vibrates.

Aron, sagging in the chair and clearly bored out of his mind, glances in my direction.

I meet his gaze only a moment before turning my back to him to read the message from Dad.

`It is. Where are you?`

I thumb back one word: `work`

I turn and slide the phone into my pocket once more.

Aron stands so close his proximity makes me jump. I follow his gaze down to the pocket where I just slid my phone. "You texted him."

"I had to," I whisper, glancing at the supervisors, managers, and directors of the department.

"Why?"

I open my mouth, leaning close, then pull away and snap my jaw shut. "I can't tell you."

Aron takes a step back and eyes me with that disarming smirk. "I didn't think you had it in you to act out in any way."

"I'm not acting out." I edge toward the corner, away from our bosses and their bosses, dragging Aron with me. "Listen. This, whatever it is, it's big. I can't tell you what I know. *I'm* not even supposed to know some of it."

"Oh, come on. Now you have to give me something." Aron keeps his voice down, feeding off my urgency. "I thought we were friends."

Though the words are teasing, they hurt. I frown. "The friendship clause does not include requiring me to divulge classified information."

Aron bites his lip to fight off his grin—and fails. My gaze is drawn to his lips for a moment before I look away.

"So, it's classified."

The two of us stare at one another. I'm afraid of saying more, afraid of what I might accidentally spill under that dark, heart-stopping gaze. And he just keeps staring at me. Is he waiting for me to slip up?

My phone buzzes in my pocket. Neither of us moves.

"Are you gonna check that?" he asks.

"Are you going to read the messages over my shoulder?"

"Obviously."

"Then no."

Still, neither of us blinks, but the curiosity is making my hands twitch. Aron knows it, too. He knows me well enough to know that if he just waits long enough my need to know will force me to act.

The phone buzzes again. Aron raises his eyebrows.

What if Dad needs me to respond directly to a question and I'm ignoring him to have a staring contest with Aron? How childish.

It buzzes again.

Aron sighs in defeat. I relax a little.

He moves quickly. Too fast for me to react. His hand slides into my pocket. It feels very personal. Too personal. The move makes me uncomfortable.

In seconds, he pulls my phone out. Then he slumps.

"It's your sister." Aron hands me the phone.

I snatch it from his grasp. What does Paige want?

Only two messages from her, but I had three notifications.

```
Where r u? Was hoping to chat
Everyone here hates me, G
```

Aron has lost interest in my phone, turning his attention back to the rest of the office with his hands tucked into his pockets.

```
Work. Can't get away. Will chat later.
Doubt everyone hates u, P
```

I send her the message, then open one from Dad, glancing covertly at Aron. His attention is still elsewhere.

```
Stay put. We are on the way.
```

We? Who is coming with him?

Not that Aron and I have been allowed to leave. The department director is afraid we will say something if they let us leave. Never mind the NDAs we signed when we were hired forbid us from talking about work outside of the office. Though I suppose Aron *is* excitable right now. Who knows how well he would stick to the rules if we crossed paths with coworkers.

I tuck the phone away again and try to wedge myself into the ring of superiors and glean anything off their conversations, but they give me no space.

"Stop trying so hard," Aron says. He has resumed his place in the chair.

I slink over and perch on the arm of the chair. My stomach grumbles, reminding me we haven't had dinner.

"I hear you, man," Aron mutters to my intestines.

The thump of feet across the marble floor toward the office draws silence into the confined space. Everyone looks toward the glass wall.

Aunt Bianca and Uncle Levi lead a group of security guards around the floor, as if they expect assassins to jump out from under the glass-topped desks. As security parts, I spot Dad in his suit, trailed by other members of the Council of Representatives. A guard opens the door and holds it as two more sweep into the room and take position in opposite corners. Everyone in the office is at attention now, no longer huddled over infographics, pie charts, and maps.

Dad's gaze sweeps the room. In a matter of seconds, he has assessed the situation. I can see it in the way his body shifts from stiff and formal to casual and curious. He knows exactly how to talk to everyone in this room—a skill I would love to learn. They won't respond to authoritative demands. These people are all like Aron and me. Curious at heart.

Dad eyes me strangely and I tense, but he turns his attention elsewhere in the room. "Director Perlberg," Dad says in his easy manner.

I release a breath of relief that he hasn't singled me out.

"Minister Powers," Perlberg says, sounding alarmed to see him there. "What brings you to the Department of Science and Technology at this hour?"

"Same that brings you here, I assume," Dad says. "Why are you *all* here so late? I would guess we would be hard pressed to find a manager not in this room."

A councilwoman steps around the group to examine the map. Her body tenses and she shoots Dad a look of alarm. "Is that a signal from the Lakes?"

Dad nudges his way toward her. His lips part ever so slightly as he watches the signal's outer ring ripple against the edges of our drone range. "What is it from?"

"We don't know, Minister," Perlberg says. "We have spent the last couple hours poring over data to discern what it could mean, but we don't have anything that goes out that far."

"Who discovered the signal?" another councilman asked.

Suddenly, sixteen supervisors, six managers, and the director all fix on me. The councilors follow their gazes to me as well. Aron shifts beside me, making the leather creak. When I meet Dad's gaze, pride softens his face with a tiny smile.

I clear my throat, suddenly sweating under all those eyes. I explain what Aron and I found—certain to point out that Aron was the first one to see it. Then I offer a brief rundown of what the two of us could discern from the signal, how we used the drone, and what my assessment is based on the limited knowledge I have at hand.

"Someone must be out there," I finish.

"And what have you learned since recording this?" Dad asks, keeping his tone professional to avoid showing favoritism.

I shift feet nervously, glancing at all twenty-three bosses in the room. It takes a moment for me to form words, and I wish Aron would speak up. He is so much better at this sort of thing than I am. I dip my eyes to my feet. "Nothing. Aron and I have just been sitting here."

"Why?" the councilwoman asks.

"We felt the two of them did not share the experience to decipher the information adequately, so we asked them to stay and wait," Perlberg replies.

The pride in Dad's eyes vanishes as he turns a sharp glare at Perlberg. "You are telling us that you took the two men who *discovered* this *and* collected the initial data, two clearly bright minds, and shut them out?"

Perlberg scowls at Dad. He opens his mouth to respond, but before he can say a word, Dad barrels over him.

"I want those two on this. Tonight. They are just as important to this task as any of us." Dad slides his suit coat off and lies it over a chair, then rolls up his sleeves. "We are all here. Let's get to work."

I grin, infected by his eagerness to solve the mystery.

5

ZEPHYR

N AT PERCHES ON THE edge of the boat. The moment we are close enough to the dock, he jumps down—along with a handful of others—then gives the signal. I toss the rope, giving the command to the rest of the men and woman on board to prepare for docking. The deck immediately scrambles with activity.

Several others join Nat on the dock, securing the ropes to the bollards. In the main cabin, the second captain cuts the engine so it can recharge.

Three others step behind me, taking hold of the same rope.

"Pull!" I shout.

The sound of tensing rope cuts through the sudden silence, punctuated by the gulls flying overhead. The muscles in my arms strain and ache, but I heave with all my might, knowing that Nat and his men are doing the same down on the dock.

"Secure the hawser!" I command, tying the rope off on the deck to tighten the hold on the dock. When the waters get choppy, a loose rope can mean a loose ship.

I pause a moment to take in the turning of leaves in fall colors across the island. Without a doubt, the landscape of the Capital is stunning year-round. In the spring and summer, brilliant blooms of colorful flowers and trees surround homes and estates. In the fall, everything transforms as leaves change color to prepare for winter. And the winters are snowy and stunning. Today, the air is crisp and clean.

Once everything on deck is secure, I head to the Sun Deck cabin bunks to retrieve my bag.

We hardly made it around the Upper Peninsula before the call to return came over the radio. I had hoped I could spend a few weeks on the open water, away from my father and his disdain, searching for a place called the Haven where religious zealots tout the coming of salvation. The Haven is in our territory but has eluded us for decades. But the Admiral called all ships back to harbor with the code for urgency. I had little choice but to order my second captain to turn *Wave Slicer* around.

"Captain." Nat sidles into the bunk room, leaning against the doorframe with his hands stuffed in his pockets. He's one of my best friends—especially when we are out at sea. His playfulness is a stark contrast to my endless tension. He knows how to unwind me.

I stuff a sweatshirt into my bag and glance back at him through the open door. "Yeah, Nat?"

"You have a carriage waiting at the end of the dock," he says. "They stressed the urgency of your swift return."

"Just me?" I frown.

"'Fraid so." Nat shrugs. "Not that the rest of us aren't ordered to head to the palace as soon as we can, but they want *you* now."

I groan inwardly. That can't be good. My dad likely wants to punish me down for something I don't even know I did. I sling my bag over my shoulder.

"Thanks, Nat." I pat him on the shoulder as I pass. "I'll catch you later, then."

"At the tavern?" he asks, following me down the stairs.

We cross the lower deck and I step onto the ramp, then the dock. A red royal carriage with black trim and rolling painted waves awaits me at the end of the dock. I fight off another groan.

"Maybe the inn, instead," I mutter. The tavern is where off-duty soldiers gather most nights. But the inn is for a particular need to drink and escape to a small room.

"That bad, huh?"

"Looks like it."

Waiting beside the carriage, my half-brother Dominic waves me down the dock. His face is drawn and pale. Just the sight of him in such a state makes my stomach twist into knots. Dad is furious about something, for certain. Somehow, I'm to blame. Again.

I march toward my half-brother. My leather boots make a hollow ringing on the metal dock.

Dominic doesn't offer his usual hug upon my return. "You smell like sweat, sea, and fish." He gives me a faint smile and climbs into the carriage.

I don't utter a word as I follow. The driver closes the door and climbs in the front, giving the horses the signal to go.

"Well, what's he about to whip me for this time?" I ask, slumping back against the seat.

"Zeph, he..." Dominic's voice cracks and he turns his gaze out the opposite window, using a finger to hold the black curtain back.

Dominic has always been the softest of my three older brothers, and quick to emotions, but this reaction does nothing at all to help the nerves twisting my stomach in wild knots.

"Dom," I say, trying to use a light voice and forcing a crooked smirk. "You're making me nervous. It's not that bad, is it?"

He shudders and my skin goes cold.

Then I realize he's trying to hide his tears from me.

"He's dead."

The words don't register at first. In fact, he says them so quietly I almost think maybe I didn't hear him say it. What if it was just wishful thinking?

I lick suddenly dry lips. It's no big secret that Dad and I have always had a mutual hatred for one another. I can't keep from picking at the dirt under my nails.

"Alric sent the message, then?" I ask.

Dominic presses both hands to his face. His breathing catches repeatedly. *He's crying!* I'm not surprised by this reaction from him. Dominic loves Dad—a feeling I can't make myself share.

I place a reassuring hand on his shoulder and give it a small squeeze. "It's okay, Dom. Everything will be—"

"They're both dead, Zeph," Dominic moans through his fingers.

I blink. There's no way I heard that right. *Alric is dead, too?* Alric is—was—the wisest, kindhearted, compassionate brother. Dominic takes a close second, but Alric... Everyone loves him. And he would make a great king one day. Or would have. *He's dead.* The shock of this hits me a hundred times harder than Dad's death.

"What happened?"

Dominic shakes his head, dragging his fingers down his face. I give him a moment to collect himself, but I'm eager to learn more. I glance through the front window of the carriage as it turns up the main road to the palace.

The Capital rests on an island in the Great Lakes—impossible to invade without ample warning. Hotels and homes from before the collapse of the old world were converted into residences. In the case of the Grand Hotel, a palace.

The sprawling white six-story structure looms on a seaside hill-top, illuminated in the dying sunlight by alternating red and blue spotlights. How did I not spot that from the water? Those colors are only lit when the king has died, or a new king is crowned.

I close my eyes and press my head against the wall behind me. With Alric dead, Cypress will be next in line for the crown. While he and I don't hate one another—I love all my brothers—Cypress and I often butt heads.

"The three of them went on a hunting expedition on the north side of the island," Dominic says, his voice thick with grief. "There was a rockslide at Eagle Point."

The area is a popular place for island natives to walk. Hunting is sparse there. Why were Dad and Alric there hunting?

"When the rockslide happened, it caught Dad first." Dominic's voice is thick with grief. "Alric pushed Cypress out of the way, but the rocks caught him before he could escape as well." Cypress was with them? "Cypress escaped thanks to Alric. He has a few cuts and bruises, but nothing major."

As the carriage rounds the corner, following the road that travels in front of the palace, I notice the line of carriages near the main entrance. I self-consciously sniff at myself and grimace.

"I need to get cleaned up before I'm paraded in front of the mourners," I say.

"Mother wants you to report directly to the throne room," Dominic says, curling his nose. "But you have a point." He brushes his hand across a cheek and steels himself as the carriage lurches to a halt. "Be as quick as you can. I'll try to buy you a few minutes, but she's getting impatient. She knows you docked."

Of course, she does. The carriage door opens and I grimace. I step out and glance along the line at the men and women climbing the red carpeted stairs into the palace. I sling my bag over my shoulder and slip through the entry on the lower level.

A guard at the door jumps alert as I open the door, lightning springing to his fingertips. Once he realizes it's only me, he relaxes.

"Welcome back, Lord Zephyr," he says.

I give him a tight nod of acknowledgment before turning right and heading along the hallway to the back elevator. The black and white checkerboard tiles glow with red and blue light from the spotlights outside. The hum of distant voices from the stairway spill down the hall as if chasing me.

The elevator takes me to my floor, and I rush to my room. As usual, the brightly colored geometric wallpaper assaults me the moment I step inside. Whoever decorated this room had little sense. Red and white floral bedspread and curtains. Red, white, and black geometric wallpaper, navy blue rug, and sea green trim. At one point in my life, I was used to it, but now I spend so much time on the water that returning to this place makes me want to rip down the curtains and burn the bedspread. But they are hard to replace.

I drop my bag unceremoniously on one of the red velvet chairs and step into the bathroom. The shower will need to be quick.

Dominic and I don't share a mother. His mother, Queen Elena, has even less affection for me than my father did. For years, she has made a sport out of ignoring my existence unless it personally hindered her. Then she becomes viciously sharp-tongued.

My mother, Lady Emry, is—was—the king's consort. His mistress. Not that he treated my mother much better than me. His abuse toward her was more emotional than physical, but still often cut her deeply. Then Baron or I would have to pick up the pieces while she excused the king's behavior. Hate is a powerful emotion, and my father is the only man I have ever hated all the way to the depths of my soul.

No doubt, with her husband and the Crown Prince both dead, Queen Elena is going to make some play for power. The question is, will she use Cypress, or will she dismiss him completely? Alric was the perfect son. Bronwyn the demure, agreeable daughter. Dominic is the kind-hearted, dedicated servant of the Kingdom. Cypress is the screw up with no clear place in the line of succession. At least as far as his mother was concerned. She was happy to ignore me—something Cypress envied as we grew up. She never ignored his mistakes and was quick to pinpoint them briskly and without mercy.

And Cypress let her. Because he adores his mother despite it all.

A few minutes later, I towel off and dress in a black suit and tie.

"Zephyr?" Mom calls from the doorway.

I slip the black jacket on, then join her in the entryway to my small suite. "Mom." I kiss her cheek. "How are you feeling?"

Her face is unusually pale. Is that from Dad's death, or her sickness? He certainly didn't seem to care about finding the best healers for her. Not like he would have done for Queen Elena. My mother is expendable.

Unfortunately for him, he died first. Maybe I can convince Cypress to find someone to help. Her illness gets worse when she uses her magic—something I have pleaded with her to stop doing. Mom can cleanse blood, which made her useful when a servant tried to poison Dad. Ironically, she cannot cleanse her own blood.

"Better, now that you're here," she says, giving me a gentle smile.

I offer her my arm to escort her down to the throne room. "Looks like I might be stuck here for a while to help oversee security for the coronation."

We take the elevator to the main floor, and she clings to me, trembling the whole way down.

"They won't let me see his body to say goodbye," she says.

I pat her hand. "I'm sorry, Mom. I'll see what I can do."

"They won't let anyone see the bodies," she mumbles. "Baron thinks something is wrong."

Uncle Baron is the Admiral, and Dad's only remaining brother. When I was growing up, Baron would teach me to fight, hunt, read. He was more of a father to me than my own father ever was. When Dad used me as a punching bag, Baron and Mom were always quick to help fix me up.

Only once did Baron try to stop Dad. Afterward, Baron left the island for months. On a mission from the king, Mom told me. But I am convinced it was some form of punishment for getting involved.

And Baron never tried again after that.

Mom gathers the flowing skirt of her black dress as she climbs the steps toward the throne room. A line of patrons winds from the doorway, down the steps, and out to the main entry. The two of us walk past all of them, and I give them solemn nods as we pass. They all know who we are. No one speaks up about us butting in line ahead of them.

The inside of the throne room is filled with people sitting in rows of chairs or lining the walls. The place is bursting at the seams, and I'm surprised Cypress didn't insist on having everyone gather in the theater. It's much bigger and better equipped for such a crowd.

Mom and I pause at the door.

Cypress sits atop Dad's throne on the green dais at the head of the room, outlined by salmon curtains and flanked by two massive bronze lion statues. At the bottom of the dais, Dominic sits in a seat beside his sister, Bronwyn. Her hands are folded over the deep gray skirt of her dress. A black veil hangs over her face, so I can't read her emotions. But I do sense her eyes falling on me.

"About time you showed up, Zephyr," Cypress says. While his words are spoken in jest, there's a sharpness to his tone as well.

I walk down the aisle, holding Mom's hand for support. The two of us feed off one another, gathering strength with each step. If I am the black sheep of the family, my mother is the outcast mistress. They all look down their noses at us. Except for the two people who matter most: Bronwyn and Dominic.

"I just stepped off the boats," I say, pressing all the confidence into my voice that I can muster. My gaze sweeps the room. Where is Queen Elena? "And I reeked of sweat and fish. I figured no one would want to spend the evening around that."

Cypress grimaces, but nods. "You have heard the news, then?"

I do my best to appear as if I'm grieving, but it's hard to grieve for a man who treated me so terribly. Cypress knows it. He knows how Dad treated me. He must. While it sometimes garnered sympathy from my brother, sometimes it didn't as well. Cypress's approach to my punishments was often pragmatic, bordering in ignorance.

"Dominic told me. I'm sorry this has fallen on you, brother, but relieved you survived the incident."

He nods, then his blue eyes flick to Mom. "Lady Emry. You may join them," he waves her toward the corner of the room where Baron waits.

Mom slips her hand from mine. I protest, eager to help her to her seat, but she gives me a soft shake of her head. Something in her eyes warns me to say nothing.

"Zephyr, take your place as well," Cypress says, waving me to stand guard near the dais. It's a clear sign he doesn't see me as part of the family during these proceedings. That, or he doesn't want others to see me that way.

I watch the room from beside the bronze lion as the line of well-wishers enter to offer condolences to Cypress first, then Dominic and Bronwyn, before moving off to speak to my mother and Baron. They all ignore me. I should be offended, but it comes as a relief. Nearly as many people move out of the room to find refreshments as join the crowd gathered.

Where is the queen? Is she so overcome with grief that she refuses to come out? That doesn't seem like Queen Elena to me. She loved my father, but their marriage was atypical. They got under each other's skin almost as often as they showed each other affection. Maybe love is too strong of a word. There might have been love at one time, but the years made them companionable equals more than lovers. Is that what all marriages end up like? Experience shows me love fades once the passion dies. I've seen it not only with the king and his two wives, but in other marriages on the island as well. It always fades.

Baron remains beside Mom's shoulder like a guardian. He cuts quite a striking figure in his formal admiral attire. The deep colors of the coat bring out the rich color of his leathered skin. His eyes meet mine a few times throughout the processional. He is trying to say something with his gaze, but I cannot figure out what it is. Trouble. That much is obvious. It makes the muscles in my body tense.

An hour in, the crowd has dwindled.

Queen Elena makes her grand appearance. She marches in, wearing a brilliant emerald dress that highlights her stately figure. Unlike Mom and Bronwyn, the queen doesn't bother wearing a veil of mourning. Further proof that love fades. Does she even care that her husband is dead?

She marches straight up the aisle toward Cypress, her face set with determination. I tense, unsure what I should do. The air around her seems to bend to her will—her magical gift. All the mourners in the room avert their gazes to the floor.

Elena has always given me anxiety. Her magic doesn't work on me. I'm immune—my own gift. But her presence is so authoritative even without her magic that she often scares me.

"Cypress, Prince of Tides," she says formally as she takes the final few steps toward the dais. "Kneel."

A hush falls over the room.

My gaze flicks past her at the maiden trailing in her wake, forgettable in every way.

Except for what she carries.

Nestled on a red velvet pillow is the golden crown my father wore everywhere he went.

Cypress raises his chin, then does as his mother commands, kneeling at the edge of the dais.

I hold my breath. This isn't how things are done. There should be a period of mourning, then plans for a coronation a week later. The only exception to this rule is when we are at war, which doesn't happen that often. There aren't many people to go to war against.

"King Alric the Third is dead." Queen Elena's voice is crystal clear. No hint of grief in her tone.

The doorway crowds as everyone realizes what is happening. Mourners spill into the room behind Queen Elena, perfectly silent. To my surprise, Donimic watches his mother with approval—no, satisfaction—in his eyes. Despite the crease of grief on his face, his eyes are intense. As Keeper of Tides, the king's right hand, if Dominic approves this move, no one will stand in their way.

The royal trio can seize control without contest.

"Alric the Fourth has passed with him," Queen Elena continues. "According to governing rules, the eldest son will be crowned unless a challenger arises." She pauses, her cool eyes sweeping the room as if to dare anyone to try challenging Cypress. Feet shuffle, but no one speaks up. Satisfied, she picks up the golden crown and lifts it over my brother's head.

I don't like this. It sets my teeth on edge. I need a drink. A line of drinks. Dominic wouldn't go into this with ill intentions, though. He knows something, some benefit to making this move quickly. I have to trust his judgment.

"As Queen Mother, I crown you Cypress the First, King of the Kingdom of Tides." She lowers the crown onto his head.

My palms begin sweating.

"Rise, King Cypress!" Queen Elena steps back.

Cypress rises, and somehow he appears taller, more formidable.

Across the room, Baron scowls at Queen Elena. His jaw is clenched so tight I can see it twitching. But even he wouldn't dare speak up to stop this. His gaze once more falls on me, and he gives a subtle shake of his head, indicating what I already know.

Something about all of this is wrong.

6

PAIGE

AFTER ANOTHER BRUTAL DAY of simulations and testing, the team gathers in the debriefing room, waiting for Camden to pick us apart. I rub the exhaustion from my eyes.

I spent last night hanging out with Mom at the house, watching ancient romance films as we made fun of the plots. The tradition began years ago when I would wake in the night and couldn't fall back asleep for hours. Dad and Gavin were out working on some project together. The two came in the door just after midnight, their voices excited. It was just another painful reminder of just how much Gavin is like Dad. And how much I'm not. I couldn't catch much of their conversation before they stopped talking. Something about the solar trucks and adding audio to drones.

Instead of asking questions, I said goodnight to all three of them and turned in. Gavin came into my room shortly after. We laid together talking about all the reasons my team hates me as he tried to reassure me it wasn't true. Eventually, the two of us fell asleep.

As the sun came up, I woke in a sweat from a strange dream about Camden promoting our team. Then Tudor had insisted I join them for drinks this time. And we kissed. In front of everyone.

Why does that dream still give me chills so late into the day? It makes me all too aware of how close Tudor currently sits to me in the debriefing room after another training session. Maybe I should have left more space between us.

Camden finishes his usual assessment. I reach down for my water, expecting to be dismissed as usual.

"I am proud of your progress, team," Camden says.

The words freeze me. I raise my gaze to see him standing at the head of the room, exactly as he had in my dream. It can't be real, though. It was just a dream. Or maybe this is déjà vu.

"Colonel Pond, the floor is yours," Camden says.

My heart stops as Aunt B marches up the aisle between our chairs to the head of the room and stops beside Camden. She pivots on her heel and her copper eyes sweep the room.

"You okay?" Tudor whispers to me.

I swallow the lump in my throat and sit up, water forgotten. I can only nod in response.

"Thank you, First Sergeant. You can take a seat with the team," Bianca says. The moment Camden is settled beside Carlos in the front row, Bianca folds her hands together behind her back. Her stance is firm. A tank couldn't push her over. "X-Team, I have been monitoring your progress for the past few weeks, and I can't help but agree with your trainer. You have all been progressing quickly and are one of our most adaptable teams when it comes to receiving and correcting criticism."

I mutter the next words along with Aunt B.

"His recommendation to promote X-Team for field work has been unanimously approved," she says in perfect rhythm with my muttering.

Tudor casts me a curious glance out of the corner of his eye but says nothing.

"Congratulations," Bianca continues, "Specialists."

The room explodes into cheers and celebration. Bianca watches me and the corner of her mouth twitches up ever so slightly.

But I'm too dumbfounded to react. Not as the others chatter on about our success. Not as Tudor throws an arm around my shoulder and hugs me tight to his side. How did I dream this just last night, exactly as it happened? Like a premonition. I shake the thought from my head. I'm too old to start developing new Powers.

Bianca raises a hand. The room falls silent. With a few quick touches on the holoscreen at the front of the room, she pulls up a map. It looks like something my brother would pour over for work.

"Last night, analysts at the Department of Science and Technology discovered a radio signal at the far edge of our trackable drone range," she says.

Gavin is an analyst at the DS&T. Was this why he and Dad were out so late? Did Gavin discover this? I watch the pulsing wave pattern curiously, and the truth sinks into my gut.

This means Dad was right. Something else is out there.

"Over the next few days, the Council of Representatives will work with the heads of various government departments to put together a team to investigate this signal," Bianca continues. "They will send us their list of requirements and we will find the best individuals to fulfill those requirements. We don't know what that will be. But your promotion is not by accident. There is a chance that they could select one or more of you for this team. I will give you the evening off to celebrate your promotion."

A smile lights up Aunt B's face. "You are dismissed, *Specialists.*"

The second she dismisses us, I snatch my water and jacket from the floor and surge to my feet. I need to talk to Dad.

Tudor steps in front of me, grinning from ear to ear. "I have to be on that team," he says, mirroring my own thoughts.

It occurs to me that all the DS Specialists probably feel the same way. This isn't just a quick resource mission. This is a real fact-finding quest that could change everything. It's my chance to move out of Dad's long shadow.

I step to the side to move around Tudor. "I think we all agree."

Tudor shifts into my path once more. "Drinks. No excuses this time, Paige."

I huff. "I need to talk to Dad."

"Why?" Easton asks as he strolls over. "So you can convince him to put you on the team instead of one of us?"

"No." That hadn't been my plan at all. Mostly because I already know what Dad would say. If anything, he would ban me from going and pull strings to keep me in the city. I just want to know what he knows about this, and what it could mean for Elpis.

"Then come get drinks with us," Easton says in an obvious challenge.

"No excuses," Tudor repeats.

And I realize he is right. There aren't any excuses that will get me out of it this time. Because if I don't go, they will all assume I circumvented the council selection to pull strings.

———— ❊ ————

I HAD EXPECTED AN evening of drinks in a quiet bar downtown. Instead, Tudor, Carlos, and Sam share a hover taxi with me that takes us to a rather questionable-looking building in Pax. The moment we open the door of the taxi, I can hear the muffled thumping of the rhythmic music inside. The windows are boarded over and someone—or several someones—has sprayed graffiti on the side of the building. It takes a moment for me to recognize the massive image. A crow's nest.

Elly is already there with the others, near the head of the line. Tudor guides me along with him to join as Elly speaks to the bouncer at the door. I can't hear anything they say, but the massive Somatic sweeps his gaze over our party of ten. Then he nods and waves us in.

I glance anxiously back at the people in line who protest as we head through the door.

"How did you manage that?" I ask Elly, leaning close so she can hear me over the noise.

"You aren't the only one with connections," she replies, grinning.

The muffled sounds from outside are nothing compared to the noise in the club. I want to plug my ears against the noise, but everyone already thinks I don't have a fun bone in my body. That won't help matters.

The club lights are brightly colored, flashing in beat to the music. Bodies gyrate on the dancefloor or brush close to one another near the tables. Along the wall to our left, a bar stretches the entire length of the club. It's just as packed as the rest of the place. All these bodies so close together makes my claustrophobia kick in.

Easton turns to me, a drink in his hand. I glance at it. He hates me. Would he slip something in my drink? He must sense my hesitation because he rolls his eyes to show me his annoyance and hands it to Carlos. He distributes a drink to each of us from the bar, where he has wedged his hip and shoulder into the mass crowded around.

Tudor elbows my side and raises his eyebrows at the next drink Easton offers me.

I swallow the growing anxiety swelling in my chest and take the drink from him.

"To the X-Team!" Easton shouts over the music, raising his shot glass.

The rest of us follow his lead, raising our glasses. As he drinks, his gaze locks on me.

I watch the others all take a drink. Easton's mouth curls up in the corner. I notice the subtle twitch of his hand and realize he is about to take my drink away. Before he can move, I down the whole thing in a gulp. It blazes all the way down, burning some of my anxiety away as it courses through me.

"Powers! Who knew?" Easton slaps me on the back, then turns back to the bar.

"Let's dance," Elly says, taking my hand and drawing me away from the familiar comfort of Tudor's presence.

By the time the song ends and the next starts, other members of the team have joined us on the dancefloor with more drinks. The intoxication mingling with the distracting rhythm of the lights and music sweep me away from the cloying anxiety. I let down my guard around the team for the first time, losing myself in the music and movements. Each member of the team joins me at one point or another, but it's Easton at my back that makes me most uncomfortable.

His body is close enough that the heat overpowers my own. He takes one of my hands as I reach toward the ceiling, then spins me around and pulls me against him. I want to pull away, but don't know how to reject him without making a scene. Instead, I continue dancing, seeking some means of escape.

Whether Tudor senses I need rescuing, or he's just plain jealous, I don't care. He nudges his way in, spinning me toward him and pulling my back against his chest. Our hips sway together.

"I should have known you could dance," he says into my ear, and his breath sends heat through me.

I pull back and turn to face him. His hands immediately find my hips.

"Muscle Memory," I say, grinning at him. "You never asked. But I was a champion dancer in high school."

Tudor responds with something I can't hear over the music. His dark eyes shimmer in the strange lighting. We inch closer to one another as we continue moving. I'm drawn to him, unable to resist. Tudor's lips brush against mine playfully, then more firmly. I return the kiss eagerly, lost in this moment with him.

Then I remember the dream and jerk back.

Reality crashes against my euphoria.

The anxiety claws its way back into my chest. I glance around us and note several members of the team staring at the two of us.

Relationships on the team are not allowed. They can hinder our reactions, cloud our judgment.

Tudor seems to realize the mistake a moment after I do. Both of us stop dancing and stand as if frozen in time in the middle of the dancefloor as the world continues spinning around us.

"Paige..." he says, realizing what just happened, what this means.

It wasn't his fault.

It wasn't my fault.

We are both guilty.

I shake my head, breaking from my trance. It all happens in just a moment.

Before I can step back, Tudor grabs my waist firmly and holds me against him. "Don't react. Just keep dancing. We will switch in a minute."

My heart is racing. Terror grips me. But I comply.

"We can pass this off later," he says. "Heat of the moment drinking mistake. Nothing more."

I don't respond. I don't know how. Panic tightens around me, suffocating me as I continue dancing, passed off to Carlos.

I've just made a terrible mistake.

We were just promoted. If Tudor is wrong and we can't convince the others that it wasn't a big deal, that it meant nothing, then Tudor and I will not both be selected for the council's upcoming mission. Except I didn't want it to be a mistake. Is that what he really thinks? Or is it just part of his plan?

The terrible truth intensifies my anxiety. His hearing will be useful on the mission. My Power will not.

They will choose him.

7

ZEPHYR

THE BAR ACROSS FROM the palace is packed from one wood-panel wall to the next. Uncle Baron meticulously scheduled guard shifts around the docks and the palace grounds to protect the island and the royal family during the transition. The shift change often lead to busy bar nights like this as men finish up their shifts and shuffle across the street for a drink. Cypress used to come here to mingle with the soldiers. Now that he is king, he seems content to raid the stash our father kept in his suite bar.

Nat brings me a second glass. The beer sloshes over the side and foamy suds seep into the mahogany table. "How have you gotten so light on shifts?" he asks as he drops into the empty seat across from me. "I would have expected the Admiral to work you like a dog."

I shrug as I pull the hoppy delight closer. "Maybe he's finally taken pity on me."

Nat shorts out a laugh. He knows as well as me that isn't the case.

The bar is just one of three places I enjoy frequenting when I want to mix with the men and not get caught up in the political games in the palace. The second is the Tea Room on the fort grounds, and incidentally it doesn't serve any tea. But access is restricted to off-duty officers and troops.

The inn—lovingly called the Gate House—is another favorite. But ever since I returned yesterday, the place has been packed to the ceiling. And unlike the bar, the Gate House has men and women all jockeying for political advancements. Apparently, every time a new king is crowned, there is a shakeup in social standing. This is the time for people to change their fortunes by aligning with the new king and gaining his favor.

I hate the games. The social clawing. The call for Tributes. The Choosing. The entire thing disgusts me. I would much rather sit in this bar with these soldiers than be part of the upper class. Thankfully, the upper class is happy to ignore the king's bastard son, and these soldiers are happy to welcome me with mugs of ale.

The air in the bar reeks of oranges and sweat. It's an odd mixture I've become familiar with. Just like I could name every man in the bar with me. I've trained with some of them for at least five years. Others I have sailed with for two years—ever since I turned sixteen and joined the navy on their expeditions to the mainland.

Someone pulls out a guitar, and the singing begins. The atmosphere is a far cry more entertaining than the somberness of the palace. I sling an arm around the man beside me and raise my glass, singing along with the rest, enjoying this moment of freedom.

It's well past dark by the time I stumble across the street and begin the long march back to my room. The toe of my boot catches on the curb and I pitch forward, affronted that the ground would rise so quickly to greet me. The grass is kind enough to catch me, though.

But it's also damp. I grimace and sit up, swiping my wet palm over the leg of my pants. Damn fall moisture. It never goes away.

"Look at the state of you, poor thing." The silky voice draws my gaze up.

Nora crouches in front of me, holding out a hand. But instead, my gaze drifts along the curves of her body. "I'm fine." But even I hear the slur in my speech.

"Let's get you back into the palace before someone sees you like this," Nora says. She slides her arm under mine and the two of us work together to get me back up.

I grab hold of her as I stumble, suddenly aware that my hand landed somewhere inappropriate. "Sorry," I mumble.

Nora has always been nice to me, despite what the other affluent girls might say to her behind closed doors. I used to think she was kind to me because she wanted to get on Alric's good side, and he was always kind to me. Took me far too long to realize it was just her. A perfect match for Alric.

Just thinking about my eldest brother makes the tension in my throat painful. Tears well in my eyes and I curse myself, fighting to blink them back.

"How're you holding up?" I ask her, resisting the sorrow and the slurring as best I can. "I know you and Alric were...close."

She tenses her grip, guiding me along the sidewalk toward the side door into the building. It's closer to the elevator and less likely for anyone to see me. I appreciate her thoughtfulness. Marching through the front door in this condition would earn me a beating—or maybe not any longer. Would Cypress or his mother take up where good ol' Dad left off? Not likely.

"I'll be okay," Nora says softly, easing the door open and glancing up the long hallway.

The guard posted at the door simply nods at me. He won't tell anyone.

"It's been a bit of a shock," she admits, helping me down the narrow hall leading to the back elevator. "I mean, I thought..." Nora releases a shuddering breath. "Cypress has been very supportive. He even offered me a room just down the hall from his own in case I need him. It's a sweet gesture, but I'm not sure it's appropriate."

The news shouldn't shock me. Nora was all but promised to Alric. He would have skipped the Tribute Season unless his mother forced it on him. He would have chosen Nora without a second thought before bringing a bunch of outside women to find a bride.

Cypress has the crown, so why wouldn't he want the girl that comes with it? I can't help a small stab of jealousy. Not for the crown. I wouldn't want that if I were the last man in the family—and I'm sure they wouldn't give it to me. But I've always been attracted to Nora. Her angular face and deep blue eyes. Maybe deep down, some small part of me had hoped that, with Alric no long an option, she might consider me.

Not that a girl like Nora would ever want a bastard like me. It wouldn't be proper for a lady of her rank to marry me. *Marriage? I must be drunk.* I have no desire to ever marry. Love is a lie.

Bronwyn paces the hallway in front of my door, her brown skirt swishing with each twist of her hips. While she and I don't share a mother, there is a likeness between us. The same sharp eyebrows and long face—just like Dad's.

"You found him! Thank goodness!" Bronwyn rushes forward to help bear some of my burden from Nora. "I can take it from here. Thank you so much for your help, Nora."

"Take care of yourself." Nora pops up on her toes and kisses my cheek. It sends a shock through me. I can't help but flush. "Goodnight, Zephyr."

"Night, gorgeous," I say, smirking at her swaying hips as she walks away.

"Animal," Bronwyn mutters.

My sister drags me inside and pushes me back on the bed, unable to bear my weight any longer. I toe off my boots and revel in the feel of the soft pillow against my spinning head.

"You can't go on like this for long, Zeph." She places a cold cloth on my forehead, and I murmur my thanks. "Just because you are allowed to drink now doesn't mean you should make a habit of drowning yourself in the glass."

My stomach lurches, killing my protest before I can even form it. It takes a moment to hold everything down. "I don't have...have much else going for me."

"Your mother needs you," Bronwyn says. My older sister with the patience of a saint. If she could use her Telepathy to read my mind, she would be furious with me. Thankfully, I'm immune to all magic.

"Yeah, yeah."

"I need you."

I crack an eye open, and it takes a moment for the room to stop spinning. "Does it ever make you angry, Wyn?"

"Your drinking?"

"No. That you can't take the crown just 'cuz you're a girl." I shift so I can see her better in the dim lamplight. "It's an archaic rule. You're older than him. Smarter and kinder, too. And you know everything about everyone."

Bronwyn flushes and dips her chin to her chest. "Not every-thing." But she does. Her Telepathy allows her to truly know people.

"You would make a better king...queen," I correct myself.

She pulls a blanket over me, then pats my hand affectionately. "It doesn't matter, really. I love my family. And Cypress isn't as bad as you might think. He has a gentle, passionate side."

I try to picture this, but all I can picture is his mouth twisted up in a grin when he beat me at archery at twelve.

"You would make a good king, too, Zeph."

I close my eyes and snort. "Please. The day I'm king of this rock is the day the world ends...again."

The mattress shifts as she stands. "Get some sleep. The king wants to see you in the morning. I'll be sure coffee and eggs are sent up right away to prepare you."

I mutter appreciation, but drunken sleep slurs my words as it pulls me under.

TRUE TO HER WORD, Bronwyn has a hearty breakfast delivered. The smell of it makes my stomach twist, but once I choke down the bacon and eggs, the sickness and pounding in my head fade. I wash everything down with the coffee, taking massive gulps once it's cool enough.

Mom shuffles in, seating herself in one of the red velvet chairs. "How are you feeling this morning? Bronwyn said you had a rough night."

"Better now." It had been a terrible night of sleep. Something about my dreams tickles at my memory. "I think...I had the strangest dream. Like, not strange really, but I was on the *Wave Slicer* with my crew, and everything seemed to be normal. Then suddenly, this girl was standing in front of me. She came from nowhere." I frown, trying to recall anything about her, but the harder I try the more she fades.

"Dreams are strange things," Mom says. She arranges her skirt as I finished breakfast, and something about the movement strikes me as off. Nervous.

"What's wrong?" I move the tray of plates and cups, now empty, to the side so I can climb out of bed.

"Probably nothing. It's just...Cypress was meeting with a few of the councilmen yesterday."

"Not unusual at all," I interject.

"No." She licks her lips. "But the heads of the council and your uncle are meeting in the lower chambers this morning."

"Also not unusual."

"He has summoned you to join them."

I freeze at the bathroom door, eyeing my mother. Why would Cypress summon me to that meeting? Dad never did. He just had my orders passed down to me through my uncle.

"I suppose I should shower and get dressed then," I say. "What is appropriate attire for this sort of thing?"

"I will set it out for you but be quick. Baron is already downstairs."

I curse and slam the bathroom door closed.

———❈———

V OICES ARISE FROM THE lower council room as I approach. At least five of them.

"...without consulting us!" Baron snaps.

"I don't need to consult you, Admiral Baron," Cypress responds. I can hear the defensiveness in his tone. He's trying to take his stand, show what sort of king he will be. But Baron isn't a fool or a pushover.

I press open the door and the room falls silent. All five men—including Cypress, Baron, and Dominic—are seated at the polished table in the center of the small room. They eye me up and down. Dominic gives me a small smile and rolls his eyes. I unconsciously adjust the sleeves of my jacket and clear my throat.

"You summoned me, Your Grace?" I say, hating the formal title and the way it makes my brother straighten.

"About time you woke up," Cypress says. His face is stern, but his tone doesn't match, as if he is amused by me. I'm not sure how to take it. "I did summon you."

Baron leans his hands against the long table as he winds up for his argument. "Cypress—"

"It's already done, Uncle," Cypress snaps. "Take a seat and help us sort through the plan."

Baron's jaw twitches, and he sinks into his dragon-backed chair.

I wait beside the door, hands folded behind my back.

"It's time to collect Tributes," Cypress says. He remains in his seat, relaxed even with that crown perched on his dark wavy hair. It almost looks natural to him.

Tributes. Cypress wants a wife. Not just any wife. If he's asking for Tributes, he wants a girl who not only compliments him, but who also has the magical strength to give him powerful heirs. It's a common practice for unwed Crown Princes and Kings. Outlying communities would send their strongest girls to compete for the king's hand. Some of the girls will be from the island, but most of the people who live here don't have magic. They depend on the ruling class to protect them. Occasionally, someone will be born with magic, and the boys usually end up training as a recruit. Girls...well those of suitable age become Tributes for the next king.

For Cypress.

Last time the Kingdom collected Tributes was over twenty years ago, before either of us were born. Not long after Father's coronation.

I say nothing, unsure if I am part of this conversation or just an observer. Why did Cypress want *me* here?

"The Keeper of Tides and I sent the call out yesterday," Cypress announces.

Dominic straightens. His role as Keeper of Tides makes him Cypress's right hand. And the two have always been thick as thieves. Where Cypress goes, Dominic follows like an eager puppy.

I tense. This is what Baron is angry about. What is the rush? We need the Tributes, sure, but not urgently. Cypress is still young, only twenty. There is plenty of time to wait until spring when the waters are safer to travel.

"I still don't see why we cannot delay until spring," Baron says. "We need to keep our focus on the Haven. We are close to—"

"I will not waste my focus on tracking down zealots my father obsessed over. They have not been a threat to us. They can wait a little longer, worshipping their Idols and the coming end of all things."

Tense silence fills the chamber. Cypress just told the council that he thought my father's entire mission, the whole focus of his reign, was folly.

"Besides, it doesn't matter," Cypress continues. "The call is out. The people are preparing their selections for Tribute. Your *only* job is to organize the men who will go out and collect. Test them. Only the best magical strengths."

Suddenly, I understand why I'm here. Not only am I immune to magic, but I can sense the strength of it in others and prevent them from using it anywhere near me. I have to try sensing the strength, but the prevention and immunity are automatic. I don't control it.

"Zephyr, you will be in charge of the *Wave Slicer*," Cypress says. I swallow as he continues. "Before anyone girl is accepted, you will check her yourself. I want only the highest quality. The people in the outlands have lived in comfort long enough. It's time for them to send their king what's due."

"Recruits as well, then?" I ask, catching his drift.

He nods. "We haven't gone looking for them in a long time. Too long. All magic-capable boys for recruitment. All magic-strong girls for Tribute." The corner of his mouth quirked up. "Only the best."

The glint in his eyes made that statement clear. He didn't want me to bring back any girls he wouldn't find attractive as well. Only the best is his polite way of saying no dogs.

I nod. "When do we leave?" My hands are clasped so tight behind my back that my nails dig into my palms.

"How fast can you put your crew together?" Cypress asks, smirking. He already knows the answer.

I don't understand the urgency. Is he so desperate to assert his authority? Or is this Queen Elena's doing? Marry and produce heirs before anything can happen to him. "My crew can be ready to cast off in an hour."

Baron growls. "We need more time than that."

"No, Admiral. You do. But my brother is capable of leading this mission. You will stay here and oversee the fleets."

I shift feet, aware of all the council eyes boring into me. "How many ships are we talking?"

"Three should do. Only the largest." Cypress raps his fingertips against the edge of the table, satisfied with himself. "Go, brother. Ready your men, gather my Tributes, and make me proud."

The comment makes my gut twist, but not nearly as much as the disapproving shade Baron throws my way as I accept the orders and spin on my heel out the door.

I make it about halfway down the hall before Cypress catches up to me. He eyes me sidelong and pulls me into the throne room.

"I've been catching flashes of things," he admits, squaring off in front of me. "A hint of something here or there, ever since putting this thing on." He rolls his eyes up, indicating the crown on his wavy hair.

Cypress can read the history of people. To my knowledge, he's never done it with objects before. Is this a recent development in his magic, or has it always been there?

The expression on his face is nothing like the joking yet serious king from the meeting room. A sadness haunts his blue eyes. "I had no idea how bad it was. I mean, I think I always knew it wasn't good, but...I should have done more to help you instead of pitting against you as much as I did."

It takes me a moment to catch on. Dad. He's talking about Dad. I glance at the crown. The history it holds. My history. I swallow. How can I blame Cypress for what Dad did to me? He was only a year older. There was nothing he could have done that wouldn't have raised our father's ire toward him instead.

I shake my head. "Let's just leave it behind us."

"When you return, we will talk about retiring old Baron." Cypress grins, bringing back the cheeky side he showed in the meeting. "As long as you find me good women."

"You're horrible." But I chuckle.

I will bring him *all* the powerful magic-toting beauties in the outer communities if it gets me Baron's job.

8

GAVIN

THE DAYS PASS IN a blur of work. The level of activity on the tenth floor of the Department of Science and Technology is distracting. Every analyst is now on the case of the area east of Elpis. Some review daily radiation levels. Others monitor local activity within a one-hundred-mile radius of where the signal stopped. The information they all collect appears random to them. No doubt, they wonder why they are being assigned new tasks.

The analysts send the data they collect to Aron and me, who work on compiling everything into coherent reports and correcting mistakes—and there are so many mistakes. Once we finish our data analysis and compilation cleaning, we compare notes to be sure our results match. We then meet with Higbee to discuss the results. From there, Higbee sends it farther up the ladder until it reaches Director Perlberg.

One thing I am certain of is that the analyst the Council of Representatives selects to go on this mission had better understand the radioactivity ionization rate of decay in specific electrodynamic environments. We have no idea what is beyond our five-hundred-mile limit.

"Maybe I should recommend avoiding Electromancers in the mission," I mutter to myself as I tap my fingers on the edge of the desk.

If the analyst doesn't know how to evaluate the data properly, and an Electromancer is in the group using his or her Power, it could result in catastrophe. The data we have on hand is inconclusive as to the results of certain Power-related interactions with such a potentially radioactive environment. Historically speaking, though, I know exactly how it will end.

I slide my final report for the day into a file on the holoscreen and send it to Higbee, then press my palm against the desktop to deactivate it. Uncertainty plagues me as I push my chair back from the desk. A few times, I shift to stand, then sit back again.

No. I'm not uncertain. I'm not wrong. I'm never wrong.

The statistical probability of negative interactions in an unknown environment with specific Powers will be highly dangerous. If they haven't figured this out already, it's my duty to report it.

I take a breath to steel myself, terrified of a confrontation when I tell the higher powers. In my experience, no one likes being told what to do. Especially when they think they know better and have a higher social standing. It isn't uncertainty that plagues me. It's anticipatory fatigue that slows my steps.

Higbee is hunched over his desk, reviewing something I can only assume is confidential based on the black-back of the screen. The only time holoscreens use redaction backing on reports is when the information is classified.

"Sir?" I say from the doorway, wincing at the slight tremor in my voice.

Higbee glances up and waves me in. "I was just reviewing your report." He turns his attention back to the screen.

I edge farther into the office but don't sit in the leather seat across from him. "Did you read the final recommendation I noted at the end?"

Higbee's frown deepens, and he scrolls his finger up the screen. I watch his gaze dart from one line to the next as he reads. Then he sinks back in his high-back chair. "You think they should avoid Electromancers on the mission?"

"Yes, because the—"

"I read it, Gavin. No need to repeat it." Is that irritation in his tone or amusement? Sometimes, I can't tell what people are feeling. Paige is so good at reading people's emotions. I wish I had that skill.

I shift feet. "I, um, actually have a list of recommended Powers to avoid using on the mission based on historical and current data. But Electromancer is at the top. The most dangerous to include."

Higbee raises his brows, staring at me in a way that makes me incredibly uncomfortable. Again, I cannot glean his reaction. "You realize that this mission will require the use of Powers to protect everyone who goes."

"I do."

"And you still think they should avoid them?"

"Not all of them. I can compile a more complete list for the Council, but I can say with absolute certainty that—"

Higbee raises a hand to silence me. His head shakes ever so slightly. "It's too late for that, Gavin."

I swallow the lump in my throat. Why?

He motions to the chair. "Sit."

Am I about to get fired? Why would they fire me? They need me. I shudder to think what will happen to the data that runs through this department without me to correct it. No one else understands it like I do.

"If you will give me a chance to explain," I say, certain now that he can hear the tremor in my voice.

Higbee's expression softens. "Sit, please."

I do as he commands, sinking into the plush leather chair. I keep my back straight, hands folded in my lap.

"I received this notice just before you sent me your report," Higbee says.

For the first time, I notice the envelope on his desk perched precariously on the far corner. He slides out a letter and hands it to me. My hands shake slightly as I accept the paper.

The official Council of Representatives header catches my eye immediately. What did they send to Higbee? Curiosity slides its tickling grasp around my mind as I read. It isn't for him.

The letter is addressed to me.

Due to your exemplary analytical skills, you have been selected to join Project Restoration.

The letter goes on to explain why I was selected. My perfect analytical record. A list of my Powers. But this means leaving Elpis. The very idea sends a chill down my spine and makes my lunch revolt. I don't want to leave the city and venture into the unknown. I like it here. I know what to expect. But out there...

"You okay, Gavin?" Higbee asks.

I can only shake my head.

"This is a voluntary selection," he adds. "They won't require you to go if you don't want to. As much as I would hate to lose you in the office, I can't argue with their logic. You are probably the best prepared to deal with the necessary calculations and analysis in the field. And if anyone can discern the source of the signal to help us determine if there really is anyone else out there, or what danger they pose, it's you. Your work *is* exemplary." His chair creaks as he shifts, but I don't look up from the paper in my hand. "Gavin, this selection comes with a promotion to Senior Analyst. Something that's probably overdue. You will be my boss when you return."

When I return... But what if I don't return? Or what if I don't go at all? Will I lose the promotion to someone else?

My gaze shifts to the glass wall looking out over the mass of desks. Most of my co-workers are headed toward the door, done with their shift. Will one of them get the promotion? What if Aron is selected instead? I don't like the idea of him going out there any more than myself. The unknowns are too terrifying.

I need to talk to Dad. It isn't his signature on this letter. Does he know I was chosen? Was he part of the decision? I doubt it. He has always been supportive, but protective as well. I can't imagine he would recommend me for Project Restoration.

I fold the paper delicately and precisely into thirds. I need time to assess the pros and cons of this offer, then analyze the resulting data.

"Can I take some time to think about this?" I ask.

"Of course." Higbee smiles at me in a way he must think is reassuring, but I find it difficult to stomach. "But not too long. You can have the evening to consider the offer. But if you haven't decided by tomorrow morning, I have to send them another recommendation. If you choose to go, just send me a message. Then tomorrow you are to report to the Department of Security for a mission briefing."

I nod, murmuring my thanks, and make my way out of the office. The letter slips into my pocket.

I want that promotion.

I don't want to leave Elpis.

Something tells me I can't have it both ways.

9

PAIGE

THE CHAIR BENEATH ME is uncomfortable plastic. The Department of Security meeting room's air stifles my lungs. The pristine white walls reflect enough light to make the sun seem dim. I struggle not to shift in my seat as I sit alone in front of a panel of Captains, Majors, and Aunt Bianca. All five of them given off an air of command and urgency that does nothing for my already growing discomfort and anxiety.

Several days have passed since the incident with Tudor. Per Tudor's suggestion, we played the kiss off as nothing, a moment of drunken weakness fueled by the excitement in the club. The other members of the team seemed to buy it. Easton had scowled at us every day since though. He's been watching us like a hawk for additional signs of a relationship. Thankfully, we gave him nothing. At work, we are all business.

The day after the incident, I had expected to be pulled aside and reprimanded. Of anyone on the team, Easton seemed most likely to tattle.

The second day, I eyed my teammates curiously. Easton in particular. Were they holding the truth in their pocket to tear me down at the right moment? After a couple more days of uncertainty, I relax. I assume it's over with and no one reported us.

Then I watch as my teammates are called away one by one throughout the afternoon, not to return. That couldn't bode well for the purpose of this meeting.

"Specialist Powers," Captain Wilson says. "Your father is Minister Powers, isn't he?" He is reading it off a report on his tablet, but I don't doubt he already knows exactly who I am. I may not look like my dad—I'm paler like Mom—but there is no doubt he and I are father and daughter.

I answer anyway. "Yes, sir."

Bianca slides into the conversation in what I can only assume is an attempt to steer it away from my dad. She knows how uncomfortable I get when people talk to me about him. It sets unreasonable expectations on my shoulders. I might be his daughter, but I'm nothing like my dad.

"We are calling in all of our top Specialists as part of the Project Restoration selection process," Bianca explains.

The news takes me by surprise. I just assumed this was about Tudor and me. But it isn't. Do they even know what happened? Surely, someone on my team reported us. Easton is the most likely suspect.

"Your test scores are some of the highest we have seen," Bianca continues. "And your fighting skills are nearly unmatched." A hint of a smirk plays on her lips.

Nearly unmatched because she is clearly a stronger fighter than anyone. But I can't be that high in my rank.

"These make you a perfect candidate for the Project Restoration mission," she says.

"However," Captain Wilson interjects, leaning forward against the dark wood tabletop, "it has come to our attention that you perhaps have your father's penchant for disregarding rules."

The grin on my face slips. Here it comes.

"We have already spoken with several members of your team and have confirmed your relationship with Specialist Ryan." Captain Wilson's lips thin.

"I wouldn't call it a relationship," I mutter. Tudor and I hardly had time to really start anything. And we certainly never put a label on anything. It's still new to both of us.

Bianca scowls at me and I know I have stepped over a line. "Specialist Powers, you will join the Project Restoration mission."

My heart leaps with joy. Why would they choose me? Test scores were of little practical application. Though Gavin might argue against that. Bianca must know this will make Dad furious.

But it's exactly what I wanted. To be included on a mission that can change the future of the entire city.

"You will report tomorrow for mission briefing," she says. "You are dismissed, Specialist."

"Thank you," I say. As I rise, I hope they can't see how the excitement has my limbs trembling.

"Specialist Powers!" Wilson snaps.

His tone freezes me in my tracks. I turn to face him.

"We expect you to follow the rules," he says sternly. "Otherwise, we will be left with no choice but to pull you from this mission and reconsider your future in the Department of Security."

The warning is a clear shot over my bow. And honestly, it feels unfair. Tudor and I may have grown close these past few months, but that kiss was our first. In training we maintain a professionalism that I can't say many of our teammates share. I certainly don't want to risk the career I have spent months training for.

I came into the DS right out of high school when I was seventeen. At first, I was trained to be a Security Private—which is just the Elpis police force. When I found out they were accepting applications for the Specialist program three months into the DS-SP job, I jumped at the chance. I didn't need Aunt B showing me any form of favoritism to earn my place—though her training over the years certainly helped with the physical aspect of the application. For the last eight months, I have worked hard every day to prepare for this job. I won't lose it over a boy.

"It won't be a problem, Captain Wilson."

I step out into the waiting room, my skin flush with excitement. I can't believe it. We were selected for this mission. All I ever wanted was a chance to show I can make a difference like Dad, to live up to the insanely enormous legacy he continues to build. This mission is my chance.

Before I head home for the evening, I set out to the locker room to collect my belongings, a spring in my step.

The second I step in, Tudor looms in my path. The anger on his face instantly kills my elation. He's angry. Why?

"You were selected, weren't you?" He isn't asking. No doubt he knows by the way I entered the locker room.

For the first time, I realize the rest of my team may not have been selected with me. And the implication of his statement makes my stomach sink.

"Weren't you?" I ask, but I already know the answer. He's far too angry to be selected.

Tudor snorts in derision. "No, Paige. They picked you over me, stating they couldn't send both of us, *under the circumstances*." The way his dark eyes sweep over me is nothing like the way he looked at me in the club. "Did you do it on purpose to get this position?"

"What?" I take a step back, angry at his implication. He thinks I *used* him to take the spot? It would have been a terrible idea. Our superiors could have chosen him over me.

"I can't believe you. I thought..." He huffs, his shoulders tensing, bracing for a fight. Then something else crosses his dark eyes. Betrayal. Disgust. He does blame me!

"Easton was right about you." His words punch me in the heart. I note the way his hands clench into fists so tight it turns his knuckles white. Anger doesn't even begin to describe his fury. "You used your connection to your dad to get a place on the mission, and probably used that kiss to keep me off of it. I won't pretend to understand why, but I thought you were better than that. Clearly, I misjudged you."

Tears sting my eyes. "Tudor—"

"Save it, Paige," he snaps, edging closer. I don't shrink away, holding my ground. Who does he think he is? "You know, I was the one who defended you against the others. I told them they were wrong about you, that you earned your place just like the rest of us, but now I'm starting to think they were right all along. You don't care about anyone but yourself."

I flex my hands into fists at my sides. "That's not true."

Tudor brushes past me toward the door. "Whatever. Sink or swim on your own, Powers."

With that said, he slams the locker room door closed behind him.

I can't hold back the tears despite my burning rage. Tudor turned against me so easily. But this isn't my fault. And I didn't use my connections to get anything. Something he would know about me if he paid any attention to anything I ever said to him.

The anger spills over as I march to my locker. I slide on my jacket, then slam the locker door closed so hard the metal around the hinges snaps. The door clatters to the ground as I storm out.

As if my day couldn't get worse, I now have to go home and face Dad.

And he won't be happy either.

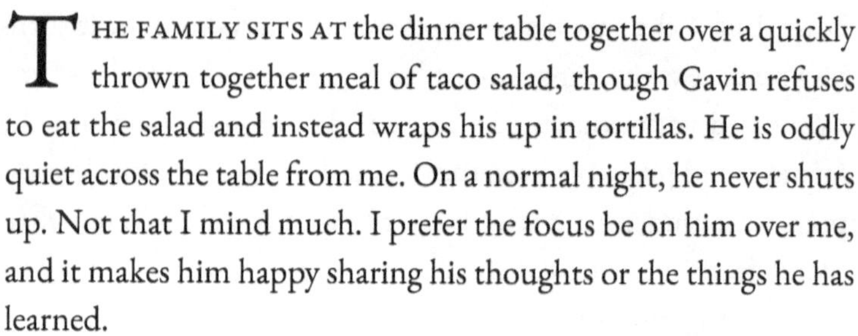

THE FAMILY SITS AT the dinner table together over a quickly thrown together meal of taco salad, though Gavin refuses to eat the salad and instead wraps his up in tortillas. He is oddly quiet across the table from me. On a normal night, he never shuts up. Not that I mind much. I prefer the focus be on him over me, and it makes him happy sharing his thoughts or the things he has learned.

But tonight, the set of his brows is studious. Something is on his mind. Something more important to him than anything any of us have to say. Something important enough to render him mute.

Not that I have much to contribute to the conversation. I find it hard to eat, picking at the salad with my fork and chewing each bite slowly. Somehow, I have to breach the subject of my selection. Part of me wonders if I could wait a few days and just drop it on them the night before I leave. Will it be right away or a few days? I suppose I will have more answers tomorrow.

"The newest batches are doing well, then?" Dad asks Mom.

She nods. "You know, I thought that entire business with that barrier was just you looking for a way to avoid a midlife crisis." There's a teasing glint in her eyes as she stares across the table at Dad.

"Enid, I'm not that old," he says with a chuckle.

I roll my eyes at the two of them. Their affection often comes across as teasing and sarcasm. For them, it's the equivalent of smarmy declarations of love. Not only that, but when Mom jokes about their youth, it's a clear jab at the rebel Dad used to be. After my confrontation with Tudor today, my tolerance level for their happiness remains minimal.

They were right about you, I hear Tudor's angry voice say in my head and begin stabbing at my lettuce as if it's a voodoo bowl of Tudor salad. *Sink or swim on your own.* Jerk. It isn't like I cost him a job. Just this mission. And it wasn't even my fault. They said it. My scores are better. What did he think, that just because he was "seeing" me he might have some better chance at a mission like this than the rest of us? How deluded could he be?

"Paige!" Dad calls, breaking me from my angry focus on the salad bowl. I meet his gaze. He frowns at me. "What's wrong?"

Even Gavin is giving me an odd look. *He* looks like Dad.

"Nothing," I mutter. How do I tell my dad that I broke up with my boyfriend who wasn't my boyfriend who I wasn't even supposed to be seeing in the first place? Or that everyone assumes Dad plays favorites for me—which is so obviously not true.

"Well, just in case you needed reminding, the salad was already slaughtered by my kitchen knife," Dad says, smirking at me. I can tell by the way his fingers tap on the tabletop that he doesn't believe me. It's a habit I don't think he is aware he has. "But I'm sure your mother would appreciate if you didn't break her bowl with your fork."

And just like that, my appetite disappears. I drop the fork on the table and excuse myself, headed for my bedroom.

A chair scrapes the floor of the dining room as I round the corner and I hear Mom hissing, "Ugene, leave her be."

He offers an unintelligible response I don't care about.

I climb the steps two at a time, then slam my bedroom door closed.

The sage walls and full-size bed make the room feel much more confining than it ever has before. Maybe after I get back from this mission, I should look for my own place. Gavin can stay with Mom and Dad as long as he wants, but I need to get out.

I sink down against my headboard and pull a pillow into my lap. Tudor's reaction shouldn't upset me so much. But it isn't as much about him basically dumping me as it is about what he said. *You don't care about anyone but yourself.*

Does the whole team feel that way? I worked so hard to prove myself to them. To everyone!

A knock on the door. Dad sticks his head in without prompting and frowns when he sees me. I know there's no point in telling him to get out. He won't listen.

"Paige, be honest," he says softly, settling on the edge of my bed. "What's wrong?"

Might as well rip off the Band-Aid. The pillow squishes in my fists. "I was selected for Project Restoration by my commanding officers."

He flinches, and his shoulders slope downward. For a moment, he just watches me. Then he reaches for my arm and gives it a reassuring squeeze. "You don't have to go. The Council agreed participation should be by choice and not demand."

I jerk my arm away and glare at him. "I'm going."

"But I thought..." It's satisfying seeing the dumbstruck look on his face. Dad is usually either a step ahead, or he picks up on things far too quickly. It's rare to catch him by surprise like this.

"My selection isn't the issue," I say. I slide my fingers into my sleeves and pull them down, taking comfort in the warmth and length. "The problem is that my entire team thinks I'm self-centered. That I use my connection to you to get things."

"Like your selection," he says. I can actually see the moment it dawns on him.

Now that I've opened this door, I can't seem to close it again. The emotions swell inside of me. Anger. Loneliness. Sadness. Inadequacy. "Do you have any idea what it's like being me? To constantly live in your shadow? In Gavin's shadow? At work, people see me as entitled or expect me to stack to up to your legacy. At home, I'm never as good as Gavin, as gifted as he is. Nothing I do is good enough."

The way a smile slowly spreads across his face only fuels my growing rage.

"Why are you grinning?" I snap. "I'm being serious, Dad. You want to know what's wrong? There it is. I will never be enough for anyone."

The compassion his eyes offer is of no relief. "You sound just like me."

"What?"

"Most of the time you are so much like your mother—fearless, determined, stubborn to a flaw—that I rarely see myself in you at all." He shifts, turning to face me fully. "I said something a lot like that to my dad once upon a time. He didn't understand how hard it was to be me, a Powerless punching bag at school. A lazy disappointment at home. He had such high expectations I never dreamed I would ever achieve. I wanted to prove myself, to have some value to him and to society. That's why I went to Paragon."

How can he possibly compare my problem to his own? They are nothing alike.

"But what I did was reckless and dangerous," he says. "It brought Elpis to where we are now, so I wouldn't change it, but I might have done a few things differently. My choices cost people's lives. It's something I can never erase or make up for. I don't want a burden like that on your shoulders. Paige..." He picks at invisible lint on my evergreen comforter. "We don't know what's out there or what this signal is. Please don't do this. It's too dangerous."

I slide off the other side of the bed and plant my hands on my hips. "You just said you wouldn't change what you did. Now you want me to curl up in a corner and let someone else put his or her life at risk? Dad, I'm not sure what Aunt B tells you, but I'm the best at what I do. And I've seen death. Don't think you're shielding me from anything!"

He rises, no longer soft and reassuring. *This* is the father I know. The one who gives me commands and just expects me to listen. I'm not a little girl anymore.

"Those deaths were simulations," he says, using his political voice as if I were someone to charm into following him. Dad slinks around the bed toward me, desperation and anger in his movements. "The real thing is *much* different, Paige. I watched powerful people tear the blood from bodies of my friends like they were a leaking hose. I saw the ground swallow up hundreds of innocent people. And all of it was my fault." His voice trembles. "You don't want to hold your friend in your arms as he or she bleeds to death."

Bianca. He's talking about Aunt B. "But she isn't dead."

Pain seizes his throat. His voice is so frail it hurts me to hear, but not nearly as much as the shocking truth of the words. "Yes, she is."

I know he doesn't mean it literally. In the fight against Paragon, Aunt B died. Her brother somehow brought her back to life stronger than she ever was before—but it cost her all her memories. Memories of her youth with Dad, of their friendship.

The words settle over us, smothering arguments with discomfort. He stares at the floor. Then he sniffles and raises a trembling hand to wipe away tears. I regret making him relive those days.

Mom will only talk about it with Dad behind closed doors. She never says anything to us aside from cursory, "You don't understand" or "Now isn't the time." Not that it's ever the time. What kind of demons does she live with?

"Dad, I'm sorry," I say softly, edging close and taking his hand. "I didn't mean to bring up old memories."

He clears his throat, and his watery gaze meets mine. "I don't want you to live with this kind of pain, Paige. It swallows you whole when you least expect it."

"I know." My words are more placating than actual understanding. Though I have watched him give in to moments of grief when he thought he was alone in his office. Unlike Mom, he is willing to share the stories with Gavin and I, but never around Mom. I'm certain he keeps out some of the grisly details.

"It's settled," he says, pleading with me.

"What is?"

"You will stay here?"

My grip on his hand tightens. Steely determination courses through me. I will not be held back or told what to do. Not even by him. "No. I'm going on the mission. And you won't try to stop me or bar me from it, either."

For just a moment, his entire body relaxes. His eyes glass over. It only lasts for a second or two, and then his brows knit together.

"Paige, what did you do?"

I drop my grip on his hand and cross my arms. "Told you the honest truth."

"No..." he says slowly.

But before he can continue the debate—something I usually lose against him—I grab my jacket off my bed and head out the door. "Yes. And you didn't like it, but you won't change my mind."

I need to clear my head, and I know just where to go.

10

GAVIN

I FROWN AS PAIGE storms out of the dining room.

"Ugene, leave her be," Mom says as Dad rises from his seat to follow Paige out.

"Something is clearly bothering her," he says. "She needs support, not isolation."

"She will talk to us when she's ready," Mom insists.

"We both know that's not always true, Enid." He marches toward Paige's room.

Dad is right. Paige doesn't always talk to them, though she does usually confide in me.

Paige has had such a rough go of things at work lately. It's probably about that.

Seven days ago, I spent the entire night trying to console her, though I'm not sure my words offered much reassurance. Maybe her team revealed their true feelings toward her—that she is entitled because of who our father is and that they think she is selfish. I'm not sure where any of it comes from. Dad hates that Paige is training as a Specialist—or she was, anyway. Her team was promoted last Tuesday. When she was just a Security Private, Dad hadn't minded as much. She was still safe inside the city limits. His overprotective nature bothers Paige far more than it bothers me.

Not only that, but Paige is one of the most selfless people I know. Growing up, I watched her protect others. It's a natural impulse in her. When a few of the poorer kids in our school didn't have enough for lunch, she gave hers up for them. She stood up to school bullies for everyone. Paige has always gone out of her way for others. She gets that from Dad, who is notorious for the same thing. I know she wants to prove herself, show everyone that she is worthy to be a member of the Powers family. Her deeply seeded need for approval is classic of a primary inferiority complex. All I can do is offer her encouragement and support.

I want to know what happened to her at work this time, but at the same time, I can't stop thinking about my selection for the upcoming mission. I don't want to leave the city limits. I like it here. I know what to expect. I have a bed and a house and a great job. But there is no doubt the promotion I want is linked directly with the mission. If I don't go, I won't get the promotion. It would make me one of the youngest Senior Analysts ever.

"You are oddly quiet tonight, Gavin," Mom says, drawing my attention toward her.

"Sorry."

She smiles. "Why are you apologizing? It's not necessary. But it does make me curious what's on your mind."

I glance at Dad's empty seat. "Just thinking about work."

"They are working you really hard."

I nod as I finish my taco, then wash it down with milk. Part of me wants to talk to Mom about the selection, get her opinion. But I already know what she will say. The outside world is harsh and dangerous. I may not be equipped to handle what awaits. It would be best if I chose to stay. Mom wouldn't take a firm stand about my staying. Nor would she tell me directly what to do. Instead, she would skirt around telling me what to do by making it sound like the choice is mine while her words still sway me. It's a pretty classic move for her.

I could almost have the entire conversation in my head.

Finished with dinner, I collect my dishes—and Paige's—then kiss Mom on the temple as I pass her.

"I like the work. It doesn't bother me at all."

"Just don't let them take advantage of your dedication," she says as I move toward the kitchen sink.

"I know, Mom." I rinse my dishes, then scrape Paige's dinner into the trash compactor and rinse hers as well.

Before Mom can layer on any of her motherly guilt, I head toward my room. Perhaps a pros and cons list will help me decide what to do about my selection. Of course, I will have to make sure that it's calculated to weigh the value of each item on the list. For instance, the promotion holds more weight than, say, our transportation breaking down. No. That's a bad example. I can fix our transport with my Matter Mutation if necessary.

Dad's sharp voice halts my steps near Paige's door. His voice trembles as he talks about his own troubles at our age, the dangers he faced, and the people he lost. One person, in particular.

Paige says something I can't quite hear, and all I catch is sorrow from Dad's tone. Why are they arguing about something that happened before we were born?

Paige murmurs an apology.

Maybe their fight isn't so bad this time. They don't realize how alike they are—which is why they butt heads so much. I wish I could get them to see it. They might fight less often if they understood.

I hear Dad clear his throat. They exchange a few more soft words. Then he says something about her staying.

My heart skips. My breath catches. My hands sweat. Stay? Is she planning on moving out? No, that doesn't fit the narrative of the argument.

Paige's voice is cold and hard, sending a chill down my spine. "I'm going on the mission."

My lips part in alarm. The mission? Paige was selected as well? It's what she trains for, but I am surprised the Council of Representatives would allow both of us to be selected for a dangerous mission. Not that I can think of a single Elpis proposition that prohibits one family to send all their children on a single, dangerous mission. Come to think of it, that seems like an egregious oversight.

I miss the end of the argument, but jump as Paige storms out, jacket in hand. I trail a few steps behind her. "Paige—"

"Not now, Gavin!" Paige snaps, descending the steps two at a time.

I stop at the top of the staircase and stare after her. We should talk about this. Does she know I was selected as well? Do Mom or Dad?

Wiping the sweat from my palms, I turn as Dad steps out of her room. We meet gazes for a moment. His eyes are red-rimmed and shimmering with tears he is fighting to hold back. The moment is fleeting. Three seconds later, he is headed to his office, slamming the door shut behind him.

I shuffle to my own room and sink into my desk chair. The room is orderly, with shelves lined with various books organized by subject, then author. The bed is neatly made. I consider this space with a new perspective.

Since birth, I have spent every night in this room. I grew up in this space, building things with linking blocks at a young age. As I grew older and my Matter Mutation manifested, I began building with scraps of metal and electronics. In middle school, Liam and I would sit on the floor, backs to the foot of the bed, and watch movies on my holotv or play video games.

The room is filled with good and bad memories. Some good memories link with bad memories. Paige helping me break down a jumble of emotions I couldn't unravel alone regarding my feelings toward Liam. The first kiss he and I shared, follow shortly after by his staunch denial and brutal rejection when I tried to hold his hand at school. My entire family loving me and supporting me and helping me pick up the pieces for weeks afterward. Paige slept in my room for over a week after that final fight with Liam, comforting me, joking with me.

Some nights, after one of her nightmares, her insomnia would kick in and she would lie awake either in this room with me or I would sleep in hers. We've always drawn comfort and strength from each other.

I lean against the desktop and press my head into my hands. Paige is a capable fighter. I know that. I know I would be safer out there with her, and that she can take care of herself. But if another analyst goes on the mission and miscalculates radiation readouts, it could be catastrophic. Paige could be hurt through negligence—or she could die. I don't know how to survive without her. She's the post I lean against for support.

Refusing my own call to action could cost our family dearly. I could never live with myself for not doing everything in my power to help her, protect her, and help see her home safely.

Fighting, she can handle.

But there are dangers out there that can't be beaten with fists and feet.

I groan as I rise and head toward Dad's office.

I *have* to go. I don't really have a choice.

The office door is ajar. I place my hand against it to push my way in, but freeze when I hear Mom's voice.

"You can't protect her forever, Ugene." Her voice is soft, soothing in a way that tells me she is trying to sway Dad. "Paige is so much like you. The more you try to pin her down, the harder she will fight to kick free."

"No one has gone so far before, Enid. What if those dangerous people Crow mentioned in the journal cube are still out there beyond our range? What if *they* sent the signal? What if she doesn't come back?"

"You should be more worried about her choosing not to come back if you can't let go of the reins a little. Paige is eighteen, not thirteen. You acted the same way when she wanted to go downtown shopping with her friends when she was thirteen. What did she do when you forbid her from going?"

I recall that day with striking clarity. And the tension in the house when they found Paige's room empty, only for Dad to drag her home, thus embarrassing her in front of all her friends.

"She snuck out and went anyway," Dad grumbles.

Footsteps make the floorboards creak. Mom's voice lowers as she replies, "You can't forbid her from going on this mission. She will go anyway."

"No, but I can use my political position to bar her from leaving Elpis."

Mom and Dad won't like what I'm about to tell them.

"That will only push her out of our lives," Mom says. "She needs this. I don't understand how you, of all people, don't see that."

I push the door open, knocking lightly to make sure they aren't alarmed by my appearance.

Both fall silent as I step into Dad's office. Mom crouches beside Dad's desk chair, her hand on his chest. Dad's face is sagging in what I can only assume to be deep sorrow. I lick my lips nervously.

"What's wrong?" Dad asks. He obviously picked up on some cue in my body language.

I glance at my hands, wondering what has given me away. I clear my throat. "Uh, just wondering. How dangerous is this mission? Like, what are the odds of something being out there to attack?"

Dad leans back. Mom's hand falls away and she rises beside him, watching me curiously. "We don't know, Gav," Dad says. "That's what makes this so dangerous. We have been locked away inside our box for over a hundred years. There's no way to know until we go out there."

I swallow hard. That's hardly reassuring. "You can't use your position to keep her in Elpis," I say, edging toward the desk. "It will only cause her more problems at work. Her teammates already think she only got her position because of you. If you intercede, it proves them wrong, but I don't think they will see it that way. And they could accuse her of being too scared to go, which will only make her problems worse. Not to mention, this time her placement actually *would* directly result from your interceding. To them, it would only prove their point—wrong as they may be. She has to go."

Curse the lump in my throat. It won't go away.

Dad drags his hands over his face, and even I can see the agony as he puzzles this all out and realizes I am right.

"She won't be alone," I add, praying they can't hear the tremor in my voice. I rub my palms against my legs.

"I know that." Dad sighs. "She will have a team with her, but—"

"I will be with her."

Mom's eyes double in size. "What?"

I reach a sweaty palm into my pocket and pull out the letter, holding it out over the desk.

Dad frowns uncertainly as he takes the letter and unfolds it. Both read the letter. Dad's expression darkens when he finishes. His jaw twitches.

"That woman," he growls. The venom in his tone alarms me. "She did this on purpose."

"Councilwoman Howser?" I ask, remembering the signature at the bottom.

"Ugene..." Mom crosses her arms.

"She's baiting me, Enid," Dad snaps.

I don't fully understand what is going on, but Mom clearly does.

"She wants my job," Dad continues, slapping the letter down on the desktop. "If I intercede, she will have all the ammunition she needs to get exactly what she's after. But if I don't..."

Mom's eyes well with tears and she shakes her head. "You have to do something, Ugene."

"I can't, Enid! Did you hear what I said?" The rising anger in Dad's voice makes both Mom and me flinch.

She drops to her knees in front of Dad and takes his hands. "Who cares? These are our children!"

He hangs his head.

I cock my own to the side, observing the exchange. It isn't a surprise that Mom values our lives over his job. I don't doubt Dad does as well. He's been far too overprotective of both of us not to.

Suddenly, Dad's gaze snaps up to me. "You both have a choice, though. You can stay, Gavin. You don't have to go. If you refuse, it wouldn't be my fault. They can't force you to go."

I shift feet. Both of my parents are staring at me with desperation and hope. I hate to kill that, but I knew before I even entered this room what I had to do to protect my sister.

Dad groans before I even speak. He already knows what I will say.

"I have to go."

Mom rushes around the desk and seizes my arms. "No. Gavin, please. Don't do this."

I shake my head and step back, but her grip is firm. "I must. Paige will go either way. And she will look after me, but I need to be there to look after her. There is still a chance of electrodynamic interaction out there due to radiation. If someone else goes and miscalculates the radioactivity, it could be catastrophic. No one is better at this than me. You both know it." My gaze flicks from one to the other. "If I don't go, she could die from negligence beyond her control."

Mom brushes a tender palm over my cheek. "My sweet boy. This is so dangerous."

"I know that, Mom." I lean my head back away from her and take a step back. "Which is exactly why I am the one who has to be there. We can watch over each other. And I'm not a boy any longer."

"I hate this," Dad grumbles. "I wish I could go." He digs through his desk drawers. "If this is happening, we need a plan." He pulls out a notebook and drops it on the desk.

I smile. Another puzzle for Dad and me to solve together.

I sit across the desk, eager to get started.

11

PAIGE

T HE SELF-DRIVING TRAM STOPS across the street from Tribute Park. I step off and breathe in the downtown air—roasted meat from a nearby gyro restaurant mingling with fresh water from a nearby fountain and flowers from a closed shop down the block. There's something comforting about the smells of downtown, even if the tall buildings all packed in tightly together doesn't help my claustrophobia.

As the tram continues along its pre-programmed route, I tuck my hands into the pockets of my jacket and glance both ways before jogging across the street illuminated in the dark by building and streetlights.

Tribute Park is a massive city block sized park with carefully manicured landscaping and well-tended smooth stone paths that wind all around the block, meeting in the same place. The center of the block where Tribute Wall overpowers the space. I stroll along a birch-lined path, noticing the way the leaves had started turning yellow. Fall will be on us soon.

When I reach Tribute Wall, I run my fingers along the glass-like onyx surface over thousands of names. The wall isn't really a wall, but a sculptured infinity symbol with no beginning or ending. In the center, an eternal flame burns. Every single name on the wall is another person my father blames himself for not saving.

When he was seventeen, he volunteered as a test subject at Paragon Diagnostics, a mega-pharmaceutical company and hospital in the heart of downtown Elpis. Everyone in the city has a Power of some sort, be it Muscle Memory like myself or Matter Mutation like Gavin. But Dad's Power never manifested. He was the lone Powerless citizen in a city full of Powers.

I can't even understand what it must have been like growing up without a Power or place. Back then, social standing was determined by what they called the Cass Scale Rank. The higher the number, the higher one's social standing. We don't place value in Powers the same way anymore. Dad proved to everyone that the strength of one's Power doesn't indicate his or her ability to contribute.

During his time at Paragon Diagnostics, he met Alex and Mom, along with several others. He learned that Paragon and the Directorate—our former governmental leaders—were using test subjects in brutal and deadly ways. Those who failed the experiments were often killed, and their bodies disposed of in a ditch well outside city limits where no one would dare look. Now it's the site of a mass grave. Another memorial marking the struggle.

Dad outsmarted all of them. Paragon. The Directorate. He escaped Paragon with dozens of test subjects, brought them to safety. Upon further investigation, he also discovered the Directorate was teaming up with Paragon to either "cure" or kill citizens with low Cass Scale Ranks. He exposed the truth, giving a speech that moved the entire city into action against the Directorate.

Tribute Park is built on what had once been the location of Paragon Tower. During the revolution, a woman named Willow led a group to the tower and planted explosives that brought down all two hundred stories. Dad blames himself for not stopping her.

I've heard his story quite a few times. It's a painful time for him to recall. I know that. I also understand that none of it was easy for him. But he must know that, just like he could not stand aside while people were abused and murdered, I cannot stand aside when Elpis could be in danger. He's right. In some ways, we are so much alike.

I find the names on the wall by instinct. I've been here so many times before. Sometimes with Mom and Dad. Sometimes alone.

Jade. Mo. Trina. Dave. Vicki. Leo. Noah. These were all friends of Dad's who died in Paragon or saving him. I owe my life to these strangers.

The only name not on the wall is Celeste. Dad talks about her a lot. The sister he never had. He firmly believes Celeste never actually died. That her Divine Power was so evolved we cannot even fathom what she was capable of or where she went during the escape from Paragon Tower.

"I thought I might find you here."

I glance over my shoulder as Aunt Bianca approaches. Her gaze fixes on the Eternal Flame of Elpis and for a moment, she appears haunted.

Aunt B was part of the fight against the Directorate and Paragon. Her brother's experimentation on her to make her stronger and better came at a steep cost. Not just her memories of her youth.

She can't have children of her own. Nor can Uncle Levi. The serum that enhanced their Powers negatively affected their ability to reproduce. As a result, Aunt B spent a lot of time in the orphanages with the children whose parents died on Liberation Day. She latched on to Gavin and me. She was the cool aunt I had admired growing up. We formed a bond over the years. She just gets me.

"I just needed to remind myself why I am doing this," I say, pulling my hand from the familiar names. "And that maybe I'm not so different from him."

Aunt B chuckles. "I'm not sure you're different at all. I see the same determination and desire to help others in you that I once saw in your dad."

I throw up my hands. "Then why can't he understand why I have to do this? I can't live in his shadow my entire life. I need to … I don't know."

Bianca shrugs as she turns to face me. "He does understand. That's what makes this so hard for him. Your dad loves more fiercely than anyone, which also means he is terrified of losing people he loves." Her words make sense to me, and it explains why he always smothers me. "The day you were born, Levi and I came to the hospital to visit. Ugene sat in the rocker beside Enid's bed, cradling you so close in his arms. The pure adoration on his face made me so envious."

I watch Aunt B curiously. She has never told me this story before. In the past eighteen years, she has told me a lot of stories, but this is new.

"Gavin was named after your grandfather," she continues, staring at the eternal flame. "Do you know where your name came from?"

I shake my head. No one ever told me. I admit, it is something I was always curious about. Gavin got a family name, and I was just Paige. No significance. I never doubted Mom's faithfulness to Dad, but sometimes I wondered if he and I were related at all. We look nothing alike—not like Gavin and Dad do. We act so different—unlike Gavin and Dad.

"Ugene stroked your tiny nose and told us they named you Paige because he could just sense you would be like him, a page from your father's book."

Tears well in my eyes. I blink furiously to control them, but to no avail. My throat clenches. Sadness rips at my heart.

Bianca tears her eyes away from the eternal flame and her coppery gaze sees right into my soul. "He was right. As usual. Great things are coming your way, Paige. I see it just as clearly now as he did the day you were born."

I can't hold it in any longer. My arms slide around Aunt B. She hugs me close, stroking my dark, wavy hair. And I cry. Why I cry is a mystery. I want to believe her. But how can I when I can't see it for myself? And how could Dad be so certain of me so quickly? Did he still feel the same?

⁂

I REMAINED AT THE park with Aunt B for a bit longer before heading home. Going on this mission is important to me, but I can't leave anger or bitterness between Dad and me when I leave. Like it or not, I have to go home and talk to him.

By the time I slip through the door, it's well past ten. It's likely everyone will be asleep by now.

But as I pad quietly through the dining room toward the living room, I am surprised to see Dad and Mom waiting for me. Dad rises from the sofa the moment I step into the room. He rubs his hands anxiously together as his dark gaze settles on me.

Mom glances at him, then strolls over to me and kisses my forehead. "I love you, Paige. No matter what."

"Love you, too, Mom," I say as she passes me and heads up to bed.

Silence falls between Dad and I, awkward and unsettling. He can't stop fidgeting.

"Paige..." His feet shuffle over the carpet toward me.

"Dad, I don't want to fight."

"Nor do I." He stops a few feet away from me. "I need to tell you something before it's too late. Something I probably didn't say to you enough."

Great. A confession of his love. I already know this. "Dad..." I groan. I resist the urge to roll my eyes at him.

He holds up a hand. "Before you leave this house, it's important to me that you know I'm proud of you. I should have said it more, shown it more."

The words stun me, root me in place, freeze me in time. "Wh-what have I done for you to be proud of?"

"Is that a joke?" he asks. He seems honestly stunned. "You have always been so courageous, so strong. And it has nothing to do with your Somatic Muscle Memory. This mission is just another in a line of examples. Doing this takes a lot of courage. Anything can happen."

"If that's your way of trying to use reverse psychology to make me second-guess my decision it won't work."

He shakes his head, smirking. "No. You have blossomed into a beautiful, strong, intelligent young woman. I need to recognize that and give you the space you need to find your own path." He places his hands on my shoulders, warmth rolling off him. "I'm proud of you."

The little girl in me takes over. I throw my arms around him and hug him close. "I love you, Dad. But this is something I need to do."

"I know. I do. It's just not easy for me letting go of my little girl."

I break the hug and step back, sniffling and swiping away a tear. "I told myself I wouldn't cry again tonight."

"Me, too." Dad lets go and takes a step back. In the dim light, I can see the wetness on his cheeks. "Get some rest, Paige. You have a busy few weeks ahead."

"Thanks, Dad." I head toward the staircase, then pause and glance back at him. His shoulders droop toward the floor as he studies the carpet. "I love you, Dad. And I'm proud to be your daughter."

He nods tightly.

I climb the steps, surprised to find Gavin sitting outside my bedroom with his phone in his hand. He glances up at my approach, then taps out another message and sends it before climbing to his feet.

"What are you doing out here?" I ask him.

"You always say I can't go in without permission," Gavin says.

I laugh as I step into my room. "Okay."

"I needed to talk to you." He pauses in the doorway. I wave him in, and he shuffles over the threshold. "I heard you and Dad fighting earlier. Everything good now?"

I wince but nod. How much did Gavin hear? Not that he doesn't know most of it already. I drop my jacket on the floor, drawing his gaze to it. He frowns but doesn't move to pick it up. Then I strip off the top shirt, leaving me in my tank top.

"Then you're going?" he asks, perching on the edge of my bed.

"Of course, I'm going."

He makes a sound and I'm not sure if it's disapproval or disappointment.

"Gav, the DS committee selected me because of my record. And you know how much I want to get out there. This is my chance." I step into my walk-in closet and change out my leggings for PJ pants. When I come back out of the closet, Gavin is focused on his phone, frowning. "What's wrong?" I sit beside him and glance at the phone. "Aron? *The* Aron?"

Gavin pulls the phone back, but not before I see Aron's message.

"Go where?" I ask.

He sighs, slouching heavily. "I received a letter—"

"Unbelievable," I mutter as it hits me. Gavin is going on the mission, too.

"What?" He looks genuinely confused.

"I can't even have this one thing." Gavin going along means everything that we discover will be credited to him. Once more, Gavin will get all the accolades and I will get nothing. "I suppose Dad doesn't care that *you're* going."

He flinches. "I thought you would be happy I was coming along. And for the record, he and Mom both wanted me to back out."

"Good. We agree for once. You stay here with Aron. He obviously wants you to stay close to him." I wave at the phone.

His gaze drops to the phone cradled in his hands and he frowns at it. "He does?" He shakes his head. "No. I think he wants the promotion that comes with it. If I don't go, he probably will." He turns to face me, dropping the phone aside as it buzzes. "Paige, I wouldn't be going at all if you weren't."

"Trying to protect me?" I snap sarcastically.

"Yes. But I also need *you* to protect *me*. I can analyze the data in real time better than anyone else, and you are the best fighter I know, aside from Aunt B. We need each other."

I want to argue, but his logic—as usual—is sound. Instead, I curl up under my blanket and pat the top of the bed beside me. Gavin stretches out, facing me.

"This will be hard work, Gav," I say, tugging the blanket to my chin—a hard feat to do with him laying on top of it. "And possibly dangerous."

"Likely dangerous, actually. I wouldn't trust my life in anyone else's hands, Paige."

It's so hard to be mad at him. Gavin is always so level-headed and open. I sigh and close my eyes. "Nor would I, Gav."

The two of us lay like that for a while longer, whispering stories about what might be out there—some fantastical and others serious. This routine is familiar. Another comfort on those nights when I couldn't sleep. But tonight, his presence soothes me and makes it so much easier.

Then I dream of being carried away on foggy waters.

12

ZEPHYR

WAVE SLICER IS A beast in the open water. On a sunny day, we can travel much faster, but when we cast off from the island, clouds covered the sky, casting a gray pall on everything. A trip that should have only taken eight hours requires an overnight on the ship. It's just one of many reasons we should have waited until the spring. Even a combination of solar, wind, and water-generated power isn't enough to maintain top speeds, and even with a Windcaller on board to keep the winds at our back, we still move slower than I would like.

Despite wanting crews to sail as swiftly as possible, Cypress had little choice but to delay departure for a day for proper planning. It had been well over twenty years since the last Tribute, and it required more organization than a quick crew and sail. Baron had been through this before with my father. He knew how to handle it. He organized three ships across various areas of the mainland: one directly across the water from the island; one up around the upper peninsula into Haven territory; and my ship around the mainland and down the second stretch of lake toward the largest area of the Kingdom of Tides.

While the Capital resides on the island, the Kingdom of Tides stretches hundreds of miles across the mainland. It covers the expanse of all known survivable territory. Dozens of communities across the mainland belong to the Kingdom of Tides. From spring to early fall, our soldiers patrol the Kingdom. In the winter, a few battalions of troops remain on the mainland to guard our position, but the rest return to the island for further training to prepare for the next season.

Only the Haven has ever eluded us—my father's endless obsession. Despite years of searching, our military has never ferreted out whatever hole they hide in. Not that it matters much. The Haven is content to remain in its own territory most of the time. Bunch of zealots, to boot, if you ask me. They have some pretty crazy beliefs. Doom and gloom about another end of the world and how an Idol of Creation and Desolation will one day come. One to destroy the world. The other to rescue it. Bunch of hogwash.

The back cabin of the sun deck was long ago converted into bunks. The seats had been ripped out and replaced with rows of bunks for sleeping. Manning the ship only requires about a dozen people, but having enough soldiers along with us for patrols is a different story.

For this mission in search of recruits and Tributes, we brought along a hundred soldiers to help in the gathering. Some communities resist. We cannot allow resistance of any sort. To remain in charge, we must exert our authority. Besides, our shipments of goods feed these people. Our military protects them from danger and keeps them from turning against one another. They need us.

Last night, I stretched out on one of the beds to get some shut-eye while my second captain manned the bridge. This morning, Nat pokes me awake before the sun rises.

"We spotted the lighthouse," he says, glancing around as others stir as well. "It's almost time to dock."

I nod and rub the sleep from my eyes. That girl was in my dreams again, staring across the aft out at the lake as *Wave Slicer* glided across the foggy waters. Why does she keep suddenly appearing in my dreams? Who is she?

The cook is hard at work in the kitchen in the main cabin on the sun deck. She nods at me with a small smile. I return the gesture, taking one of her muffins on my way up to the bridge.

By the time I step up beside the second captain, the sun is breaking colors across the horizon to the east.

"All quiet for the night?" I ask.

"Nothing out here," he says, handing me the boat comm. "Power is running low, but we should be ready to dock in just a few minutes."

"I'll be sure the carriages are ready to disembark," I say, attaching the comm to my hip. It's an old handheld wave radio we use for communication on these trips. Someone found them long ago and used their mechanical magic to fix them up. "When we are docked and powered down, I leave you in charge of the ship with a few of the men while we travel to the communities. We shouldn't be more than a week. Make sure she gets enough sun to get us home."

He nods. "Roger, Captain."

I pat him on the shoulder, then head to the lower deck. It seems I don't need to give my men orders. They know their jobs. Already, the horses are being secured to the carriages. Long ago, the military attempted commandeering old vehicles from the mainland to get around. But the vehicles ended up being more of a liability than a blessing. They broke down often, requiring parts that were often hard to come by. Or they didn't get enough solar power to go very far. Fuel is a nonexistent relic. In the end, the carriages on the island proved more effective than vehicles.

"Ready for mooring," I command.

Two of the men rush to the rear railing of the ship. From there, they will be able to reach the ropes to secure the ship to the dock. A third will hop down to the dock to lower the ramp for the carriages.

I move to the upper deck, sliding the comm off my hip as the ship begins moving slowly in reverse toward the dock. When we are close enough, I send word to the second captain. He holds the ship steady as the crew secures the mooring to the bollard on the deck. The other end of the ropes are fastened with metal and loops to the dock.

In just a few minutes, the ramp is secured, the rails are removed, and the carriages begin plodding onto the mainland.

As my carriage lumbers along the broken roadway, I check the radio that will allow me to communicate with the island in case of emergency. The channel is left open, only used when absolutely necessary. The frequency is boosted by a tower built about ten years after the Collapse to extend the range of the radios. Some magical powers still amaze me.

Not everyone has magic. Most of the common people we encounter don't. But all the royal family have some form of magic. In fact, a king won't marry a woman without magic. It's necessary to keep our bloodline strong so we can continue protecting the people.

"Maybe you'll find a powerful woman who will floor you and take your mind off Nora," Dominic teased before I left the island. As if I needed a reminder that she caught Cypress's attention, and my chances are even worse than they were before.

Not that I would ever be allowed any of the women selected as Tribute until Cypress dismisses them. It's just the way things are done. Usually, marriage happens by birth order. The oldest first, then the second, down the line—except for the Keeper of Tides, who is married to his job.

I'm last in line.

Not that I'm in a rush. Women are nice to look at, but a distraction all the same. It serves me better to remain focused on my job as Captain of Tides and ensure the safety of our island. My priority is first to the safety and security of the Kingdom of Tides.

We pass along the streets of a once massive city. In the center of the skyscrapers, an enormous crater serves as a landmark to the battle that once took place here. I've been along these streets enough times to know the best route, as have many of my men. We traverse the toppled buildings, mounds of rubble, broken bridges, and skeletal remains of unusable automobiles without any difficulty.

One of the buildings we pass always catches my eye. The dome of the building is collapsed and the glass doors long-since destroyed, but the metal birds on the side remain steadfast in flight. Despite the terrible state of the building, they continue evermore.

I stopped on one trip through the abandoned city a year ago. The inside of the building is ruined. The floors are either caved in or unsafe to cross. Ancient relics lay wedged amidst the rubble either broken, bent, or hidden completely from sight. I couldn't tell whether the skeletal remains of people and animals were from the Collapse or part of the once great museum.

The building did have snowshoes that proved useful on several occasions, though. And my long gray overcoat was pilfered from the wreckage inside as well. The overcoat fits me perfectly, as if it were just waiting for me to come along and collect it.

Others have taken items from the building as well. Nat is quite proud of the gun he stole. An original, he is certain. And it came complete with the wooden box and pieces. Not that it works any longer.

It takes nearly two hours to maneuver around the crumbling city and reach the outskirts. By my best estimation, we will reach the first community by nightfall. Nearly nine hours by carriage, with frequent stops to water and rest the horses.

13

GAVIN

THE DEPARTMENT OF SECURITY building is close to the northern edge of Elpis. It's just one of many reclaimed buildings since the expansion of the city. The concrete building is very symmetrical with its rigid lines that stagger downward. It reminds me of the top of a building from before the collapse that I read about once. The Empire State Building, but without the pointed tip.

Paige marches alongside me, dressed in her Specialist uniform. I glance down at my own clothes as we enter the rotating doors. My navy-blue dress pants and pale blue-gray dress shirt must look strange beside her. Am I overdressed? This is what I would wear for work meetings, but is it overkill here at the DS? I look like Dad.

We approach the reception desk in the wide lobby. Paige has clearance to enter the building, but I have to check in.

Once I'm cleared to continue, Paige and I take the elevator to the fourth floor where our designated briefing room will be.

Everything about the inside of this building is clean and clear of clutter. No table or floor plants like in the DoST building. The walls are plain beige stone with matching marble floors polished to a shine. There aren't even pictures or paintings or any sort of décor on the walls. My office is littered with them.

As we walk toward the briefing room, my stomach twists in knots. I suppose it's too late to change my mind.

An older woman in uniform stops us at the doorway into Room 411. I try peering over Paige's shoulder to see more, but the room is hard to see past her. The uniformed woman checks our names against her list, then uses bioprints to verify our identities. We each press our index finger to a tablet to certify ourselves and activate the tablet. Then it is handed over.

Paige enters before me, emitting an air of confidence with each fluid motion. I trail in behind her hoping no one looks at me, hugging my tablet close to my chest. I want to see what's on it but assume we will be given further details in the briefing.

The room is set up much like a theater, with five tiered rows of seats spread out on either side of the center aisle. Each row has twenty seats, and each seat has a fold-up desk arm on the right.

Paige makes her way to the front row, and I wish we could melt into the back somewhere. But I follow her, determined to stick close to her side.

Only four others are in the briefing room when we enter. Are there more coming?

A boy in the right front row looks up as Paige turns left. He scoffs at her—a look that completely destroys the handsome, chiseled features of his face.

"Both of you, huh?" he says.

I frown, wondering why that makes him so disgusted. Before I can reply, Paige takes my arm and pulls me away from the man.

"Don't," she commands under her breath. "It will only encourage him."

We settle into chairs beside one another, and I try my best to ignore him, but he keeps staring at us. My throat tightens as I scan the room to see the other three eyeing us in a discomforting way as well.

"I knew it," he says, playing to the audience now. "Didn't I tell you the Powers kid would be along? Looks like we get both of them."

"Kid?" I frown. I'm easily older than he is.

"Gav, stop," Paige mumbles. But she ignores her own advice and leans forward, smiling sweetly at the boy. "I'm surprised to see you here, Easton. I thought they wanted the best on this mission."

Easton. Ah. Now I know who he is. I can't help analyzing him, the boy who gives my sister such a hard time at work. He is on the mission with us? That will complicate matters. He's Somatic, without a doubt. His massive shoulders and the strain on his uniform around his muscles makes it obvious. A Strongarm, by my best guess.

"They do," Easton retorts sharply. "Some of us have to actually work for our place."

Paige just rolls her eyes and presses her back into the seat, crossing her arms over her chest. "That argument is getting real old. Can't come up with a better quip?"

As the two of them continue arguing, I activate my tablet with my bioprint and quickly scroll through some of the data—particularly that which relates to Easton. It's a good idea to know as much about our team as possible. Whether Paige likes it or not, he was chosen just like we were.

My brows climbs as I see Easton's dossier. Paige has always complained about him, called him an idiot, but the information before me doesn't reflect her assessment. Which means whatever feud is between them is personal—or that they are a couple of Alphas fighting to be the top dog.

"Couldn't handle this mission alone so you had to drag your big brother along, huh?" Easton remarks.

I don't look up from my tablet as I continue scrolling through information for the other team members. "According to the dossiers, her assessments are above yours in all but..." I slide my finger along the surface. "...brute strength. Easton Sinclair, Strongarm, eighteen, raised in Pax House, second highest Specialist of your class."

Paige glances over my shoulder.

I raise my gaze to meet Easton's, noting the venom he is shooting my way. "Your response to our position makes perfect sense, but I assure you, when we are out there, you will need me. No one else is as accurate as I am when it comes to electrodynamic and radioactive analytics, and I have a perfect base knowledge of the landscape we will be visiting as well as the technological capabilities to discern the message and its source. Our placement here holds as much merit as anyone else in this room."

Easton gapes at me.

"Perhaps more so," I add.

Easton shakes his head, but I'm already scrolling through the dossier for another teammate. The woman two rows behind Easton—Olivia, age twenty-eight—who watched the entire encounter with wide eyes and is now scrolling through her tablet just as I am. A Psychometrist. I suppose that could be a useful Power on this mission. Based on her own professional advancement listed, she's quite capable and came by personal recommendation from Dad's friend Lily.

Three seats over from Olivia is our healer—Doctor Eli Adams, twenty-seven, advanced medical scores indicating a strong base knowledge. His Healing Hands Power seems to focus on both disease detection and cleansing. Both useful skills if we do end up with radiation poison in the field. He watches the exchange with apparent discomfort, shifting in his seat and drumming his fingers on his tablet. His long face and hooked nose remind me of a bird.

The last member of the team sits in the second row behind Paige and I. Harper Blue, twenty. Her blonde hair marks her out as an oddball in this group of dark-haired individuals, but her eyes are very keen as she stares at me. I chew my lip and avert my gaze. Harper's Power list is impressive. Her Enhanced Vision is classified as FlexVision. Three-sixty vision, night vision, short and long-distance sight, and soundwave perception. Having so many variations of a single Power is rare. Not as rare as my resume, but impressive still.

"So, you think you're better than the rest of us?" Easton snaps, drawing my attention back to him.

"What?" That wasn't what I mean at all.

"Leave my brother alone, Easton." Paige sighs.

"He is better than we are," Olivia says, eyeing me once more. "Do you really have Powers from three of the Four Branches of Powers?"

I click off the tablet and gaze at the white screen at the front of the room. "Yes." Suddenly it feels like the entire room—the people, the chairs, the walls, everything—are all staring at me. It's an unreasonable reaction I can't control.

The door to the room closes with a *thunk* that silences everyone and draws all eyes to the aisle.

Levi—the Department of Security Director and one of my dad's closest friends—marches toward the head of the room with another woman I don't know. Based on the stripes on her uniform, she is a Major. Both are all business as they reach the head of the room and activate the massive holoscreen behind them. The Department of Security logo spins in place.

All banter amongst the team members halts as we pay close attention.

Levi starts by welcoming everyone and thanking them for volunteering for Project Restoration. I'm not sure I would call it volunteering, but I don't argue with him.

"For the time being, everything pertaining to this mission will be deemed highly classified," Levi continues. "Leaking information will result in severe punishment. Only the Council of Representatives and Department Directors have details. You will discuss this mission with no one outside of this room. I will give you one last chance to leave. If you stay, you accept the terms."

He pauses, eyeing each of us in turn, saving Paige and I for last. It seems he lingers longest on the two of us—on me—like he wants us to leave. Did Dad ask him to apply a little pressure to see if we would change our minds? Unless Paige gets up, I'm not going anywhere. I will her to do just that. If she leaves, I don't have to travel beyond the borders of Elpis.

Everyone remains firmly fixed in their seats, eyes forward. No one even shifts.

Levi nods.

The Major taps a button on her tablet and the holoscreen display changes. A bird's eye view of Elpis appears, including the road to the Greenhouse a few miles outside of the city and the red ring created by a series of laser lights forty miles around the perimeter of the city in a perfect circle. Paige, Easton, and I are the only ones who don't appear surprised by the red ring. The other three lean a little closer, squinting at it.

"Five years ago, the Minister of Elpis and I discovered a barrier around the city we previously did not know existed," Levi begins. "After some investigative work, we learned this barrier was created to protect the city from the dangers of the outside world.

The Council of Representatives voted to keep the barrier down and increase security around the city limits. The Department of Science and Technology has been watching the area for signs of danger. Leaving it up was too dangerous to the citizens of Elpis."

Voted. He makes it sound like such a peaceful thing. Dad fought hard to sway the vote to keep it down. The barrier is powered by a green crystal called a Power stone. It absorbs Powers and stores them for gradual emission. But whomever touches the stone will lose their Power and die. Dad also discovered the stone was gradually drawing on Powers just through proximity to maintain its job—keeping the barrier up and running. If they left the barrier up, the Power stone would have run out of Powers, leaving the city vulnerable if something was out there. The only way to recharge the stone is to have people sacrifice themselves to give their Powers to it. That was not a conversation Dad was willing to have with the people.

Instead of leaving the barrier up, they trained Specialists like my sister, as well as a whole floor of security analysts, to watch as far out from the city as we safely can. Not that security has ventured much beyond the barrier limit. Returning to safety means sticking close. Anyone outside the barrier when it goes back up will be trapped outside of it.

I glance at Easton. He would have been thirteen when Pax House was moved from its previous location over the old Crow Homestead—ancestral home of the founding father of our city and secret location of the Power stone. Dad had worried the children living there would lose their Powers over time. How long was Easton there before the orphanage was moved? He certainly doesn't *look* like he lost any Power.

"A new training program was created in the Department of Security," Levi continues. "Paige and Easton here are two of our top graduates from that program. Their training is focused on patrolling and venturing beyond our known borders."

The Major taps her tablet and the image on the screen changes to the signal Aron and I discovered a week ago.

"Last week, the need for the barrier changed. Gavin was among the first to discover a signal which just reaches the edge of the furthest sector of the wasteland beyond the city." Levi points at the pulsing signal. "The Council and I agree that this signal could be a sign of survivors in the wastelands—and a potential danger to Elpis. Project Restoration will be an ongoing series of missions coordinated between myself, the Major here, and Colonel Pond."

As if on cue, the Major taps the tablet once more and a trail animates from the eastern edge of Elpis all the way to the edge of the signal's range. Levi carries on without missing a beat.

"Your first mission is data collection only. Harper will drive the team to the designated location marked on your devices. The drive should take no more than a day in the solar truck. Gavin will use his location tracking skills to ensure you stop at the right location. Paige and Easton will be the security team, ensuring the safety of team members while beyond our range. Olivia will use her Psychometry on the landscape and any items the team may encounter, then record her findings for later review. Doctor Eli Adams will be along in case there is a medical emergency."

Levi continues his speech, showing everyone what we know about the landscape—and the bits of grassland surprise everyone but me. I've seen all this before. The orders are clear. Go to the designated location, gather as much information about the landscape and the signal as possible, then return to Elpis with the reports. After that, Levi makes it clear that future missions will be coordinated based on the information we collect.

"No one has gone so far from the city before," Levi cautions. "It's important to understand that you will be alone out there. We can hear signals up to five hundred miles out, but no farther. The closer you can stay to our range, the better. All security emergencies will be dealt with in the field by Paige and Easton. We expect this should take you anywhere from three days to a week, depending on the data collection."

Paige glances past me at Easton, who puffs up with self-importance in his seat.

"Any preliminary questions before we get deeper into the details?" Levi asks.

I can already sense the impending battle of wills between our security detail. Nervously, I raise my hand and chew my lower lip.

Levi raises a brow. "Yes, Gavin?"

"I, um, well it seems important to know who the senior officer will be among us," I say, cursing the tremor in my voice as all eyes turn to me. "I mean, in case there is a disagreement, we should all know who has final say."

"Barring a medical emergency—which would put Doctor Adams in charge—it will be up to the Senior Analyst to keep the mission on track," Levi says.

The room suddenly shrinks, along with my lungs. My head spins. "Me, sir?"

"You are the Senior Analyst," Levi says flatly, though I swear I hear a touch of amusement in his tone. "You are the one who will know when you have enough data and where the team might need to move to gather more. Doctor Adams, as I mentioned, will take over if medical attention is critical."

I open my mouth, but no words will come out. It's as if my throat has closed itself off.

Easton is leaning forward now, a hand pressed against his knee. "Sir, what if there is a security emergency? You can't seriously believe an analyst is best equipped to handle the issue."

Levi's lips thin in a tight line as he turns sharply to take in Easton, then Paige. "I expect my *highly trained* and skilled Specialists to be able to work together and coordinate security under any and all circumstances. If you feel that is not something you can handle, we can find two replacements easily enough."

"Yes, sir," they reply together.

Though they agree with one another here, I wonder what will happen in the wastelands. It's obvious these two hate one another. Perhaps I will have to find a way to get the others to help me act as a buffer between the two.

Levi seems satisfied enough with their responses. He continues explaining the next few days of preparing—physical exams, equipment gathering and loading, individual requirements in the field. I fight off a yawn as my stomach grumbles for lunch. Is this what Paige's job is normally like? I've been bored out of my mind for hours as the details are broken down.

We break for lunch, provided to us so we don't have to leave the Department of Security building. I watch as Olivia and Doctor Adams sit in silence together. Paige reluctantly strikes up a friendly conversation with Harper about each of their jobs before this. Easton sinks into the seat beside me as I check my phone for a message from Aron. He was pretty upset with me last night. But there's no signal in this building. Probably on purpose.

"So, looks like it's you and me buddying up, Powers," Easton says softly before ripping very indelicately into his sandwich.

I wince. "The name is Gavin. And we are all 'buddied up'." I glance at him curiously as he devours his lunch. "Why do you hate my sister so much?"

He rolls his eyes. "Like I would tell *you*. And I don't hate her."

"Then I guess we have nothing more to say." I finish my food and make my way back into the briefing room.

It isn't long before everyone else returns. Paige is last in, but she looks like she wants to ask me what happened as she sits.

Levi doesn't give her a chance. He picks up right where he left off.

The only entertaining part of the briefing is when Levi asks me to explain what we know about the land beyond Elpis and what we are looking for.

No one else in the room seems interested in anything I have to say, but my excitement still pours out as I break down the data we have and what we need to gather. Radioactivity. Topography. Wildlife. And, of course, information about the signal and what it could mean for Elpis or the world.

Despite my excitement as I explain all of this in detail to the rest of the team, Easton nearly nods off. Paige rubs at her eyes several times. Only Olivia seems interested, scrolling along on her tablet and making notes or nodding in response. She even asks a few intelligent questions.

Once we are done for the day—each with a better understanding of what we are to do and what is expected of us—I make my way to the exit quickly. I just want to get home and do something to stimulate my brain. Reviewing my individual responsibilities on the tablet seems like an ideal way to study before tomorrow.

In just two more days, Paige and I will be leaving Elpis. The prospect is frightening.

14

ZEPHYR

THE MEN CONTINUE CHECKING all the makeshift log homes in the small settlement as I wait beside the blazing bonfire. At this time of year, cold snaps can happen quickly even this far inland. The bonfire keeps everyone warm enough as we wait for the all-clear.

The men move efficiently, pushing into homes in pairs and extricating any who dared hide inside. So far, nearly two dozen men, women, and children kneel in the dirt of the community square. All the log homes circle the large square. The weathered outer walls would blend with the forest around us if it weren't for the open space in the center.

I pace languidly along the line of subjects, hands clasped behind my back. This is not a part of the job which I enjoy. But if I don't show strength and confidence in this, we could end up under attack. I won't risk my men.

This particular community has been part of the kingdom for just over sixty years. Long enough for most of them to have experienced the Tribute two or three times already. Long enough for most of the residents to forget a time when they were not ruled by the King of Tides. But a couple of the subjects here remember.

The community elder raises his chin, glaring at me in defiance. "We were told we had another year until it was time for Tribute. We are not ready."

I ignore him. Giving him a response might make him feel like he has an advantage or opportunity. I can't give it to him. He is one of only two here old enough to remember a time before we swept through and rescued them from destruction. The farther a community is from the island, the longer they had to survive without help from the Kingdom of Tides.

"We don't have anyone strong enough to qualify as Tribute or recruit," the elder continues. His unshaven face and thick eyebrows are peppered with silver that shimmers in the bonfire light.

I march closer to the line as a family is forced to join the cluster of kneeling subjects. For a moment, I close my eyes and breathe deeply. The scent of campfire and body odor slide across my senses.

I continue along the line, reaching out with my magic, hoping to sense someone strong enough to make the journey back with us. Cypress said only the strongest.

A few women whimper. Some of the children cry, hushed by mothers. In all, I can sense every one of them. The elder isn't wrong. While I do sense a few with weak magic, there are not many. And nothing noteworthy.

Deep despair and pleading to leave them alone slams into me. I freeze in my tracks. My eyes snap open, able to sense strong magic.

Before me, a boy of twelve cowers beside his mother. She holds him protectively, trembling violently. But he glares up at me as if determined to turn me away.

I crouch in front of him and frown. I hate to use my magic on a child, but it seems I have no choice. As I reach out toward his youthful face, he jerks back. His mother releases a startled cry.

"No. Please," she sobs.

"Just leave us in peace," the boy says. Despite the determination on his face, his voice quivers.

"I won't hurt you," I say softly. My fingers brush his temple. The moment I contact his skin, he relaxes, dropping his gaze to the dirt. "You have some strength. What's your name?"

He licks his lips. The determination in him evaporates swiftly at my touch. "Finrik."

"Nice to meet you, Finrik."

"Leave him alone!" the elder growls. But when he tries climbing to his feet, Nat grabs his shoulder and shoves him down hard against the dirt.

I carry on, ignoring his outburst. "I am Lord Zephyr, Captain of Tides. Have you heard of me?"

The boy's eyes widen. He nods.

For the past two years, I have reached out to these communities in peace. If the subjects are compliant, it makes life easier for everyone. Last time I was here, this boy didn't show any signs of magic. It must have been a recent development.

"Have you ever wondered what it would be like to sail across the Great Lakes?" I ask.

"You can't take him," the boy's mother says sharply, desperately.

I glare at her. She shrinks away. "Finrik is nearly a man. He can speak for himself."

"He is only twelve," she whimpers.

"Old enough." I dismiss her and return attention to the boy. "See that man there?" I point over at Nat, still looming over the elder, holding him down. Finrik nods. "He was just like you. Exceptionally adept at Absorption. It took ten men to stop him once he had the energy stored to fight them. And he was only ten. In the end, he went along with them. Do you know why?"

Finrik sniffles and shakes his head.

"Because he knew he could achieve greater things, live a better life in the Capital." I offer him a smile, which seems to calm his nerves. This time, I raise my gaze to meet his mother's. "Isn't that what you would want for your child? The best life he can live?"

"Not with you lot!" the elder snaps.

"He would never have to worry about his next meal," I continue, ignoring the old man. "Or how to keep a roof over his head. He would be warm, fed, housed, and welcomed."

Silence settles over the group, punctuated by the snapping of the bonfire. Dozens of subjects kneel in a cluster, surrounded by my men. All eyes are locked on the mother. I don't have to read minds to sense their desperation to keep Finrik here. He would be a useful weapon to help protect them, no doubt.

War wages in the mother's eyes as she considers the offer. Life out here in the wild is unpredictable. If the elements don't get to you, starvation will. These communities don't remain small because we come and collect the strongest among them. They remain small because survival out here is nearly impossible. Nature keeps them contained. That's why they need the Kingdom.

Finrik would be much better off than any of them could dream. And he would likely live a long, healthy life.

I raise my chin and call over my shoulder. "Soldiers, if you were saved by the Capital, show your devotion!"

A loud round of "ah-oo!" thunders through the camp. The subjects whimper and cower closer to one another. A few jump in alarm. Well over half my men came from communities like these. Just last year, I discovered a young man who could walk through walls. He was hard to catch, but once we did and I offered him the same future, he accepted. Now he is happy on the island and one of the top cadets.

"You see," I say in the most reassuring voice I can manage. "What do you say, Finrik?"

"Wh-what about my mother?" he asks, glancing at her.

I sigh, casting a sympathetic smile at him. "She cannot come along. But I can offer her a healthy reward."

At a snap of my fingers, one of my men grabs a sack from a carriage and marches over. He drops it at my side.

"This is just the first of many," I say, opening the sack wide enough to show the stock of food, seeds, and bread. "Each year you serve, another delivery will arrive for her. She can help this entire community with these deliveries."

One man roughly my age snorts in derision, sneering at the promise.

I glare at him. "Is there a problem?"

"Those deliveries never come," he says sharply. Anger rolls off him in waves. But I don't understand where it stems from.

"I have helped load these myself since I was a boy," I reply calmly.

"Maybe you should ask your *king* where they actually go, then, Lord of Tides." His intense hatred and cynicism aren't unexpected, but I don't understand this particular point.

It also doesn't escape my notice that he referred to the king as mine and not his. I rise, marching toward him with a hand on my knife, still tucked safely in my belt. The crowd between us parts to give me space. When we are inches apart, I stop, glaring down at him.

"You mean *our* king," I correct, voice laced with steel. "He is yours, as well."

He raises his chin, nose curling in disgust. Then he spits at my boots. "I don't serve a king I've never met." A steely resolve firms his face. "For all I know, it's you, *Lord* of Tides."

Suddenly, he lunges forward, reaching for my knife. The men launch into action as other subjects attempt fighting back.

I throw a punch in the man's jaw as he grapples for my knife. He takes the punch surprisingly well. The knife is free from my belt, his hand clasped tight over my own as we struggle for control. He twists my wrist out, trying to force me to release. Pain lances up my arm. I bring my knee up into his chin. This time he lets go and falls back. I add an extra kick to his ribs for good measure. The blade of the knife presses against his throat as I kneel on his chest.

"My mother gave me this knife," I growl.

He glares at me as blood spills from his nose.

All around us, the soldiers use their magic to pin subjects to the ground or knock them out cold. A few are wrapped up in a mess of vines. The fight is over almost as quickly as it began. The people are no match for our magic-enhanced soldiers.

"Tie this one up," I command.

Vines shoot up out of the ground, pinning the man down. I back out of the way and slide the knife back into my belt.

The crying has begun anew. My gaze sweeps the crowd. Everyone is either pinned down or cowering in terror.

But Finrik stands over his mother and the sack of food. Though he is slight of frame, he exudes a confidence I admire for a kid his age. His hands are clenched into fists at his sides, jaw set. He would make a great soldier. I can see it clearly.

"The Crown will not tolerate disobedience," I say loudly, taking in each of the subjects in turn. "I will leave you to decide proper justice for this man. But he must be punished severely before we return in the spring."

I turn to the boy. "What do you think, Finrik?" I motion around the meager community. "Do you want to stay here and carry on as you always have? Full of loathing and hunger. Or will you come along with us to live a life of fulfilment and hearty meals?"

The boy swallows, examining the aftermath. Bruised limbs and bloodied lips. No casualties—for which I am thankful—and no one left to resist. Then his eyes meet mine.

I smile.

15

PAIGE

THE SIX OF US stand beside the solar truck—already loaded with equipment for the mission—as Levi, Aunt B, and the Council of Representatives stand together behind the Minister of Elpis. He eyes each of us as he speaks. I ignore most of what he says. It isn't for my benefit, but to inspire the others with me.

This morning, as Gavin and I prepared to leave, Mom hovered over us, ensuring we had everything we needed ready to go. I had to beg her to stay home and not make our departure more awkward with the motherly farewells in front of the team. Then she gathered our phones. In the wasteland, we won't have service, so everyone is to leave them behind. Instead, the team will have old hand radios Gavin tinkered with to extend the radio frequency. Why he couldn't do that with our phones, I don't understand even after his lengthy explanation.

Beside me, Gavin stands stiff as he hangs on every word Dad says. Sometimes, I wish I had more of his curiosity.

Dad goes on to explain why the barrier was deemed necessary over a hundred years ago. "We were not alone in the world, like we were taught. There is every chance we *still* aren't. The purpose of Project Restoration is twofold. To learn if there is any chance we can begin restoring the world broken by war and Powers, and to prove, beyond a doubt, that we are not alone. The six of you will be at the helm of this discovery. Take that privilege seriously. History will tell your story, for better or worse."

Harper shuffles feet beside me, her arms folded over her chest in a manner that is more self-comforting than anything. I glance from the corner of my eye at Easton at the end of our line. He stands tall and proud, chin raised high and chest puffed out, hands folded behind his back. For all his harassment about my father, he certainly displays a need to give off an air of determination and importance. As if he wants Dad to notice him. I resist the urge to roll my eyes.

"The greatest journey in your life is not where you stand as much as in what direction you move," Dad says. His gaze falls on me for just a moment and I swear I see his expression soften, but it passes so quickly I'm not sure if I truly saw it at all. "And it begins with a single step. So take your step, venture into unknown, learn something about the world, and about yourself." This time I'm certain his meaningful gaze is trying to tell me something. "Then return to us swiftly and safely."

Levi claps his hands once. "Load up, team!"

Gavin breaks away, shuffling toward the truck and climbing into the front seat. Harper climbs in beside him and closes the door. I make my way around to the passenger side. Olivia joins me.

"There's something about him that really gets my blood pumping," she says, leaning close and keeping her voice low as she glances back over her shoulder.

"Who?" I try to follow her gaze. Is she talking about Doctor Adams?

"The Minister." She opens the back door and smirks at me.

I scrunch up my nose. "Gross. That's my dad, you know. You can share that kind of crap with Harper." Before she can say more, I climb into the front seat beside Gavin.

"What about me?" Harper asks, eyeing the two of us.

"Paige can't handle the idea of her dad being a good-looking guy," Olivia says, sliding into the seat behind me.

Gavin laughs for a moment, then chokes on his amusement when he realizes they aren't joking. At least I'm not alone.

I glance toward Dad and frown. He is huddled close to Easton, and the two are exchanging words. Easton nods at whatever Dad says, and my stomach twists in knots. I hope he isn't asking Easton to look after me. That won't help anything between Easton and me. A moment later, Easton shakes Dad's hand, then climbs into the backseat behind Harper in the driver's seat. His gaze lands on me and I abruptly face forward.

"Let's move out, Harper," Easton says.

It only takes us a few minutes to reach the eastern edge of Elpis. Gavin already has his tablet activated and is tracking our location as we approach the barrier. No one speaks. All six of us fall into anxious silence.

As we approach the red lights marking the barrier, the truck slows to a stop. A drone hovers nearby. I know it's recording us, and I do my best to keep my face forward and appear impassive about this entire endeavor, even though my insides are twisting endlessly.

"Barrier is down," someone reports over one the handheld radios. "Go for crossing."

Easton opens his door and mutters, "Like hell."

"What are you doing?" I call to him.

He pauses after hopping out. "No offense, but if they are wrong, I would rather not die today."

"Throw a stone at it," Gavin says, eyes glued to the tablet.

I realize that, while the drone is recording, Gavin is the one controlling it. He slides his finger over the screen, and the drone flies up and lands on the magnetic holding pad on the roof of the truck.

Easton does as Gavin instructed, hefting a stone he found on the ground at the barrier. It passes the red lights without dissolving. Satisfied, he climbs back in. I won't tell him that I'm grateful for his forethought. It will only inflate his ego, and he doesn't need help with that. Jealousy worms into my stomach, mingling with the already writhing nerves. I wish I had thought of double-checking.

Harper guides the truck forward. I hold my breath as we approach the red lights. Once we reach the other side, a collective exhale resounds in the truck cab. Turns out, I wasn't the only one worried about it.

"We're through," Easton reports, glancing behind us. "And clear. Reinstate the barrier."

A minute later, we receive confirmation that the barrier is back up. Until we return, it will remain up to protect the city.

"I don't understand why they don't just leave that thing up all the time," Olivia says from behind me. "The DS Director said it's been down for a few years now. Why is it such a big deal?"

Gavin and I exchange a glance. Should we tell them? They have a right to know, considering what we are doing and why.

"Who knows why the Council does what it does," Doctor Adams says flatly.

"These two do," Easton adds.

I shift in my seat so I can see those in the backseat. Easton's gaze is locked on Gavin and me. He noticed our own uneasy glance.

"Only by accident," I say. Hopefully, he can hear the sharp edge in my tone. "Right place at the right time, you know."

"You mean at home," he adds with a grimace.

I roll my eyes to add extra emphasis to my words, "Get off it, already. None of us controls who our parents are."

Harper must sense the tension between the two of us because she adopts a light, cheerful tone. "So why is it such a big deal, then?"

Gavin clicks off his tablet and watches the backseat in the rearview mirror. Neither of us speaks. I'm not sure I even fully understand the why of it, but I understand enough to know that Dad was adamant about what happened.

"The barrier has limited Powers left," Gavin finally breaks the silence. "To preserve that Power, they decided to deactivate the barrier until it was deemed necessary. There really was no alternative."

I prop my chin on my fist and smirk at Gavin.

Easton says, "We have more than enough resources to generate power."

Gavin licks his lips. "It—it isn't that simple. It draws power from... well, Powers. To feed more Power into it would require ... well, it would be costly. Anyone who feeds their Power into the stone dies. Dad never would ask anyone to sacrifice themselves like that when we don't even know how long that sacrifice would add Power to the barrier, or how necessary it even is any longer."

Once more silence settles over the team. Easton stares out the window. Doctor Adams fidgets with his jacket sleeves. Miles pass by the window as we all contemplate what might happen if the barrier fails and there *is* danger in the outside world. Or at least, that's what I can't stop thinking about. What will we find out here? What sort of danger will it pose to our people?

"I remember the night before Liberation Day," Olivia says softly, her gaze fixed beyond the window at the arid landscape. "I was six. My parents couldn't keep me in bed at bedtime. I kept having nightmares about when the DMA took my uncle in for retesting."

Retesting. I heard Dad's stories a hundred times. The old Directorate had instituted a Proposition that required anyone with low-ranking Powers to retest and submit for application to join the Department of Military Affairs—the DMA. They used brute force to arrest anyone who qualified. Not everyone survived retesting.

"This boy suddenly appeared on every holotv in our house," Olivia continues. "He was so young, and I was curious why he was on the tv." Olivia hugs herself tight. "But his words... even at six they moved me. I curled up under my blanket and cried as I listened to his speech." Her voice tightens. "And the images he showed us... other people being treated like my uncle ... or worse." Olivia releases a breath slowly.

I know what she is talking about. Dad's broadcast to the entire city the night before he and the Protectorate tore down the Directorate. It's part of our history class now, and I've heard the speech so many times I have it memorized.

"I begged my parents to do something," Olivia continues, "but they refused to go to the Administration Courtyard the next day. They said it wouldn't be safe. I resented them a little at the time, but ...after... I'm glad they didn't go."

Most of the protesters in the courtyard that day had either been swallowed up by the earth—quite literally—or killed when Paragon Tower and the Admin Building fell.

"My dad went," Doctor Adams whispers. "I didn't understand what was going on, but my mom begged him to stay home. He said something about not being able to do nothing. He never came home."

Olivia reaches over and takes his hand, giving it a reassuring squeeze.

Tears prick my eyes and I face forward. Gavin slides an arm around my shoulders and hugs me against his side. I rest my head on his shoulder. Dad was against what happened to both buildings, but he had been the one who inspired all those people into action. The weight of his decisions presses down on me. I understand why he said he didn't want me to bear such a burden. His actions changed the lives of everyone in Elpis—and not all were for the better.

"My parents were there, too," Easton says. "One of those Power-removing bullets the DMA had hit my mom. She survived but lost her Power. The depression never went away. Then one day she just...gave up."

I prop my chin on Gavin's shoulder and eye Easton, but he is sneering out the window. Does he resent his mother for quitting? Uncle Alex told us that having a Power removed is like having a piece of oneself ripped out. It breaks you, turns you into a husk of yourself. That Easton's mother managed to overcome long enough to have him reveals her true strength. Most people don't survive a year without finding some new purpose.

Does he blame me for what happened to his mother? Is that why he hates me so much? She lost her Power because of my dad, then gave up like most people who lose their Powers do. If that is why he resents me, I don't know how to overcome the hate.

"That day changed everyone in some way or another," Doctor Adams says with deep compassion. "It was an ugly day that gave birth to something beautiful. Sometimes, before we can fix something, we have to tear it apart."

His prophetic words end the conversation by some unspoken agreement.

Gavin turns his tablet back on, scrolling through data and checking Harper's speed periodically. When he looks up, he examines the terrain in front of us, then nods and mutters something to himself before tapping a few commands on the screen. I don't understand what he is doing, so I busy myself watching the wasteland pass.

Harper drives the truck alongside the remains of an ancient highway. The old concrete is broken down and unsafe to navigate over, but it still serves as a guide heading straight east. A few chunks are buckled by earth or heat compression. Others are forced toward the sky where a tree grows. Abandoned and rusting vehicles break up the roadway. Tires are long since gone, leaving behind only cracked, rusted, or broken rims.

After nearly two hundred miles of the same scenery, the landscape bores me to sleep.

———— ❧ ————

MUSHROOM CLOUDS OF SMOKE rise into the night sky. A mountain rises from flat earth right before my eyes, growing toward the clouds so quickly boulders tumble toward my feet. Water rises from within the earth, creating a river winding down from the mountains. I watch in awe as the world is remade before my eyes.

"Paige, it's okay," a man says from somewhere behind me. His hand falls on my shoulder, then slides down my arm toward my hand.

Red energy pulses in my palms, growing so powerful it takes my breath away. My heartbeat increases. Panic clenches me as tears roll down my cheeks.

"I can't stop it!" I cry.

"I'm here," he says, but when I turn my blurred eyes to gaze at him over my shoulder, all I can see is his tan skin. The features of his face are obscured.

The red light spreads up my arms, shifting like fog as it swirls around my limbs.

"I'm here," he says again, more gently as he takes my hand.

⁂

I WAKE WITH A start, heart pounding. Gavin's hand is in mine, squeezing it.

"We're here," he says, eyeing me as if he has said this already.

But I can't steady my racing heart. That nightmare felt so real. Was I recreating the world? That's not possible. I don't have any Naturalist Powers. And certainly nothing on that scale. But the panic as that intense red Power enveloped me seemed so real. It still does.

"You okay?" Gavin asks. "Another nightmare?"

Who was the man in the dream? Is it a premotion, like the promotion? What happened is impossible. It's probably just a nightmare fueled by this new adventure into the unknown and my own inadequacy issues.

I only nod in response to Gavin's question. Nightmares caused my insomnia a lot growing up.

"Wanna talk about it?" he asks.

I glance around the truck cab. Everyone else is already unloading the equipment from the back. Perhaps I should tell my brother. I've done it before, and he has always talked me down. Plus, he's clever. He might know what it means—if it means anything at all. But I can't bring myself to explain it. I'm not even sure how to start. Instead, I shake my head.

Gavin pats my hand once more, then slides across the driver's seat and out the door.

I take a moment to collect myself, observing the landscape around the truck. Harper and Doctor Adams are setting up the thermal tent, attaching it to the truck like we did in training, and laying the heated flooring. The tent turns the back of the truck into a sort of camper-tent hybrid to keep us out of the elements and safe from potential radiation. Olivia helps Gavin move the computer and data collection equipment into place. Easton scouts the area to secure our location.

The truck is parked on the southern side of the highway, surrounded by long grass and trees—so many trees! Their colors blaze with life in stark contrast to those we saw a few hundred miles back. Brilliant shades of red, purple, and yellow leaves glow in the light of the setting sun. While it's not my first time seeing color-changing leaves—we do have them in Elpis—I never expected to see them in the wastelands. And they're so *tall*.

I slip on my mask before opening the door and stepping out. Until Gavin gives us the all-clear, we are required to wear protective masks. Our uniforms are already fitted with protective fabrics.

"It's something else, isn't it?" Doctor Adams says as he joins me gazing at the flaming trees. "A wild, untamed earth. The other side of the highway is a different story." He nods behind us.

I step around the truck and climb the embankment to stand on a slab of cracked and overgrown highway.

The skeletons of dilapidated buildings to the north have become part of nature again. Crumbling remains. Piles of rubble. A large building with a collapsed roof and missing windows actually has greenery spilling out, as if the earth is attempting to swallow all signs of former civilization. It looks just as wild and untamed as our side.

"I was wondering," I say, eyeing the landscape around us. "How does a doctor qualify for this mission over another? I mean, aren't all doctors basically the same?"

He raises a brow at me, bemused. "No. We are not all the same. Each of us have different skill sets and experience. We choose what kind of medicine we want to practice." He gives me a half-hearted shrug. "I think I was inspired to become a doctor by Liberation Day. I've always wanted to help cleanse people of illness and mend broken bones. It's why I became an orthopedic doctor. I can set bones and cleanse any potential infections before they become dangerous."

Before his Power even developed? "But what if you ended up with a Power that didn't allow you to become a doctor?"

Doctor Adams watches the clouds as he contemplates this. "I don't believe I ever considered it a real possibility. I just...knew it'd work out." His attention turns to me. "Do you ever wonder if sometimes Powers manifest because we will them to be? Like, what if some people can just *be* something so deep in their bones that the Power manifests to fit it."

I snort and roll my eyes. "No. First of all, you should know that's not how it works. Secondly, if that were the case, I wouldn't have Muscle Memory."

"Are you sure about that? The science is still unclear on how exactly it does work. It can't be predicted before it starts to manifest. There was a whole section of research dedicated to uncovering the truth and all they could determine is that they can't determine it before puberty." He grimaces, then glances back at the others milling around the truck. "I read your dossier. Impressive scores. Even more impressive history. From what I gather, you were close with Bianca Pond growing up. Maybe that closeness made some deep desire in you want to be like her."

Willing our Powers by some subconscious choice? No. That can't possibly be right. I had a lot of role models growing up. Bianca, sure. But also Uncle Alex, Dad's best friend. I was always fascinated with his Electromancy. Mom is pretty powerful creating mist, which served her well working in the Greenhouse.

Dad never had a Power. According to what he learned of himself years ago, he is a carrier for a whole new breed of superpowers. I look down at my hands. I certainly don't feel super.

"Anyway, I was one of ten doctors selected," Adams continues, oblivious to my contemplation. "Most of them backed out." He smiles ruefully. "I was the last on the list. And I have nothing to lose out here."

"You don't have a family back home?"

He shakes his head. "Not that I don't want one, but I can't seem to keep a woman interested in me long enough to take the next step. I could either remain in the city wishing for more, or I could come out here and find something more."

I understand his sentiment. It's a big part of the reason I willingly came along.

"Paige!" Easton calls. He stands in the middle of the highway, his gun holstered on his hip as he points to the dilapidated buildings. "I'm going to scout out the area and make sure nothing is hiding there. Keep your radio on."

I nod, wishing I could go with him, but one of us has to stay with the truck and the others. I pull the radio from my hip and check the frequency, giving him a sound check. He confirms, then pivots north and marches away.

While Easton scouts the city, I patrol around our camp, watching the distance for signs of life. Will there be animals out here? Did animals survive the fallout?

A breeze blows past, and I wish I could remove the mask and smell the air. What does it smell like out here? I raise a hand to let the wind caress my skin.

"Gavin, any news on the readouts?" I ask over my shoulder.

"Almost," he calls from inside the tent.

In the distance, birds call to one another. I spot one as it takes flight from a far-off tree, away from our location. Animals live out here. It must be safe.

"All clear," Gavin calls back.

I remove the mask, already smelling of sweat and plastic. Cool, crisp air rushes to my lungs and I take in a deep breath. Earth and woods. That's what it smells like. I can even taste the damp earth on my tongue. The warmth of the setting sun bathes me. I tip my head back, basking in its glow, praying the ultraviolet rays are safe out here. If they weren't, I know Gavin would have warned us of it before we even left Elpis.

We left Elpis.

The reality of those three words fills me with wonder. I dreamed of grand adventures but never imagined I would be allowed beyond the safe borders of our city.

Yet here I stand.

Five hundred miles from home.

16

GAVIN

FOR THE LAST HOUR, Paige has tried coaxing me out of the tent to "enjoy the wonders of the world around us." But the inside is comfortable and safe. Everything I need to see or know displays on the holoscreen secured to a metal arm on the truck's bed. Besides, the entire reason I'm here is to analyze data and seek the signal. If I ignore it to traipse around outside, I'm not doing my job.

With a few keystrokes in my tablet, I activate sentry mode on the truck. Now the sensors around the vehicle will act as our eyes in case anything comes too close.

"There's nothing out here at all." Easton's voice crackles over the handheld radio I have propped on the desk. "It's pretty eerie, honestly. My only encounters so far have been with a rat and a few skeletal remains. I've cleared a couple of small convenience stores, some housing complexes that might have once been hotels, and several restaurants. This place looks like it was abandoned long before the fallout."

Harper climbs onto the truck bed with me, offering a blanket and a bottle of water. I take the water and set it aside, then spreads out the blanket over me, leaving space for her. It's cold in here despite the heated flooring. She settles beside me, sitting so close I can feel her body heat, then offers me a shy smile.

"*There isn't much more out here.*" Paige's voice sounds over the radio as well. "*A few birds, but not much else. Maybe you should double back so we can set up shifts for night watch.*"

I activate the sensors that will seek out the radio waves, but all it catches is Paige and Easton.

"*Negative,*" he says. "*There's a building ahead with a mostly intact roof. Looks big. I want to clear it before heading back. It would make a good hideout.*"

The lines on the holoscreen rise and fall in tune with their voices. I grimace and snatch up my handheld, pressing the button to activate it. "Let's leave the radio waves open unless we have to communicate. I can't get a read on the mystery signal with our own interference."

I hold my breath, but neither of them says another word. My gaze is glued to the screen for so long, waiting for the radio waves to move, that my vision blurs and my eyes sting. What if we don't catch the signal again? The analyst department only caught it one other time since that first one, and it has been nearly eleven days since.

Just in case, I fiddle with the box the DoST sent along to record the audio of the radio waves. If something is out there, this will record it even if I fall asleep.

Another twenty minutes of silence pass. Doctor Adams enters the tent and sets up his sleeping area. It's cramped on the heated floor laid out on the ground, with just enough space for everyone to sleep close together while leaving a clear path to the exit. Adams glances at me and nods in recognition before settling down for the night.

I pass another half an hour calculating the radiation levels and crosschecking them against the data we received from drones before leaving on the mission. Everything is as we anticipated. The levels appear safe enough, but the radiation is still hiding in plain sight.

Olivia strolls in with her own tablet, tapping a message. A second later, a report appears in my inbox on my tablet. Olivia doesn't bother giving me a rundown before she lays down in a sleeping bag beside Eli. I grimace and open the message.

Harper and I sit in agreeable silence. She watches the equipment with curiosity. During training, everyone was given cursory lessons on how to operate the equipment, but reading the data is a whole other beast that cannot be taught in a few days. Harper asks a few questions as we monitor the data together. Her curiosity stokes my own need to share knowledge with others. I eagerly tell her what I know. There's a comfort between the two of us I don't often experience around others. All her questions are intelligent, which I'm ashamed to admit surprises me a little. She was so quiet and shy in training that I made some assumptions that were clearly unjust.

"Do you know why I came on this mission?" she asks quietly, glancing at the slumbering forms of Olivia and Doctor Adams. I simply shake my head. "The city is overwhelming."

The statement draws my attention away from the monitor. I can understand what she means, finding myself often overwhelmed by everything as well. It's the reason I prefer to go to work and directly home. It's cramped and loud and so busy everywhere.

Harper tucks a strand of her short dark hair behind her ear and leans forward, hugging herself. "Everywhere I look, there are people and flashing signs and moving traffic. Not to mention all the little creatures that scuttle along the streets. I thought coming out here would offer me some relief. I didn't know anything about this mission until I was pulled aside and given my letter from the Council of Representatives."

She pauses, chewing her lower lip. Her dark eyes shimmer as she glances at me. "Honestly, I wasn't even sure I could hack it when I showed up at that first meeting. Figured I would go and find out more, then decide." She reaches over and places a hand on my arm. I resist the urge to withdraw. "It was you, Gavin."

"What was me?"

Harper sighs, then looks back at the monitor. "You were clearly uncomfortable in that meeting, as well, but you stayed. I figured if you had the courage to do this, I could find it in myself as well."

I jerk back. It's hard not to take that as an insult. She thought I was too much of a coward to do this? Does she think so little of me?

Harper yanks her arm back to hugging herself. Her eyes widen and she shakes her head. "I mean no offence. I just meant, well, I admired you that day. Your strength gave me the strength to stay. And I'm glad I did."

Strength... Well, that's something no one has ever associated with me before. Paige is the strong one, the brave one. I cannot reconcile that word with myself.

A yawn forces its way out of Harper. She stretches. "I think I'm on second watch, so I should get sleep."

I mumble goodnight to her, but there is no way I will sleep yet. Not when every little noise draws my attention back to the radio wave monitor. Still nothing.

"Easton, come in," Paige says. I can hear her speaking from right outside the tent. "You've been an hour since checking in. Everything alright out there?"

Silence.

I grumble inwardly about their interference as I scroll through the initial report from Olivia. The news is disheartening. She cannot trace anything more than a few animals so far. Mostly birds, three deer together, and a fox. Nothing for us to worry about. Nothing to indicate other human life out there.

"Easton, check in." Paige ducks her head into the tent long enough to snatch her jacket. She slips it on, then checks the gun.

"What are you doing?" I ask.

"Going to find him."

"Alone?" I straighten. "Paige, you should take someone along."

"You wanna come?" Her umber gaze bores into me. But she already knows the answer.

I back down.

"I thought not." She checks her radio. "I shouldn't be long. If I'm not back in thirty minutes, lock down the tent."

My heart lurches. Thirty minutes and she could be missing as well? Then not only will we be without security, but my sister will be gone. Before I formulate an argument to stop her, Paige ducks out again, securing the flap.

"I'm coming to find you, Easton," she says into the radio. "Don't shoot me again."

Again?

"*Stand down, Powers.*" Easton's voice cracks like a whip over the radio. "*I'm almost back.*"

"That's a relief," Harper mutters as she lays on the truck bed near me.

I frown down at the girl. Why is she sleeping up here with me and the equipment? It's already cramped enough with just me.

Booted feet thump against the ground outside.

"What the hell, Easton?" Paige snaps, not bothering to lower her voice to let anyone inside rest. "You're supposed to check in."

"Worried about me, huh?" I don't have to see Easton's face to imagine the smirk.

"Get over yourself," she says. "This is about protocol. You are supposed to check in every thirty minutes."

Will they come to blows over this? The two certainly don't like each other, but I had hoped we could make it more than one day before they started fighting.

"The boss called for silence unless there was an emergency, which there wasn't," Easton says, oozing nonchalance in his tone.

I wince. He isn't wrong. Though I don't know how I feel about being referred to as "the boss." And I certainly don't like being used as the excuse for his lack of communication. I suppose I will have to remedy that and let him know that he needs to stay in contact periodically, according to their protocols.

Fabric shuffles, and I wonder what is going on, if I should interrupt.

"You have first watch," Easton says. "Keep an eye on the horizon, Powers."

The tent door opens, and Easton's broad shoulders slip through.

"I know how to do my job," Paige snaps, looming behind him. "Just remember how to do yours."

Easton says nothing as he closes the tent flap in her face and secures it. For a moment, he stands near the door staring at me. His broad shoulders are imposing, and I involuntarily shrink back.

"Your sister's a real piece of work," he says, shattering the silence as he turns toward his sleeping bag.

"I can hear you," she snaps from outside.

Easton puts his gun under his pillow and slides into his sleeping bag, then flips her off. Not that she can see him.

I chew my lip. Why would the DS choose these two to go on a critical mission like this? I'm starting to wonder if they will both survive. If the elements don't kill them, they will kill each other.

17

Zephyr

None of the communities are close together. Each requires at least a full day of carriage riding. The results have been abysmal so far, and I wonder if Cypress will be upset by the low number of Tributes on offer this season. Maybe it will encourage him to wait another year.

Some part of me has always wondered how well I could survive out here. As a boy, I would fantasize about running away to the mainland and making my own way. But I've witness enough now to know better. I never would have survived long as a child out here. And it would have meant leaving Mom behind, something I never could have done. She's the entire reason I keep going back.

Now that Dad is dead, I have a chance to establish myself in a better, safer position on the island. Cypress implied heavily that, should I excel at bringing back worthy Tributes, he would encourage Baron to retire. Which meant a promotion for me.

Baron has been training me to take over for him since I was little. But for me to become Admiral of Tides, he would either have to retire or die. Can Cypress force him to retire and give up the position to me at last?

As the carriage rocks along the uneven ground, I glance back at the men seated on the rows of benches behind me. Each carriage can carry up to forty adults—assuming we are packed in tight.

One other carriage like the one I ride in leads the way. Ours takes up the rear. In the center, a third carriage lumbers along.

` The back of the third carriage has metal walls and a door on the rear. Only two windows look out from the interior of that carriage. It was designed to hold up to twenty people, and somehow the entire box inhibits the use of magic. Anyone we place in that carriage can feel their magic, but not use it to escape. The design is clever, dating back to the very first gathering of Tributes—which had been on the island and along the nearest coast of the mainland at the time. Since then, the Kingdom of Tides has expanded over a thousand miles west and south.

So far, we have only found Finrik and a young woman named Holly. She nearly escaped my notice as she huddled among her community. They had gathered around her as if trying to hide her from us, make her blend more easily into the crowd. It had nearly worked.

Holly had been huddled close to a young man in the community as he clung to her. As my men began loading up, she suddenly surged to her feet, crying for him to stop.

But the young man hadn't moved a muscle yet. When I spun around, the tension in his entire body made it clear that, even though he hadn't moved, he was ready to.

"Holly, no," he had said desperately, reaching for her.

Tears welled in her eyes, and she shook her head. "If I don't, you die."

It had been at that moment when I felt the magic pulsing within her like a light smothered by a shade. I edged toward her, holding out a hand. She had picked her way through the mass of subjects carefully as they pulled at her clothes to stop her. Tears streaked her pale face. Her cold, clammy hand slide into mine.

With only a glance over her shoulder, she joined me in the march toward the metal carriage.

"Holly!" the young man had screamed, held down by several of his friends.

She had paused in the doorway, peering back at him. Her chin trembled. "I will always love you," she had said.

That didn't bode well for her chances as a Tribute. Cypress would be upset. Especially since she was the only one I had managed to gather. Hopefully, the other teams in the far north and the nearer mainland had better luck.

I close my eyes as the scene replays in my mind. Holly, bravely offering herself to the Kingdom to save the man she loves, knowing she will never see him again. I understand why this system is necessary—maintaining the magical strength of the royal line so we can protect these people—but it does feel a bit unjust. Surely, there were plenty of qualified women on the island who would be happy to stand beside the king. Cypress was a charmer, after all.

"Only the strongest women can make the strongest children," Baron had explained during my tutoring lesson. "This is why Tributes are necessary. While we have women with magic on the island, there are more on the mainland, and some of them are even stronger. Being chosen as Tribute is the highest honor a woman can receive. Especially if the king chooses her."

It made sense. My mother was a Tribute. I've never been to her old community—it's a long way to travel—but she reassured me that her selection ensured more security and wealth for her community.

"I may not have been his chosen wife," she had told me, "but Alric still loves me in his own way. And love brought you into this world. I wouldn't change a thing if it meant losing you."

My eyes snap open. For the first time, those words she spoke years ago finally sink in. *...if it meant losing you.*

Dad may have loved her, but he never much cared for me. I suffered his abuse for years. Mom took care of me in the aftermath, and sometimes I resented her for not stopping him. Had she threatened to leave if he didn't stop? Father was just possessive enough to use me a threat against her. Did he threaten to hold me hostage if she tried to leave? Or would he have threatened to kill me instead?

That angry young man in the first community had said they never received the service rewards, but I distinctly remember loading them onto ships every year for the soldiers to take to the mainland and distribute. I've helped distribute some of them to thankful communities for nearly two years. What happened to the shipments that didn't reach some of the other communities? Where did the loaded goods go?

I'm being ridiculous. It's all conspiracies. Hearsay. Assumptions.

Yet deep down, I itch to return to my mother's community and find out if they were, indeed, rewarded for her selection.

I lean forward and pull the map from the bag at my feet, then unroll it. Once I identify where we are and which communities we have already visited, I trace a finger along the map to find the place of Mom's birth. An old town on the map marked out as St. Louis.

After the next community, I will change direction and cut across the mainland. Perhaps we will find fresh Tributes there.

And just maybe I will meet Mom's family—if they still live.

18

Paige

With each passing day, Gavin's frustration becomes more apparent. After the first full day in camp with nothing substantial to report, I watch as he struggles with the switches on one of his devices. Not that he ever complains, but I've spent a lifetime around him, observing the way his mood comes out with odd little ticks.

The second day, when Olivia sends her report to him, Gavin emits a growl of frustration.

"That's it?" he barks.

Olivia frowns, then shrugs at him. "I'm not sure what you want from me. Nothing has changed since we arrived. I can't find anything new. No signs of human life any time recently. Maybe it's time to face the fact that all of this could be for nothing."

Gavin surges to his feet. "No!"

I jump at the sharpness in his tone.

Easton ducks his head inside. "Everything okay in here?"

"Yes," I say.

"No, it's not." Gavin stomps across the tent and begins rolling up his sleeping bag meticulously, but with unnecessary force as well.

"What are you doing?" Harper asks, setting down the radio she had cradled in her hand.

"We need to go elsewhere." Gavin tugs the cloth of the bag tight.

Easton mutters beside me, "Do something."

I'm not sure what he expects me to do, but the tension in the air is thick. Everyone has frozen to watch him. I sidle toward my brother, then place a calm hand on his arm.

"Gavin, we can't travel at night," I say gently. "The truck needs to be able to charge as we drive. You know that. Without the sun, we run risk of draining our source of power."

His fingers twitch, gripping the sleeping back in his white-knuckled fist. "Paige, there is someone out there. There must be. I have run through a hundred different scenarios in my head to figure out what that signal means, and I can't come to any other conclusion. It's human. Which means there must be humans somewhere."

I give his arm a reassuring squeeze. "I hear you and I trust you without a doubt. But you know I'm right about the truck." I pause to give him a chance to respond. His shoulders slump. "We can break camp at first light and head farther east."

Gavin's gaze darts around at each of our companions. Finally, he nods. "Okay. First light. I will send everything we have back to Director Pearlberg tonight and let him know we are going beyond the radio zone."

Easton's jaw slackens. He takes a few urgent steps deeper into the tent. "You heard what the DS Director said. If we go any farther, we will be out of range and out of help. We will be on our own."

I round on him, planting my fists on my hips. "Are you scared, Easton?"

"No, I'm reasonable," he snaps. "Not everyone here has been trained for this." He steps closer to me, leaning in and lowering his voice. "Paige, if there are people out there, you and I might be able to fight back. If one of us falls, everyone is screwed. And no one will know what happened to us."

Easton is right and I hate it. I also don't like how close to me he stands. It requires immense willpower not to retreat.

I raise my chin and glare at him. "Our team leader has made up his mind. He's in charge, and we follow his orders."

Easton retreats a step, alarmed by my response and—is he hurt that I didn't take his side? Did he really expect me to? He glances at the others as if seeking support. Harper stands behind Gavin. Olivia studies the floor. Doctor Adams watches everything with an emotionless expression. No one is coming to Easton's aid. I fight off a smirk.

Grumbling under his breath, Easton stomps back outside for his watch. Everyone else shuffles to their sleeping bags. Gavin climbs up to the equipment on the bed of the truck and begins his work, already oblivious to the uneasiness in the air.

My brother is right. We came out here for answers. But that doesn't make Easton wrong. Going out of range will be dangerous.

I settle down beside Olivia, watching my brother work in a bubble all alone.

"Do you really think he's right?" Olivia whispers.

"Who?"

"Gavin." She is watching him as well, hugging the lip of the sleeping back close to her chin. "Are there other people out there?"

I offer a small shrug. "Maybe. He's right. The signal had to come from something, but it could also just be an old looped signal." Though the logic doesn't entirely work.

"If it were, wouldn't the analysts have discovered it again?" Doctor Adams mumbles from his own sleeping bag.

A lump swells in my throat as I stare at my brother. He is undoubtedly the most brilliant person I have ever known—Dad included. If he is convinced someone is out there, he's probably right.

But what will we encounter when we find them?

"My dad has always believed that we can't be all that's left in the world," I say softly. "He believes that, if we ever want to fix the broken world, we need to start by going out into it and finding others who might be like us. It's been a driving force for him for twenty years. If Gavin is convinced someone is out there, he is probably right. But he also has a serious hero worship complex when it comes to Dad. If Dad said it, it must be true. Unless we can prove otherwise, Gavin won't change his mind."

Olivia heaves out a sigh. "That's a tall order. I mean, it's a huge world out there and we can't possibly explore it all." Her face pales. "That's not what he is trying to do, is it? Explore all of it?"

I laugh softly and shake my head. "No. I'm actually surprised he wants to venture beyond the safety net of our communication with Elpis. Gavin is much more comfortable at home than anywhere else. He doesn't like change."

Olivia's eyes drift closed. Behind her, my gaze meets Doctor Adams'.

"A man determined to gather enough evidence to prove his theory will step outside his comfort zone a hundred times," he says softly. "Whether Gavin is right or wrong is irrelevant. Whether he would rather be home doesn't matter. Right now, he is that man, and I'm worried he won't stop until he proves both he and the Minister are right. Just be prepared, Paige. It may fall on you to talk him off a ledge for the sake of the team."

He rolls over, ending the conversation. But his words etch into my heart. Gavin wouldn't go that far, would he? Not after everything we have learned about Doctor Cass and her experiments years ago. Gavin must understand that there are limits, that people are more important than knowledge.

But his outburst tonight doesn't leave me feeling reassured.

Brilliant as he is, sometimes his mind kicks into overdrive and can't shut down. He gets stuck with his foot on the gas to the point that it sometimes hurts him. I have been there for him, talked him down. Will I have to do that again?

He came on this trip to ensure my safety—or so he told me. I need to do the same for him.

Gavin's insatiable thirst for knowledge could be his undoing.

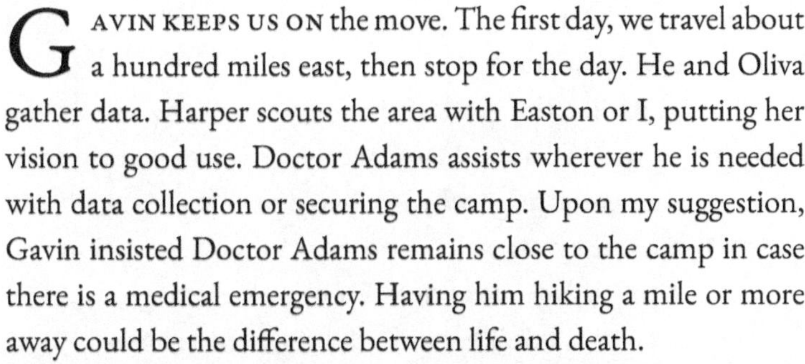

AVIN KEEPS US ON the move. The first day, we travel about a hundred miles east, then stop for the day. He and Oliva gather data. Harper scouts the area with Easton or I, putting her vision to good use. Doctor Adams assists wherever he is needed with data collection or securing the camp. Upon my suggestion, Gavin insisted Doctor Adams remains close to the camp in case there is a medical emergency. Having him hiking a mile or more away could be the difference between life and death.

Most of the cities we pass the first day are relatively small and have already been reclaimed by nature, making them hard to distinguish as we bump alongside the broken highway.

On the second day, we barely make it thirty miles before reaching our first major city. Near the outskirts, Harper stops the truck at Gavin's request. Easton and I get out to examine highway signs overgrown with grape vines. A massive, faded, green and rusting sign lies on the highway. Easton and I climb over a slab of concrete, then stop side-by-side, gazing down at the sign.

He smirks at me, then hops down from the slab. His Somatic density makes the ground crack—though it is admittedly brittle already. He crabwalks over the sign, yanking on the vines and weeds. Once the faded white words are exposed, both of us gaze into the distance at the skyscrapers covered in green. A few lean against others.

"Kansas City," he calls back to me. "How far out did Gavin say we are?"

I chew my lip, trying to recall. "A little over six hundred miles from Elpis? A hundred and thirty from our first camp."

Easton wobbles a little on the uneven ground as he straightens, dusting his hands together. "That city could be a death trap. We need to go around and keep moving."

I nod in agreement. Buildings in the city would be unsafe. They *look* unsafe even from here. And who knows how hard it will be to traverse with the truck.

Major cities like this were at the forefront of the war against those of us with Powers. Many had bombs dropped on them or suffered severe damage when Powered people rose against the Non-Powered. Skyscrapers that escaped that destruction succumbed to the negligence of time. Or so we were taught.

And the curious mind of our leader will need to know.

"Gavin will want to see for himself," I say, holding out a hand to pull Easton back up beside me.

He scowls. "We can't go in there. Who knows what's awaiting us."

We make our way back to the truck. "Which is exactly why he will want to know. Data, Easton. It's all about information."

My assessment is correct. When we return to the truck, Gavin insists we try driving closer as safely as possible. The whole time, his eyes are glued to his tablet instead of taking in the world around us. He flies the drone as close to the city as he dares, recording as much as possible, using the infrared scanner to sweep the area.

The city is a mess. Roads are buckled upward with fresh earth spilling out, covered in weeds and vines, or have been decimated by whatever tragedy struck during the war. All of us have eyes glued on the horizon, taking in as much as we can, but it's so...green. Crumbling or toppled buildings whose windows long ago were destroyed now have trees, shrubs, weeds, vines, or any other manner of green weaving through the gaping holes.

Rusted out vehicles are everywhere. The sheer number of them is overwhelming. Why did they need so many vehicles?

"Imagine the repurposing we could do with all of this," Olivia mutters behind me.

I hadn't considered it, but she has a point. All these materials could be useful to help Elpis grow. Getting them back to the city would require coordination and skills well beyond my understanding.

The journey around the city takes the entire day. By the time we reach the east end, the sun is sinking. Harper pulls into a vast parking lot which—like most things in the city—is overgrown. The lot surrounds two buildings with decaying façades. I'm drawn to them, curious about their purpose. To my alarm, Easton appears at my side, marching toward them alongside me.

Spiraling ramps on either corner of one building have collapsed down into the layer beneath them. A giant oval sign lies on its edge on the ground, cracked and embedded in the façade. At one time, the building appeared to have a bowl-like shape. An overwhelming sense of déjà vu washes over me.

I climb some of the debris, jumping deftly from one hunk of collapsed concrete to the next until I reach the sign, hugged by vines. I yank the vines off the oval sign and cock my head to the side. Some of the sign is broken away, but I can still see enough to get the gist. Arrowhead. What a curious thing to have on the sign.

"Paige!" Easton calls.

I glance down and see him disappearing through an opening. What is he doing? In a few moments, I reach the ground again and follow where he led.

The inside is much like the outside, collapsed and reclaimed by nature. But amidst the rubble, I can see strange objects. Rotting helmets. Circular bits of foam. Broken frames. Racks of clothing that are bent out of shape with the garments unraveling into the earth like they are melting.

"It reminds me of Fitness Stadium, a little," Easton says in hushed tones.

I blink in alarm, realizing he is right. The only stadium in Elpis is the home of our only sporting event, where the strongest Somatics compete against one another to prove who is the strongest of all. It's a pretty exciting event. I've gone to several games with Aunt Bianca since I was a little girl. But I wasn't aware that they played those games on this level before the collapse.

The two of us cautiously pick our way deeper into the stadium, careful to avoid moving any of the rubble. We have no clue what is supporting this structure any longer. Moving the wrong thing can bring it all down on us. We learned that the hard way in our training simulations. A few times, we double back to find another way through.

Then we step out of a tunnel onto an enormous field. Tall grass waves in the breeze across the field surrounded by faded red and yellow walls. And above those walls, thousands of vacant seats wait in orderly rows. On each end of the field, yellow y-shaped posts have crumbled and rusted. I feel like I've stood here before.

Easton steps onto the field, running his hand over the grass. "I know what this is. I read about it in high school for a Somatic Studies history project. Back in the day, major cities like this had football teams. They would fly out to compete on these fields and have huge tournaments at the end of a season. It was a really big deal. But the name for their final game was funny."

He turns to me, grinning. That grin isn't like the mocking one he usually wears. It's innocent, youthful... handsome, even. If he had acted like this around me more, I might not hate him so much.

I edge out onto the field with him, feeling the soft grass against my hand. "Okay, you have my attention. What did they call it?"

"The Super Bowl."

I laugh for the first time in weeks. An honest, deep, pure laugh. "Come on. Be serious."

Easton chuckles and turns away, gazing across the long field. "I am," he says. "There was also a Peach Bowl, Sugar Bowl, Citrus Bowl—"

"No wonder they needed a super bowl to hold all that sugary fruit." I run over, playfully punching him in the arm. "Knock it off. Those are dumb names. You're making this up to mess with me."

"Wish I was," he says, rubbing at his arm. "No need to punch me. You can look it up when we get back. Or ask your brother. He seems to know everything."

The open sincerity on his face makes me believe him. What a strange world this was before.

"We should get back before the others worry," I say. "I'm sure the camp is set for the night and the sun is going down fast. We won't have much light to get back through that mess." I wave toward the tunnel to indicate our exit.

"Let's really stretch our legs. One race," Easton says, raising his finger in the air. "To the far end of the field and back."

"What do I get when I win?" I ask, stepping beside him.

"*If* you win, I will take your night shift. If I win, you take mine."

"Deal."

We count down together, then take off through the tangle of long grass. Unlike most of the ground we have traversed these past few days, the field is flat. Easton's muscular legs press him a nose ahead, but my legs are longer, allowing me to chew up more ground to keep pace. We run side by side to the far end of the field. My pivot is a hair faster than his and I pull ahead. Cool wind whips across my cheeks. The grass catches on my boot and I stumble. I can't break my fall, so I tuck and roll like Aunt B taught me. But as I come back to my feet—so close to the finish line—my ankle twists and I pitch forward.

Easton blows past me across the finish line, then immediately circles back, standing over me with that arrogant smirk on his face.

I grip my ankle, prodding at it tenderly. "Congratulations, you win," I snap through gritted teeth.

"How bad is it?" he asks, crouching beside me.

"It's swelling," I say as my fingers brush the puffiness of my skin. "Go get the doc."

"I'm not bringing him back through that maze in the dark," Easton says sharply.

I huff. He's right. It's too dangerous in the dark. "Fine. Help me up."

He shakes his head. "You can't walk on it until we know more."

"What do you—?" I cut off as Easton slides one arm under my legs and the other around my back. He hauls me up easily.

Instinctively, I wrap my arms around his neck to help with balance. This is almost as dangerous as walking through the rubble in the dark. If he slips, both of us are screwed.

"Just one race," I say, unable to control my simmering anger, "no big deal."

"Will you stop for two seconds, so I can focus on carrying your heavy backside?" Easton snaps. His breath ruffles my hair.

I fall silent, pouting and hating that I injured myself in a footrace against him. Easton might act kind now, but when this is all over and I'm fixed up, he will never let me live it down.

He takes his time, picking his way through the stadium with each cautious step. When a slab appears less stable, he tests his footing and weight before putting all our weight on it. His heavy breathing rolls across my face. I tuck my head back out of the way so he can see clearly. And I definitely *didn't* notice his musky scent.

It shouldn't surprise me that his grip is so strong, being a Strongarm, but the level of strength in his body is higher than I anticipated.

"How can a skinny thing like you weight so much?" he asks once we are out of the stadium and crossing the parking lot.

I scoff. "I'm Somatic, dummy. All Somatics are heavier."

"Call me dummy again," he says through heavy breaths, "and you can get yourself the rest of the way."

"Call me heavy again and you will be grateful you can outrun me right now."

To my surprise, he chuckles. The sound vibrates in his chest. I flush, once more involuntarily breathing in the musky smell of him.

"I outran you even without this injury," he retorts.

Olivia rushes over when she sees the two of us approaching. "Paige! What happened?"

Easton ducks into the tent as she holds the flap open for us. Then he set me down on a sleeping bag. "She couldn't handle losing a footrace, so she injured herself to save face."

"Paige?" Gavin joins the crowd gathering around us. His face is terribly pale, and he wrings his hands.

I shove Easton away. "Jerk. I had you beat."

He stumbles back. "If you say so." Despite the cocky anger I'm used to hearing in his tone, Easton's face falls a little. "I guess you got my shift another night."

Before I can reply, he ducks out again.

Doctor Adams sets to work, asking what happened, examining the ankle, then he places his hands on it. The muscles in my leg tighten. An intense Charlie horse seizes my calf. But the swelling in my ankle reduces before our eyes.

"It's healed," he says. "But you should stay off it for the night. I'll take your watch shift."

Guilt washes through me. Not only do I owe Easton—a fact I loathe—but the doctor is now going to be responsible for all our safety in the middle of the night when I should be on watch.

I lay back on the sleeping bag and press a hand over my face. Feet shuffle across the heated floor.

"What happened?" Gavin asks, his tone hushed.

"It was stupid, Gav," I groan, matching his whisper. "He wanted to race across the field. I tripped. You know, for a hot second, he was actually human." I slide my hand away from my face.

Gavin is watching me curiously, his tablet perched in his lap. "We are all created by our circumstances, Paige. He's been dealt a tough hand. Maybe you can try talking to him about it."

"So he can blame me for being the Minister's daughter again?" I snort and close my eyes. "Not likely."

"Get rest. We are leaving first thing." Gavin pats my shoulder, then heads back to the den of equipment he has lived in for days.

I stare after my brother, dumbfounded. Was he just telling me to give Easton a fair chance? Fat chance of that.

But today, for a little while, Easton did act normal around me. Kind and caring, even.

The thought takes me into sleep. Once more, I dream of red Power consuming me whole. And the same mysterious man reaches out to help me.

19

GAVIN

E ACH DAY, WE TRAVEL a hundred miles or more due east, toward the potential point of origin for the signal. Then I choose a place to stop and collect data. The closer we can get to the old cities, the better. I've noticed that these areas have much more data available. Everything extra we gather will help paint a clearer image of what we face upon return.

My assumption is that, once we can double our range with the drone—traveling five hundred miles from the safety zone—I will be able to send the drone even farther to expand our map and our data. And possibly find the source of the signal.

So far, the levels of radioactivity have been safe enough for us to avoid wearing masks. I had worried that the big city we passed through would have been dangerous. While the levels were slightly higher there, it was nothing dangerous to breathe. Once upon a time, these areas had been radioactive dangers. When that danger passed, I could calculate with enough time.

One morning, the truck ended up stuck in mud. Paige and Easton had to climb out and push as Harper eased the vehicle out of the ditch. Another night, a storm passes overhead, shaking the foundations of the tent until we all had to work together to secure it as one of the posts broke. I used my Matter Manipulation Power to fix it.

Olivia has collected a database of animals who have survived the fallout from the war. It's much more impressive than I had expected—deer, foxes, coyotes, hawks and more. We have a few animals in Elpis domesticated or used for farming. Cows, pigs, chickens, sheep.

One day, Paige called everyone outside to get a better look at one of the creatures.

A white-tail deer stood, frozen in place as it regarded us. The animal's size was impressive. It stood at least as tall as me, with broad hind quarters that would have made any Somatic envious of the muscular structure. Harper had attempted drawing closer to it, but it twitched a few times, stamped its front hoof, then ran a little farther away before stopping to regard us again. We haven't encountered deer in Elpis.

Paige edged closer to it, her hands up in supplication as she murmured reassurances—as if the deer understood. It twitched its tufted ears but didn't run. It even tensed as if ready to sprint away. Paige closed the distance, holding out a hand as she crept closer. No one said a word. Not as it huffed at her. Not as she stopped beside it. Not even as she slowly stroked its neck.

Others were able to edge closer as well to touch the animal, but I hung back. Before the war, deer were everywhere. Males would protect their does and fawns, but this was not a male. There was no rack or antlers of any kind. Still, who knows what such a creature is capable of anymore. Everything evolves to adapt to the environment. We did. Who is to say what over a hundred years could do to the animal's temperament?

That night, everyone had been excitedly talking about the encounter, remarking how the fur was much coarser than they had expected. I simply logged the encounter to add to our final reports. The next morning, we packed up and moved onward.

As the sun rises, the team sets to work breaking down the tent around the truck. They have become terribly efficient at the task over the last few days. What at first took us about an hour now takes less than thirty minutes.

I sit on a folding chair, watching the drone sweep the area one last time. The camera on the drone reaches the outskirts of another major city only 22.3 miles from our current location. I straighten. We didn't find much life in the last one, but that doesn't mean this one will be the same. Excited at the prospect of exploring another city, I fly the drone in closer to the buildings—or what remains of them.

The city is much like the last one, overgrown and in ruins. Seemingly abandoned. Then the drone reaches a river. I zoom in on the bridge and the excitement pumps hard through me.

The bridge had obviously suffered some damage but had somehow been stitched back together. Could it have been done with Powers? That could prove there were others out there!

I open my mouth to call Olivia, but the words lodge in my throat when I hear something from the bed of the truck.

Everyone freezes, staring at the truck.

No one is there.

But the sound is clearly coming from the back.

Easton slides his hand over the gun holstered on his hip. He gives Paige some signal. She nods and the two of them edge toward the truck.

The sound crackles, broken up by static. *Voices!*

I surge to my feet. "The radio!"

"Gavin, wait!" Paige calls.

But I ignore her, sprinting to the truck bed and climbing on.

The frequency equipment is buried under tenting materials. It takes a moment for me to fight it off, throwing the thermal tent aside. One of the posts hits the edge and bounces out of the bed.

"*...return to the island...*" a male voice says over the radio.

I wrestle the frequency recorder out from under a stack of sleeping bags. Paige and Easton are on the truck bed with me now, helping me uncover the necessary equipment.

The sound of crackling and voices grows louder. I flip on the switch for the recorder and lean in to watch the tracker pinpointing the location of the signal.

"*...one more community to visit, then we will head back,*" another man says. "*I hope your luck has been better than ours. Over.*"

"Holy..." Easton's words trail off, but the sentiment seems to be shared by everyone gathered. The stunned look on his face is dopy but not without merit.

"Other people?" Olivia is standing beside the bed's hatch, eyes as wide as saucers.

I shush her as the conversation on the radio continues.

"*Only three worthy Tributes,*" the first man says. "*It will have to be good enough. See you on the island. Over and out.*"

I sink back on my heels, fingers racing across my tablet as I play back what we recorded. All six of us crowd around, listening to the playback. As it plays, I watch the locations. One is really far away. So far, I'm surprised we picked up on it at all. The other is closer though.

Much closer.

"Island?" Paige mutters, frowning down at the equipment.

"The original signal came from the Great Lakes," I say, thrilled by what we just discovered. This will change everything. Dad was right. We aren't alone. "It stands to reason that the signal actually came from an island on the lakes. In fact..." I flip through my files and pull up the original signal, overlaying it on the map we have currently updated.

I measure the distance from Elpis to our location—eight hundred thirty-one miles—and compare it to the distance from our current location to the origination point of the signal—seven hundred forty miles give or take.

"We are closer to the signal than we are to Elpis," I mutter.

"We need to go back and report this," Easton says quickly. "The Council of Representatives will want to know about this."

My gaze shoots up to him. I shake my head. "No. We need to find out more."

"Gavin, if they are this coordinated, we have no idea what we are facing," Easton says. "There are only six of us. We can't approach them with so few."

"We can't approach them with an army either," I snap, hugging my tablet to my chest. "You go back. Let the Council know. I'm going on to see if we can open communication with them."

Paige inches toward me. "He's right, Gavin. I know you want to gather as much information as you can, but this isn't something we should do without consulting with our superiors first. Our orders were clear. We are out here to gather this information and take it back for reassessment and another mission. Besides, we will need supplies to go much farther."

"But we are so close, Paige!" Don't they understand? If we go back, we will have to travel twice as far next time, and the weather is getting colder. Who knows how long it will be before we can no longer travel so far? We don't know what the winter is going to be like in these lands. No. They can go back if they want, but they can't force me to. We brought enough food and water to feed the six of us for at least two weeks. We have more than enough to go a little farther. I have more than enough to go it alone, if need be.

I stuff my tablet into my bag, then gather some provisions to bring along with me. If I assume eight hundred miles of travel on foot, it will take me about forty days. By the time I reach the signal, this island, it will nearly be winter. I grab one of the sleeping bags and head to the exit.

"What are you doing?" Paige asks, trailing along with me. She and Easton cut off my path. "You can't really think this is a good idea."

"I'm not going back." I straighten, daring the two of them to stop me. "I agree that you should go back and report. Let them know I'm headed to establish communication with the island. They can send people after me if they want, but I'm going."

Paige shakes her head. "This is a terrible idea. You're smarter than this."

"She's right," Easton says. "Even if you walk all the way there, by the time we got back and came to get you, you wouldn't even be there. We are better off going back."

He has a point. The truck could make it back to Elpis in three days if they push the limits of the charge each day. Another four or five days to get back to me. Unless I reach the source of the closest signal first.

Paige must sense some change in me because she groans. "Gav—"

I step toward her, hoping she understand my urgency. "I can do this. On foot, I can reach the closest signal by the time you get back to Elpis. I can convince them to bring me back with them, petition for peaceful talks. But if it does go wrong, we still need to send someone back to the city to inform the Council. This could be our best chance to get close if they live on an island. We don't have any way to get there without their help. Elpis doesn't have boats to send."

Easton crosses his arms and firms his stance, prepared to stop me.

"He has a point," Doctor Adams says. "If they make it back to their island, who knows how long it will be before they cross to the mainland again. Sending one or two people to attempt establishing a connection might be in our best interest. And they can let these people know who we are and that we are coming in peace."

"And what if they aren't peaceful?" Easton asks. "For all we know, these people could be hostile."

I swallow. It's a real possibility. What would Dad do? He wouldn't run back to the city. I know that much. He would continue.

Harper chews her fingernails, then drops her hand, hugging herself with one arm as the other hangs limp at her side. "We have to go back. If they are hostile, the Council needs to know so they can prepare for the defense of Elpis. Once these islanders know who we are and where we are, the city could be in danger. The Minister needs to know."

I give Easton my most imploring gaze, begging him to see the logic in my plan. It may not be perfect, but it leads to the best results for the city in the long run. "They are close, Easton. How long before they continue exploring in our direction? How long before they find us?"

"Wait." Paige holds up a hand. "Dad said that we were in some sort of box before, right?"

"Pandora's Box," I say, encouraging her to talk faster. "Yes."

"Because the outside world was dangerous and the men who lived in it were violent and greedy."

Olivia pales. "What?"

"Your point?" I ask.

"How do we know these people aren't descended from those?" Paige asks.

I wish I had a good argument for this point. Paige is right. They could have moved farther from Elpis. It's been a long time since the founders established the city and the barrier. If the violent men retreated farther away over time, once they realized the city was no longer accessible, it could be reasonable for them to be on this island.

"He mentioned communities," Olivia says. She shifts, glancing at the landscape at her back. "Do you think one of them could be close?"

Silence falls.

They won't let me leave. Easton and Paige could stop me easily if they wanted to. There is no way I'm leaving, so I need a new argument to change their minds. But what?

I have to explore this further. Find out what kind of people are out here, what they want, how they live.

Doctor Adams stares at the ground. Olivia wrings her hands. Harper resumes biting her nails. Easton stares at me as if he can read the answers to everything on my face. Paige is studying the contents of the truck. What are they all thinking?

Then an idea hits me. "Okay, another proposal. We try to find the nearest community and ask them about these islanders. Clearly, the visits are fairly regular. We can travel there with caution, hope it's a small community, ask our questions, and learn what we can about the islanders. Then we can reassess. If we can tell the Council who these people are, it will help them plan their next mission."

They all exchange uneasy glances.

I huff. "Come on. The purpose of Project Restoration is twofold. To learn if there is any chance we can begin restoring the world broken by war and Powers, and to prove, beyond a doubt, that we are not alone. The greatest journey in your life is not where you stand as much as in what direction you move. And it begins with a single step."

Paige and Easton now stare at one another. Some silent communication passes between them. For two people who loathe one another, they are effective as a team.

Finally, Easton nods. Paige raises her chin and addresses the team. "The Team Leader has spoken. We will find the community—cautiously and smartly—and see what more we can learn."

"How?" Doctor Adams asks.

I smirk. "The drone. I can use it to seek this community. It has a range up to five hundred miles. Surely, we can find something nearby based on where one of the signals came from. I will send the drone in a line toward where that signal emanated and hope that we will find something along the way."

"Okay, let's get the drone in the air, load up, and drive," Easton says.

Everyone launches into action, closing up the truck bed and climbing into the cab.

Easton grabs my arm as I make my way to the cab door. "You had better be right, Powers. I won't risk this team or the mission unnecessarily."

"Nor will I." I pull my arm out of his iron grip. "This will work." It must.

My body trembles with excitement. It's an energy that buzzes through my veins.

We have proven what Dad always suspected.

Elpis is not all that remains.

20

Zephyr

THE MEN SET UP camp as the Firestarters create bonfires to ward off the evening chill. I sit on a stump nearby, using my what little power my solar flashlight has to study the map in the dying light. We passed through a community yesterday where I found another young woman with big, beautiful eyes, and a thirteen-year-old boy who had been eager to join us. His mother had died two years ago, and his father is a drunk. He yearned for something better. I'm still not sure his magic will make him a suitable candidate for recruitment, but I leave that final decision to Baron.

My radio crackles, and the eastern team leader's voice calls to me. "Captain Zephyr, this is Second-Class Captain Peppers. Checking in."

I pull the radio off my hip and press the button. "Captain Zephyr here."

"We have completed our rounds and have been called back," Peppers says. "Admiral Baron is worried about the waters and wants everyone to return to the island."

My gaze is locked on the map in my lap. It's a long journey back to the *Wave Slicer*, but we aren't far from my mother's old community. I can't go back until I see it for myself. As King's Consort, her placement should have put the community in a good position for stability. I can't go back yet.

"We have one more community to visit, then we will head back," I say. "I hope your luck has been better than ours."

"Only three worthy Tributes," he says. "It will have to be good enough. See you on the island. Over and out."

Five Tributes and a handful of recruits? How many did the northern team find? If they had similar luck, we are only looking at six to eight Tributes total. Not great stock. Cypress won't be pleased.

My mind drifts to Nora. Her flawless skin and alluring eyes. No doubt, she has added her name to the list of Tributes from the island. Part of me jealously wants to steal her from Cypress before he can sink his teeth into her. Her magic is strong. Neither of these women with my team are as stronger as Nora. It bodes well for her chances at becoming queen...and slipping away from me for good this time.

My father's voice returns to me unbidden. *Do you know why I named you Zephyr and not Elijah? Because you are the last person anyone would ever choose.*

I close my eyes and squeeze my fist tight. Maybe it's what Nora deserves. Something better than me.

Since the first King of Tides declared the kingdom, all royal children have been named in alphabetical order according to birth. Every first-born son has been named Alric, just like my father and my eldest brother. Bronwyn is second. Cypress, third. Dominic, fourth. And as the fifth, I should have been given a name starting with "e". Mother had wanted to name me Elijah, but father had refused. I could never be king, and he wanted to be sure everyone knew as much by naming me with a "z". The last letter in the alphabet. The last choice.

"Another community?" Nat asks, settling beside me.

His sudden appearance startles me. I fumble to catch the map before it hits the ground.

"What?"

"You told Peppers we had another community," Nat clarifies. "But we just passed the last one." He leans forward, resting his arms on his knees as he regards me curiously. "So where are we going, Captain?"

I swallow the anxiety climbing my throat. Slowly, I fold the map to tuck it away. "There is one more. An old community we haven't visited in a long time."

He raises a brow. It's apparent he will not let me off the hook so easily.

I sigh and click off the flashlight. "We only have two women for Tribute. But twenty years ago, Baron found one in the furthest community from our border. It's reasonable we might find another."

Nat's face falls. His body goes rigid as his gaze flicks around the camp as if worried about who will hear us. "You mean where your mother came from? Zephyr, you know you aren't allowed to go back there. Just like none of the royals are allowed near the communities where their mothers come from."

"Why?" I ask, heat rising in my voice. "Why can we not go back and meet them? Why is it prohibited, Nat? Why do none of us *ever* go back?"

"You know why, Zephyr," Nat hisses. He leans closer to me. "You know what happened when one royal went back. The community tried to kill him."

I remember the lesson as well as Nat, but it doesn't seem wholly right. It was the second Tribute in the Kingdom of Tides. Brennen, second prince and Keeper of the Tides, returned to his mother's community when he was roughly my age to try converting the people. But instead, they turned against him. The resulting retribution ended with the entire community being wiped out. From that moment on, no royals were allowed to return to their mother's old communities.

But there has to be more to the story than that.

"You know me," I say, placing a hand on his shoulder. "You know I'm not weak."

"No." Nat nods once in agreement. "But you do hate your father. It wouldn't take much to make you question him."

"He's dead." I need Nat to understand this. If he isn't on my side in this, he could report me when we return. My actions could be construed as treason. "Nothing they say will matter. Nothing they do will change anything. But we can't go back with only two Tributes. No one has been there in years to collect. Who knows what sort of magic we will find there?"

Nat's lips thin. He studies his hands as he contemplates the argument. "We were told to return because of dangerous waters. This would be in direct disobedience to the Admiral's orders. It's borderline treason to disobey his command."

I rise and step around the stump. "I haven't received any orders from the Admiral. Peppers said *they* were to return. Not every-one."

The disapproval Nat throws at me almost makes me flinch. He is usually quick with a quip of some sort, but the way his brows knit together makes it obvious he doesn't agree with me. "That's a big assumption. You are putting all of us at risk if the waters are too treacherous to sail. We could end up stranded on the mainland."

I straighten my gray overcoat and raise my chin. "I'm your Captain, Nat. Who is questioning whom?"

Nat rises, challenging me. "I'm telling you this as your friend. Do this and you risk mutiny if we are stranded."

My limbs stiffen. Would he lead a mutiny against me? I stalk toward him, glaring at him, challenging him to stop me. "Watch yourself, First Mate. I am in command. We will visit this one last community, then turn back for home. It will only be an extra two or three days."

I stop, toe to toe with him. Nat wilts under my withering gaze.

"Threaten me with mutiny again and see what happens," I growl.

Anger pulses through me, pure and hot. How can Nat, of all people, not understand? He won't raise mutiny against me. Not yet. He will give me a couple of days. If we aren't turned back by then, I will have to keep a close eye on him.

"Zephyr..." His voice trembles.

I brush past him toward the boxed carriage where the Tributes and recruits await. Until I turn back for the *Wave Slicer*, I will have to keep the radio on me at all times. If anyone else gets a hold of it and contacts the island, my plan to visit the old community will be destroyed.

The fury burns in me as I wrench open the carriage door. A cry of alarm from within is followed immediately by a surge of environmental magic. The magic fizzles out as the earth around me rumbles, but the ground under my boots remains steady.

"Careful," I say, my voice much sharper than I intend. "These walls are designed to protect you. If this carriage topples, it could mean injury...or worse."

The new girl—Alice—trembles violently on one of the benches, hugging herself. The new boy, Ian, shifts toward her and slides an arm around her shoulders to reassure her.

"It's okay," he murmurs. "We can trust him."

This startles me. It's rare for any of the recruits or Tributes to trust anyone from the Capital. But Ian is so sure of his assessment.

"I thought you all might like some fresh air," I say.

Leaving the carriage is not a luxury usually offered to those within, but around me, none of them can do any harm. Their magic is useless, and my men are well-trained in defense. Even if they attack me, it will end badly for them.

Ian is first to move toward the door, another sign that he truly believes he can trust me. I should find that reassuring, but instead I'm more wary of him. He hops out the rear door, then turns to hold out a hand and help Alice. Finrik comes next, with Holly at the rear.

She is still pale and shaken. As her feet touch the ground, I offer her a kind smile.

"Are you feeling okay?" I ask her.

She gives me a tight nod, but I press the back of my hand gently to her cheek to check her temperature anyway. Holly flinches back before realizing my intention, then she relaxes.

"You don't seem to have a temperature," I say, mostly for my own reassurance. "But you are pale. I'll be sure you get an extra meal and water."

"Thank you, my Lord," she murmurs.

Finrik begins wandering toward the campfire.

"Stay close to me, everyone!" I call.

He pauses. I can't blame him for being drawn to the fire. It's a chilly night. If the waters are getting choppy, we could be facing an early winter.

Holly's breath mists with each exhale. She hugs herself for warmth. They all need the fire. I lead the way, sure to keep them all close enough that they cannot use their magic, then help Holly settle on a fallen log. I snap my fingers toward a cluster of nearby men. One of them rushes off to get extra blankets for the four of them.

"Bring her an extra bit of food and water," I order when the blankets are wrapped around her shoulders. "She's pale and I can't have her getting sick before we arrive."

The four of them remain close together, the two women nestled between the teenage boys. None of them says a word as they breathe in the crisp air. Every now and again, I catch Ian eyeing me.

"There's a new king?" Alice asks in a timid voice.

I nod.

"I-is he kind?" she asks.

The men nearby chuckle. I shoot them a look that silences their amusement. When I look into Alice's eyes once more, they have doubled in size. She pulls the blanket tight around her body.

I can't say I consider Cypress kind, but he also isn't cruel like my father could be. He adores his mother and has a very protective streak toward Bronwyn.

"He is a passionate man," I say, deciding to be as diplomatic as possible, "and he loves the women in his life very dearly."

Holly tenses at this. "Women?"

I cast a reassuring smile at her. "His mother and sister. And he has always been respectful to the ladies in the royal court."

A few of the men whisper in amusement across the fire, grinning crookedly at the last comment. I'm aware that Cypress has certain...passions. He's a flirt, for certain, but he has never harmed any women to my knowledge.

Ian stands in front of Alice, glaring at one of my men. He doesn't say a word, but he clenches his hands into fists at his sides. His Aurology might be useful after all. The man he is glaring at has a reputation for being a touch too violent at times. It has me worried about why Ian is so defensive suddenly. And how strong is the reading of Ian can sense it even with me around?

I watch my man. Something about the way he is eyeing Alice doesn't settle well with me either. Alice needs cleaning up, but even dirty with matted hair she is nice to look at. I will have to be sure my man and his friends are not on carriage watch. I wish I could trust them more, but some men are not the most honorable.

With a quick command, I send him and his friends to patrol the southern edge of camp—far from the carriage.

"Let's get you all back inside," I say as the men stomp away.

They follow without complaint, but when we reach the carriage, Ian hangs back as the other three climb back inside.

"What did you see?" I ask once the last of them as climbed back in.

"Darkness and red with pulsing yellow," Ian says.

I frown. "What does that mean?"

He scowls. "Nothing good. Especially for the women...or for Alice."

Darkness and red. Bad intentions, for certain. Probably bloodshed. But what is the yellow for? A warning? I close the carriage door behind him and turn to find Nat watching me from a distance. Curiosity shimmers in his dark eyes.

Nat wouldn't launch a munity against me. It was foolish to even consider it. But he might know more about what some of the men would do than I would. Perhaps Ian's vision was a warning that those men might be at the helm of the mutiny.

And I will need Nat to keep things under control.

I stroll toward him. "I'm sorry." I lower my voice. "You might be right. I only want the men we trust most guarding this carriage from this point on."

"I would never fight against you." He sounds wounded by my earlier accusation.

"I know. I'm just...tense. I can't place why, but everything feels wrong."

He nods. "Three days, Zephyr. After that, the men will know the Admiral called us back and you disobeyed the command. We can't keep this secret for long. You had better do what you need quickly."

21

PAIGE

T HE TRUCK CRAWLS ALONG the broken roadway slowly. Harper keeps her eyes open for signs of danger ahead while she drives. Gavin mans the drone. The rest of us remain silent as we make slow progress, following a short distance behind the drone.

When we reach a broken bridge, the truck stops. Gavin uses the drone to investigate. Most of the bridge has collapsed into the river, but one lane is patched together with chunks of concrete. A piece of collapsed steel reinforcement has been repurposed to support this single lane across.

"Let me out," Olivia says, nudging Easton in the backseat.

The two of them hop out and edge toward the bridge. The rest of us eagerly follow. Gavin still clutches his tablet, giving a few commands to the drone. It flies across the bridge to the other side as he continues scoping out ahead of us.

Olivia crouches beside the mended lane and touches the re-inforced concrete. Easton hovers over her, watching for signs of danger.

All of us remain silent as Olivia attempts using her Power to sense the use of Powers on the bridge. Finally, she looks up at us. "It seems like the bridge collapsed a really long time ago, but maybe twenty years ago someone restored this lane for safe crossing."

Easton stands rigid, arms crossed over his massive chest. "Which means there isn't another place to cross nearby, otherwise why bother."

"Is it safe to cross?" I ask.

Gavin slowly edges farther toward the bridge as if tethered to the drone.

"It seems so." Olivia chews her lip uncertainly. "But something terrible happened. This was fixed so people could flee."

I gaze back the way we came. Where could the people have gone if they fled. Twenty years isn't so long ago. It would have been right around the same time Dad led the city against our old government. We saw no signs of life anywhere nearby.

"Gavin, far enough," Easton calls.

"There's another city up there. A *big* one. Almost exactly as far from us as we were from this bridge when we first heard the radio call." Gavin points farther east. "We should check there. I wonder if the community is there somewhere."

Easton shakes his head. "Going into cities like that is too dangerous. There's no way a community lives there."

"How would we really know?" Gavin asks, marching back toward us. "We only have seen one city and didn't travel into it. Everything we know was taught to us by people who had no idea what the world was like outside. We can gather the *right* intel and bring it back to Elpis, teach people the truth as it is now."

Easton turns his dark eyes on me. "There's no stopping him is there?"

I shake my head. "He's a lot like my dad when he digs in his heels. Short of tying him up, we have little choice."

"I'm happy to try."

I almost laugh. "If Olivia thinks the bridge is safe to drive across, I don't see what it can hurt to go a little farther. It's only, what, twenty miles?"

The wheels of the truck crunch gravel and loose rock as it rolls close to us. Harper had gone back to get the truck already, driving it to us.

"Let's go then," Harper says, leaning out the driver's window.

We all pile back into the truck and continue driving cautiously across the bridge toward this city as Gavin continues using the drone to scan for signs of life. He directs Harper when to turn or veer away from the main road because something bars our passage.

"Keep going," Gavin says when Harper stops.

"I can't. There's a collapsed bridge in the way."

He looks up, scanning the landscape. Dead in front of us, the road is blocked by an overpass that long ago fell from disuse and disrepair. He points up the grassy slope.

"We can go that way. It will get us around it and on track."

Harper guides the truck carefully up the grassy embankment, across another road, then we connect to a main roadway once more. Gavin directs Harper straight. After only a few blocks, the broken skyline of the former city looms straight ahead. Just like in the previous one, the buildings are rotting away. Even from a distance, I can see nature attempting to reclaim the raw materials.

To our left, a broken old Ferris wheel leans against a brick building, partially embedded in the crumbling stone wall. A few more blocks, and the road is blocked by a fallen stone clocktower. Harper guides the truck off the road, through what was probably once a park, and back onto the road on the other side.

"I can't believe there are other people out there," Olivia says breathlessly. "What do you think they are like? Do you think they have Powers like us?"

If only I had an answer. Dad spent so much time insisting there had to be others out there that I always thought he was a little crazy. Too obsessed with the idea for it to ever be reality. But there is no mistaking what we heard. Nor can we ignore that they are coordinated and spread far apart. I see both sides of this argument very clearly. They could be hostile, descended from the very men the Founders had feared. If that's the case, would they remember Elpis? Would opening our borders invite destruction?

At the same time, what if we can establish peace between the communities? It's possible that we could find ways to restore the broken world. Just as this mission hopes to do. It's in the name. Project Restoration. If there is even a chance we can succeed at this, we have to take it.

"I don't see how they could have survived so long without Powers," I admit. "It's the only reason Elpis survived."

"I wonder if their society is anything like ours," Doctor Adams says.

I hadn't even considered this. Elpis became what it is out of necessity. That doesn't mean any other cities would be the same. What would necessity have turned them into? Olivia's comment could have a thousand answers. Now, I'm curious as well. Will we get to see it? My stomach flips with excitement that slowly bleeds outward to my limbs. I need to see it.

As we creep deeper into the city, I find myself holding my breath, taking it all in. Harper deftly weaves around fallen poles. The closer we draw to the downtown, the more curious I become. I wonder what it was like to live here before the war. What part did this city play in the events? Did the people here support Powered people or ferret them out for the government? A few cities built underground havens for Powered people to hide in during the war. I try to recall which cities those were from our history lessons.

Gavin likely knows the answer. I consider asking him, but he is engrossed in the drone readings.

The buildings downtown are not as tall as the skyscrapers in Elpis, but they are still impressive. A few windows remain intact along some walls, reflecting sunlight. The road is wide but clogged with long abandoned vehicles. Once more, I marvel at how many cars used to be on the roadways. The whole of Elpis probably only has a fraction of what I have already seen in this city. They line the streets, block intersections. The closer we get to the tall buildings, the more rusted vehicles I count.

"Look, that one was a library," Olivia says, pointing at a building along the cross street.

Most of the building is overgrown with ivy and green, but I spot the part of the word "library" on the side of the building as well.

"I wonder what kinds of books we would find in there," she murmurs.

"They've probably all rotted away by now," Easton says. His tone does not reflect the same awe as the rest of us. "Stop here, Harper."

She brakes and switches the truck off. Ahead, a white stone building has fallen in a heap across the road, pinning abandoned cars beneath it and blocking the truck's passage.

"The downtown will likely be hard for the truck to navigate," Easton says. "If we have to carry on, we do it on foot. Then we can easily get out of here if we need to."

"I can still get us around using the drone to navigate," Gavin protests.

Easton shakes his head. "Too risky. Harper and Doctor Adams can stay with the vehicle. We can't leave it alone here when we know someone might be nearby." He unbuckles his safety belt. "If you have trouble, start the engine and drive away, then radio us and let us know. We will establish a rendezvous point. We can't lose our data. It has to get back to the city, no matter what."

The four of us climb out of the truck, shouldering only a small pack of rations, just in case. When we insist Gavin call the drone back and leave the tablet behind, he protests fiercely. But Easton is right. We can't lose our data, and that tablet is a key to all of it. With a huff, my brother secures it in the back with the rest of the equipment.

"The whole point of this is to collect data," Gavin mutters as he stomps along behind Easton and me.

I glance at Easton, but his gaze is fiercely focusing dead ahead. Gavin will remember everything he sees anyway. The tablet won't change that.

We climb carefully over the rubble in the road and continue straight, keeping our eyes open for any signs of life or danger.

The blocks are much longer than they seemed in the car. The four of us make slow progress.

"What do you suppose that was?" Easton asks me, nodding toward the broken archway straight ahead of us. It must be blocks to it still, but I have a hard time gauging the distance from the street. I can only shrug in response.

Olivia freezes behind us. "Stop!"

The three of us turn to her. She is focused up the street to our left.

I edge closer to her, trying to see whatever she sees. "What is it?"

"I sense something," she whispers. Trembling, she crouches on the street, placing her hand against the pavement. Suddenly, she stands and begins picking her way through the rubble in the roadway, away from our original course. We cut across a park overgrown with trees that have broken through the old sidewalks until intersecting with another road to our right.

We follow in silence, as if making noise will prevent her from using her Power to track the history of this...whatever she senses. I'm a little disappointed that we have veered away from the mysterious broken arch. I had hoped for a closer look.

A sky bridge blocks the road. Easton seeks the safest path around it, leading us carefully to the other side as I cover the rear of the group. The buildings grow taller. The streets pack in tighter. It makes my claustrophobia kick in.

"I don't like this," Easton grumbles, keeping close to Olivia at the head of our group. "These buildings are in worse condition the farther we go, and they are packed even tighter against the street. We should go back."

Olivia shakes her head. "I feel it. Something was here. Recently."

"Can you tell what it was?" Gavin asks, jogging a few steps to catch up with her.

She meets his gaze. "People. I can't tell how many."

"I wonder if it's part of the community," Gavin muses aloud.

I trail behind them, keeping a sharp eye on everything. There are too many places for someone to watch us here. Are the buildings safe? Would the natives know and climb higher to get a look at us? We are sitting ducks out in the open like this. Do they have guns?

Olivia stops at an intersection, then turns slowly in a circle. "Their presence is everywhere here. More than one, for sure now. I can only recognize three unique identities."

"Can you tell us anything about them? Or how long ago they passed this way?" Easton asks. His hand rests on his holstered gun, reassured by its presence.

Olivia hesitates, chewing her lip as she scans the surrounding area.

An overwhelming sense of pressure on my head makes me gasp. I press a finger to my temples, hoping to abate the pain.

Then I see it.

The ghost of a cloaked figure rushes toward Olivia and Gavin. I'm about to scream out a warning when the ghost passes through them, running down a set of stairs beside them. It disappears.

I break into a sprint toward the steps. What did I just see? And how? At the top of the steps, I peer down into the darkness below. Panic compresses my lungs. There's no way around it. We have to go underground. My mouth goes dry. My heart hammers against my ribs.

"He went down," I mumble.

Olivia appears beside me, touching the top step. After a moment, she rises and nods. "She's right. I can feel him much more clearly here. Male. Roughly nineteen. Passed by here less than ten minutes ago.

Easton shines his flashlight down the staircase. "It looks like an old metro. This thing could be collapsed."

"But he went that way, so there must be passage to somewhere," Olivia adds. "We have to follow. Right?"

Easton sighs, but nods in affirmation. "That's why we're here, isn't it." He takes the lead, unclipping his gun and holding it ready ahead of him.

Olivia takes cautious, dainty steps down close to his back. The two of them disappear into the underground station below.

But I can't make my feet move. I'm hyperventilating, unable to control it, unable to stop my spinning head. I've done this in training before, gone underground, but Tudor was always there to walk me through it.

Gavin steps in my way, blocking my view of the steps into darkness. His hands slide into my own. "Paige, breathe in." He does so with me. "And out." We release together.

After a few repetitions, I manage to regain control of my anxiety.

"Together. Yes?"

I give him a small nod.

Gavin clicks on his flashlight, casting light down the steps. The first few we take slowly. But I can't have Easton knowing I suffer from a fear of being smothered to death. I've had this fear all my life. Ever since I was a toddler in the underground Greenhouse with Mom. There had been a cave-in not far from where the two of us were. It had taken recovery crews more than an hour to get the two of us out.

Gavin and I reach the bottom where Easton and Olivia are already investigating the area. An old metro platform rests empty. Easton had been correct. It reminds me a lot of the metro in Elpis, even with decades of dirt, dust, water damage, and rust. The overall setup is the same.

Light from the early evening filters down the stairwell, stretching our shadows. Everything down here smells of mildew and copper.

I pull out my flashlight and click it on, scanning the dark platform. "Someone came this way."

"How do you know?" Easton asks tersely.

How do I explain to them what I saw? I don't have any sort of abilities like Olivia to justify it. I'm not even sure entirely what I saw. I flounder for the words.

"It doesn't matter how she knows," Olivia says, brows climbing her forehead. "She is correct."

"Which way?" Gavin edges closer to her.

She points toward the east tunnel. "That way."

I won't let my claustrophobia hold me back. We are on a mission. I put all my focus on the task.

Easton moves to cut the three of us off as we take our first steps toward the tunnel, using our lights to illuminate the space. "Wait. We don't know how dangerous it is down here."

"Scared?" I tease, smirking at him. I'm deflecting and I know it. Fear rages in my veins.

"Sensible," he snaps.

Olivia giggles, and I wonder why. But she steps forward and places her hand on his arm. "It's okay. You're safe with me."

Easton shakes her arm off. With a huff of irritation, he hops off the platform to the rails and leads the way deeper into the arching tunnel.

It's odd that Easton, of all of us, is scared of what might lie ahead. If anything, I would have expected Gavin to hesitate—or myself. But Gavin plunges forward with a determination I have never witnessed in him.

Doctor Adam's warning rings in my head as the two of us lead the way. "He won't stop until he proves both he and the Minister are right." From the corner of my eyes, I glance at my brother.

In all the time I have known him, Gavin has been comfortable at home. He has avoided difficult situations and change. He has found his comfort zone and refused to step a toe out of line. But he volunteered for this mission. Now, he is eagerly plunging into the darkness ahead. Is this just because he wants to prove Dad right? If that's the case, he could have turned back any time once we heard that signal. Going back would have allowed him to return to his comfort zone once more.

No. This must be something else. What is driving him onward? Just his curiosity?

We walk along the tunnel for what seems like forever. The darkness is deep. Occasionally, I hear a trickle of water nearby but nothing to be alarmed by.

Despite the destruction above, this tunnel remains remarkably stable. How did it withstand the brutality of war and time when the rest of the city did not fare as well?

Suddenly, our flashlights all go out, plunging us into darkness. I click the button on my flashlight, then smack it against my palm a few times, but it won't turn back on. Gavin begins asking a question, but Easton shushes him.

Now I wish we had brought along Harper. She would be able to see in this darkness.

We all remain still. The silence around us is so deep I can't even hear my own breathing. Only my increasingly fast heartbeat. A hand suddenly grips mine and I yelp, but no sound comes out of me. What is going on?

It's a trap. It must be. And we walked right into it.

Expecting the hand to be Gavin, I give him a small squeeze, then slide my finger along the clip holding my gun at my waist.

The first sound I hear is Easton cursing beside me. The hand in mine is his, not Gavin's. I shake him off.

"Body Count," he whispers. "Paige."

"Here."

"Olivia."

"Here." She is closer than I expected. I jump in alarm.

"Gavin."

Silence.

"Gavin," he repeats.

Nothing.

All the fear I managed to hold at bay breaks free. I reach a trembling hand out in the darkness where my brother had been, but nothing is there.

Then our flashlights blink back on and confirm what we already fear.

Gavin is gone.

22

GAVIN

ONE MOMENT I'M WALKING behind my sister, examining the construction of the tunnel to try and figure out how it has remained intact. The next moment, all the lights go out. I reach out for Paige, worried about her reaction, but something seizes my outstretch arm and pulls me back. I yelp, call for help, scream. But no sound passes my lips. I hear nothing at all. It's the deepest silence I've ever experienced, and it sends a bone-cold terror throughout my body.

My heel catches on a rusty train rail. I stumble, but someone catches me and drags me away. I realize I'm being kidnapped. Are they taking all four of us, or only me?

My captor pulls me up onto a ledge I can't see. My shin slams against the concrete, sending sharp pain all the way to my toes. I give up on calling for help. No one can hear me. *I* can't even hear me.

Suddenly, I worry that this captor who pulls me along is a descendant of those evil men who used to attack Elpis long ago. What will they do to us? I close my eyes to fight off tears, praying Paige is safe. What will they do to her if they get their hands on her?

Rusty hinges creak loudly nearby. It's the first sound I hear for quite some time, and it hurts my ears.

Blinding light spills through the doorway as it opens with a horrendous groan. I flinch away from the bright light and clench my jaw against the noise. My captor shoves me forward. I stumble over my own feet a few steps before catching my balance on the far wall. Cold hits my palms as they scrap across the bricks.

When I spin around to confront my captor, I expect to find a lumbering Somatic like Easton, instead I am greeted by a young man about my size. His face is shrouded in the shadows of his hood, making it hard to discern much about him. The gray cloak hangs low around his body, but not so much that I can't tell he is certainly not a Strongarm. Am I that weak that I couldn't fight him off?

I wince, rubbing my arm where he had used his iron grip all the way here. The door clangs shut.

None of the others are with me. Were they taken to a different room?

My gaze sweeps my surroundings. An old electrical panel. Conduit pipes. A window over a river. An engineering room of some sort?

"Why are you following me?" he asks sharply, but I hear the slight tremor in his words. He is just as scared as me. He sounds about as old as me, too.

"I don't even know who you are," I say slowly.

"You won't take us to the island." He crosses his arms under his cloak, making it billow across the dusty floor. His accent throws me off. While he speaks normal English, the inflection of each word is fascinating, like nothing I've ever heard before.

I cough and wave a hand to move the dust away from my face. Gross. I use this moment to gather my thoughts. He doesn't want to go to the island, which means he must be from a community. How far away from it are we?

"I'm not from the island," I reply. "I come from the west." It doesn't seem wise to tell him everything. Not until I know more. "Hundreds of miles."

He laughs in a way that reminds me of the kids who mocked me in school. It's a sarcastic sound.

"What did you do with my friends?" I ask.

"It's safer to take one of you than all of you," he says.

And I was the easiest pickings. Paige and Easton are clearly muscular. Even Olivia looks stronger than me. He picked the weakest in the quartet.

Then it hits me. "The sound barrier. That's your Power. You can shut out all sounds."

"Power?" He shuffles a step back as if I'm a predator striking out at him. He scrunches up his face, then something dawns on him. "Gifts. What do you know about them?"

Gifts. Of course, they have a different name for Powers. Why would it be called the same thing? "What do I know? Everything. Or near enough." I raise my hands to show I mean him no harm. "Listen, my—"

"Then you *are* from the island!" All his fear evaporates in a flash. He rushes forward, pinning me against the wall. The cool metal of a knife blade touches my throat.

Reflexively, I swallow. My heartbeat hammers against my ribcage. He can probably feel it with his arm pressing against my chest. I need to calm him, get the knife away from my skin. Fighting him isn't an option. I'm not trained well enough. A few lessons from Paige and Bianca won't help me here.

"No. I swear. I just...if you are from a community, we want to talk in peace, but you kidnapped me from my group. Please. Listen to me. They have a tracker who will find me. The other two... I can't vouch for what they will do. But it won't be pretty. And it *will* be quick. Let me explain and I can smooth this out when they arrive. I don't want anyone to get hurt."

This close, his dark eyes peer out from the depths of his hood, studying me. His hand is steady, but he loosens the pressure of the blade against my throat. Slightly. The smooth, rounded angles of his face become clear. He smells of damp earth and forest. Everything about him is fascinating—yet terrifying. Will he use the knife?

"He speaks the truth," a man says from somewhere in the shadows. Just like the boy, he has the same strange accent.

My heart hammers against my ribs. Has that other man been here this whole time?

He steps out from the corner of the room, lowering his own hood. Gray hair peppers his temples. He must be at least Dad's age, if not older. "You say you came from the west. What more can you tell us?"

I hesitate. What should I tell them? I don't know anything about either of these men.

"It's okay, Drake," the older man says. "Give him a little space to breathe."

The one holding me backs up but keeps the knife in his hand. I get my first look at the blade. Chipped and somewhat rusty. That thing carries tetanus for sure.

"Well? Why are you looking for us?" the older man asks.

I lick dry lips, smoothing out my thermal jacket to cover the tremor in my limbs. "We come in peace from a city to the far west. Over eight hundred miles from here. We are looking for other survivors," I say in the most reassuring tone I can manage. "You are the first we have discovered. We just want to talk."

The graying man laughs. The sound sends a chill down my spine. "Nothing exists that far west. It's barren wasteland incapable of life."

"That's what we thought about this far east," I reply. "Yet here you are. Our council sent us to see if we can find survivors to rebuild the world. We are only here to negotiate peace. Does your community live nearby?"

"No." The man falls silent, weighing something. "The Kingdom is looking for Tributes and recruits with gifts. I suggest you go back to wherever you came from."

I take an eager step forward. "Is that the island? Is that where you are from?"

"No."

These two are on edge, which means whoever does live on the island must not be anyone we want to encounter. "You are a Lie Detector, right?" I eye the older man.

He frowns and nods as if he doesn't want to admit it.

"Everyone has gifts where you are from?" I ask.

"Only a handful of us," Drake says. "Leaders. Guards. Acolytes. Scavengers."

So that is their purpose. Wherever their community is, these two have Powers, so they are sent out to find resources for their community. It makes sense.

"Where I come from, we *all* have Powers, gifts. We built our society on it. But we have been contained in our own borders for too long and taught that no one else lived out here." The words rush out of me as I sense our time running out. The others will not be too far behind. "My father, the Minister of the city, sent a few of us out to see if it's true. He believes that there are other survivors, and that in order to fix what was broken, we all need to work together. That's why we are out here."

The older man taps his finger against his lips as he considers my rushed speech. Something in his eyes is guarded.

The boy, Drake, has no such reservations. He cocks his head as he listens, but in the silence afterward, his eyes widen. Something akin to awe crosses his face. Drake throws back his hood and turns to the older man. "This is it, Emil! Just like we were promised."

The older man, whom I assume is Emil, scoffs. "His words are true, but your assumption isn't. The garbage they stuff down your throat at the Haven is nonsense. No one is coming to save us and rebuild the world."

I edge toward Emil, excitement pumping in my veins. "Yet here we are, eager to do just that."

Drake suddenly stiffens and spins toward the door. "They're coming," he hisses at Emil.

"Get behind me," I say, rushing forward so I can act as a barrier. "They are powerful and trained. But I can stop them." Paige and Easton will be fast, but if I am between the two sides, I can slow them down.

Neither Drake nor Emil protest.

Olivia's voice is filtered through the closed door. "In there."

Boots shuffle against concrete, then a few seconds of silence. Did Drake do that? I'm about to ask him to stop when the door crashes open.

I raise my hands in front of me, feeling the Matter Mutation Power pulsing through me—just in case. Easton thrusts the door open as Paige sweeps in, gun raised. Seeing me between them and the new people, she hesitates. I seize the moment before this turns into disaster.

"Stop. It's okay. No one hurt anyone."

"They kidnapped you, Gavin," Paige says sharply. She shifts her aim to Drake.

I lean in her way. "They were scared. We were following Drake and he panicked. They only want answers, just like we do."

"Drake?" Easton sneers. "On a first name basis already, Gavin?"

I glare at him. Now is not the time for his sarcasm. "Yes. Because we both want the same thing. Put your guns away."

Easton shuffles toward the window as he holsters his gun, never taking his eyes off Drake and Emil. Drake watches Easton with obvious mistrust. When he reaches the window, Easton pulls out his radio and attempts contacting Harper and Adams.

"We tried calling up to them," Paige explains to me as Easton contacts Harper and Adams, still waiting at the truck. I can't hear what they say over Paige. "Once we realized what happened to you. But these tunnels block all signals."

"That's why we stay down here," Emil says. He relaxes, sinking down on an overturned bucket. "The Kingdom has a harder time tracking us here."

Drake nods. As he speaks, his attention is on me. Clearly, he thinks we have formed a bond of trust. "That's why I was so worried when you were tracking me. If they changed their gifts, it could mean trouble for everyone we love. We could never go home."

I take a moment to introduce everyone. As we share our story, careful not to be too specific with the details of Elpis at this point, Emil begins to relax. He knows we speak the truth.

It doesn't take long for all of us to get comfortable with each other. Emil invites us to follow him to their campsite. An invitation we eagerly accept.

On the way, Drake tells me about the place he lives. It's a small village hidden from the world—much like our own city must be, he is quick to add—but only a few people are born in each generation with gifts. These are the scavengers and guardians of the Haven. Their job is to ensure everyone has food and water that is safe to eat, and that no one ever finds their location.

"It's pretty far north," he says. "There are a few cities along the river that are good for finding resources when we need them."

"How large is the Haven?" I ask him.

"Pretty big, actually." Drake puffs up as if proud of this. "We have nearly a thousand."

A thousand! What would Elpis seem like to them? Last I checked, our population was edging toward three hundred thousand. Just one borough of our city would swallow the Haven whole!

"A little over twenty years ago, the scavengers rescued a bunch of people who lived in a community here in St. Louis," Drake continues, oblivious to my alarm.

Olivia leans toward me and mumbles in my ear, "The fixed bridge."

I nod, already having made the connection between Drake's time frame and the bridge mended in haste to avoid some sort of terrible attack.

"Emil came from the old community," Drake says. "They took his sister, made empty promises to support the community, and he knew they were lying. Not long after his sister was taken, the Kingdom sent more men and attacked his community."

Olivia gasps. "Oh, no. How many of your people survived, Emil?"

He says nothing, picking up his pace through the tunnel toward a light at the end of it.

"He doesn't like talking about it," Drake whispers to Olivia. "But there were nearly a hundred people in his community. Two were taken by the Kingdom. A handful made it to the Haven, Emil included. The rest..." Drake sighs sadly. "He comes back whenever he can, hoping to find some way to get his sister back."

I watch Paige as she marches after Emil. What would I do if something like that happened to her? I do have location tracking. I could find her, one way or another. But then what would I do? How would I get her back from what sounds like a superior force? Without Elpis declaring war on the Kingdom, I don't know how I could do it.

The tunnel opens to another platform. This one has rolling archways that overlook the river on both sides. Along one of the tracks, the long-abandoned metro sits on the tracks like the bones of a dead beast. Movement inside catches Paige's attention. She edges closer.

Drake steps through the open door onto a train car. "It's okay," he says to the two waiting inside. "They aren't from the Kingdom."

Both women relax, but only slightly. One is in her late twenties, the other closer to our age. Paige and Olivia make the first move toward the women, introducing themselves, then Easton and me. I settle on one of the metro benches, relieved to sit for a little bit.

"Gavin, was it?" Emil says as he settles on the bench in front of me. He turns sideways in the seat and rests his arm on the back. I nod. "You can't be any older than Drake. All of you look so young."

"Olivia is the oldest," I say, nodding to her as she talks to one of women.

"But you are in charge, I gather?"

I swallow. What would Dad do? "I suppose. The Director put me in charge of the team, as the Senior Analyst."

Emil reminds me a bit of Uncle Alex, but not nearly as fun. It isn't the way he looks. It's the same skeptical look in his eyes. The same way he carries himself. If Uncle Alex were uptight and had no sense of humor, he would be Emil.

"What do you analyze?" he asks, resting his chin on his arm.

I launch into the full explanation. Data collection. Radiation. Topography. Genus and species of plants and animals still on the earth. The more I tell him about my job, the more he smiles at me.

"I can see you love what you do," he says when I finally lose steam. "That's the most animated explanation of global analysis I have ever heard, for certain. I can see why your father wanted you out here."

I bite my lip, glancing at Paige as she confers with Easton near the door. No doubt they are discussing security. "No. He didn't want either of us out here, really. But he couldn't stop us."

He follows my gaze to Paige. Has he realized we are related? "I thought you said he was a Minister. Doesn't that put him in charge?"

"Well, yes." I hesitate, then add, "But he has a council that helps him. He doesn't just get to do whatever he wants. Our last government did that, and it was so bad. When Dad was my age, he led the revolt against the corruption, then he helped rebuild something better and more equal for all of us."

"He sounds like a good man."

I beam. "He is."

"What else can you tell me about your homeland?" Emil asks.

I open my mouth to respond, but Paige slides into the seat beside me, beaming at Emil sweetly enough to give me a sugar rush. "What is our plan?" she asks, glancing between the two of us. "Easton says Harper and Adams haven't seen another soul. They have locked down the area."

"I thought that, in the morning, we can talk about opening these lines of communication and trade Gavin mentioned," Emil replies.

Paige rests her arms on the back of his seat, giving him a level gaze. She is staring at him in a way that makes me uncomfortable. Is she upset with him? What has Emil done? "With the leaders at the Haven, I assume?"

Emil's jaw twitches. He narrows his eyes. "You think we will just take you to our leaders?"

"It would help if we knew who we are working with when we report back to the Minister." Paige doesn't even flinch.

Emil's voice deepens. It gives me chills. "Are we working together?"

I might be slow to pick up on emotions, but the tension between these two fills the air. It's stifling. I don't understand what just happened, but Paige doesn't seem to trust Emil. He doesn't seem to like her much either.

"That's the entire reason we came out here, Emil," she says a touch sharply. "You know I'm telling you the truth."

He shakes his head. "That's not the entire reason. I would love to trust you all, but the Haven needs to be protected. We cannot have another Kingdom hunting us down."

"They hunt you?" I ask, appalled but the notion.

"Not literally hunting," Emil says, not breaking his staring contest with Paige. "But they are looking for us. If I tell you where the Haven is, you could tell them. Or you could turn against us. You haven't really told me much about your community, except that there is corruption and revolts."

I flush. I hadn't meant for him to see those things as a negative. We are past that now.

"How large is your community?" His eyes sweep over the two of us, calculating some equation in his head. "How advanced is it? What does your council expect from us?"

The uneasiness that settles in the air makes me anxious. I shift in my seat and avert my gaze.

Drake is talking to Easton near the door. I can't hear them, but Drake is clearly asking about some of Easton's gear and training. Per usual, Easton's responses are brief and clearly unsatisfactory for Drake. He looks annoyed.

"You said the Kingdom was looking for Tributes and recruits," I say, breaking into whatever conversation Emil and Paige were attempting to engage in. "Is that what happened to your sister?"

Emil's jaw twitches.

"Please." I use my gentlest voice. "We want to know more about the Kingdom."

Paige sinks back against her seat and crosses her arms, raising a brow at Emil.

"Yes," he growls. "Every year, they send out soldiers to collect the boys with the strongest gifts to take back to their island for training. Once every generation, they call for Tributes. Young women with powerful gifts who might be worthy of marrying the King, strength the royal gifts for future generations. If they are calling for Tributes, it either means the king's wives are dead, or he is, and his heir is looking for a wife. We never see any of the girls again."

Paige's face turns red. I pat her arm in attempted reassurance.

"That's horrible," she spits. "Why don't you fight back? Refuse?"

A darkness clouds Emil's face. "We tried. Their soldiers are well-trained and powerful. Rumor has it, the new Captain of Tides can negate use of any gifts near him. He can also sense strong gifts. I don't know if it's true, but I don't feel like taking the risk. Odds are they won't come back here to find Tributes since everyone fled last time. But I would rather not stick around any longer. That's why we are leaving in the morning. I suggest you turn around and go home." He rises from his bench. "Nothing good awaits you farther east."

The news leaves me stunned. Just a day ago, I was ready to plunge into the unknown to find these islanders. Now, I am glad we decided to use caution. What would they do to the six of us if they got their hands on us? I glance at my sister. All the anger has flushed away, making her usually tawny skin appear pale. I reach over and slide my hand into hers. Paige takes it, squeezing. For a moment, we remain silent, taking comfort and strength from each other.

No matter what, I cannot allow the Kingdom to get a hold of my sister. Even if it means pushing the limits of my Powers to protect her.

23

ZEPHYR

IT'S WELL PAST DARK by the time the carriages reach the banks of the Mississippi River. Crossing the river in the dark is too dangerous—the bridge could crumble under the weight of the carriages; horses could go lame tripping over rubble; a wheel could break if we miss a hazard in our path—so the men begin setting up camp under a crossing bridge where the rubble makes a nice makeshift shelter against the cold wind.

The past two days grew tense as we continued toward St. Louis. No one questioned my orders to my face, but I caught wind of the rumblings of doubt. I noticed the mistrusting glances they cast my way when they thought I wasn't looking. We had a predetermined route. I've taken the carriages off-course.

Someone will report me when we return to the Capital. I have no doubt about this. Thankfully, I have more than enough time to come up with a good explanation. Or at least, I hope I do. The fact that returning to our roots is against the rules will not look good no matter what sort of spin I put on it. My only hope is that my brother will be more forgiving than my father ever was. Dad wouldn't let it go. He would punish me for certain, perhaps demote me or strip me of my rank completely. But Cypress might be lenient.

With any luck, I will find at least one or two more Tributes and recruits. Returning to the Capital with so few will be an embarrassment. Not that I expected to find a lot, but I had hoped to gather the largest number. Cypress clearly expects a lot from me. More Tributes from old St. Louis might smooth out any anger about my returning here.

Queen Elena is an islander by birth. My brothers and sister could visit their mother's family whenever they wanted. It's only the mainland roots we are forced to forget.

Why, then, did Mom tell me where she came from?

Finding the old community will be a challenge, and I have exactly one day to do it before the men turn against me.

All I have to go on are a few scattered stories Mom told me as a child. How she and her brother used to play hide and seek in a partially collapsed red building near the water. That they often took shelter underground to avoid the dangerous winters. She remembered, as a child, sleeping in a dirty white pod under the fallen arch.

I don't know what the arch is, but I intend to find out.

Part of me considers leaving the men behind with the carriages and venturing across the river tonight. A head start could go a long way.

Heading into an unknown city alone in the dark is a terrible idea when a community is hiding there somewhere. I know this, which is what holds me back. But the temptation draws me closer to the river.

Cold wind swirls around me, biting through my overcoat. I stuff my fists into the pockets and hug my arms tight to my sides.

Across the river, moonlight catches on two giant, angled spikes when the clouds part. I squint into the darkness.

The towers of the city are broken and crumbling, just like every other city we passed through. But those two spikes stand tall and proud.

Then I spot what looks like a massive arch angled against the spikes. It's hard to make out the details in the dark. The clouds once more cover the moon, taking with it all the light I have to see clearly. The world plunges into deeper darkness. Could that have been the Arch?

I shiver against the cold, eyeing the river. It's hard to see anything in the dark, but I can hear the waves lapping against the shore. The scent of fish is pungent this close to the water.

This river connects to the upper lake. Would I be able to make this journey on the *Wave Slicer*? Could that be faster than crossing the land?

Defeated by the cold, I make my way back to the camp. The moment I step inside, the heat from the campfire and protective walls of rubble buffer away the biting wind. Winter is coming early this year, if the bitter cold and sound of the slapping waves is any indication.

All eyes fall on me as I enter the cramped space, though the gazes are indirect. Men watch me from the corner of their eyes. I know what they think of me. That I only attained my rank as Captain of Tides because of my father. I can't deny it's true. But no less true than it was for Baron when he was my age.

How many of these men see themselves as more worthy of my position than me? Would they use that motivation to turn against me? These men are as likely to take my title as I am to become king. Which is unlikely. If I died or was removed from my position, it would be given to one of the councilmen on the island, or one of their sons.

Our recruits and Tributes remain in the carriage. Its walls will protect them from the cold wind and keeps their magic at bay. It's the safest place for them. Or it should be. I still don't trust the intentions of some of my men.

"Gentlemen, this is our last stop before turning home," I announce.

Now all of them stare at me openly.

"Thank you for having faith in me this far. My hope is that we will discover the community that has given us queens and consorts in the past, that we will find worthy Tributes for King Cypress."

I pick my way through the cramped space, making a mental note of which men avert their gazes, who stares me down, and who nod in agreement with my words. It should give me a good indication of where each of their loyalties lie.

"At first light, the Builders will take the Tribute carriage across the bridge. The rest of us will follow on foot. I won't risk all the carriages on the bridge."

Reactions are a mixture of ascent, disappointment, and discontent. Those who appear discontent with the news are certainly part of the group I need to watch. One of them is the man who eyed Alice a bit too fondly a few days ago. Since then, I have made sure he and his fellows were not in charge of the Tribute carriage. A fact that ruffled their feathers.

"We won't spend more than a few hours in the ruins looking for the community," I continue. "I want to be back across the bridge long before dark tomorrow. If anyone knows where the community was found in the past, please report to me. Perhaps we can expedite this stop. I fully expect to be back on the water in six or seven days. Hopefully with a better haul than we currently possess." I turn and march toward the door. "Sleep well, men. I plan on making quick time from here on out."

A cool breeze drifts in from the door. I find a place just inside to curl up and rest. Being near the door will make it more likely I will wake if anyone tries to slip out. I hate mistrusting my men, but some of them have given me no choice.

I close my eyes, hunkered down in my overcoat for warmth, and struggle to find sleep. Every cough and rustle of clothing sounds like a drum in my ears, bringing me back to the present.

———⁂———

THE GROUND BENEATH MY feet is scorched, broken earth. It rumbles beneath my feet, and I spin in a circle, heart hammering. *Where am I?*

A girl cowers in a cage, her back to me. Her entire body trembles violently as pulsing red light emanates from her hands. While this may be a dream, I still sense the immensity of her magic pulsing from her entire body. It's overwhelming, heady, blinding. It does nothing to calm my already racing heart. I've never dreamed of feeling the magic in others before. I can't even discern what the magic might be.

Her dark hair ripples in waves over her shoulders as she dips her chin toward her chest. I edge toward the cage, drawn toward her fearing I'm the only one who can contain her magical power. Or worse, that I can't.

After a few steps, I catch sight of her face and nearly trip over my feet. I've seen her before. In other dreams. The girl on the boat.

She holds her hands in front of her as the red mist begins winding up her arms. I've never seen anything like it before. So much intense, visceral, raw power! Terror pulses through me.

But she needs my help.

"I can't..." she moans.

I edge around the cage. There's no lock. I open the door and take a knee in front of her, reaching a hand out cautiously, like I would when approaching a skittish animal.

"It's okay," I murmur in reassurance.

Tears roll down her tawny cheeks. Makeup streaks from her eyes. I hate myself for thinking about her beauty when she is so miserable. But there's something about her vulnerability that makes her lovely. I'm a horrible person.

"I can't stop it," she moans pitifully.

"I can help," I say, holding my hand out. "Just take my hand."

Terror resides in her umber eyes. My heart breaks. What this poor girl is going through!

Our eyes meet and my heart stops. Her own eyes widen, as if she recognizes me.

It's a dream. It isn't real. But it *feels* so real.

A nearby tree, which moments ago clung to life, bursts into flames from the roots upward. The ground quakes beneath us. Is she doing this? The intensity of her magic hurts my head.

"Please, take my hand," I say more firmly, desperation bleeding through. Why is my magic not working when I am so close to her?

Her slender hand reaches toward mine, crossing the gap between us painfully slow, hesitant.

━━━━ ❁ ━━━━

I JOLT AWAKE AS Nat drags me through the doorway out into the cold. The ground beneath us shakes violently. Chunks of the bridge have collapsed.

My pulse quickens as I scramble back, rubbing sleep from my eyes. The earth really is shaking! Is that why it was part of my dream?

The sounds of agony echo through the air. As I climb to my feet, I spy the horrible truth.

Our hiding place has collapsed.

"How many men were in there?" I ask sharply.

"Most of them woke at the first tremors and bolted for the exit," Nat says. He rushes back toward the door.

"Stop!" I tackle him to the ground near the doorway just as a slab of concrete and metal slam down on the doorway.

The shouts of men inside cut off.

Nat pushes me off, then climbs to his knees and gapes at the makeshift shelter.

"I need numbers," I say. "I want every man able to walk ready to cross."

Nat surges to his feet, stumbling as another tremor rocks the ground. "Cross? You can't be serious. Captain, the sky is falling! It isn't safe."

In the distance, the river splashes as chunks of the bridge fall into the dark water.

That raw magic I felt in my dream remains. Very real.

Is *she* real, too?

"Gather the Builders, now!" I race for the carriage.

Cypress will reward me handsomely for this one. Hell, he might even name me an official heir to the throne.

The terror in her umber eyes hammers against my heart as I rush to the ready the carriage. Should I turn her over to Cypress at all?

No matter what, if her magic is as strong in the real world as it was in my dream, she will need me close. For the sake of herself. For the sake of all the world.

24

PAIGE

I KNOW HIS VOICE, but not his face. It's the first time I've gotten a good look at his features. The angles of his strong jaw. The stubble on his face.

He reaches out to me, offering help as the red mist consumes me, burning me, leaching out into the earth around me. A tree spontaneously ignites as this deadly Power pushes out. The ground rumbles. But he remains unaffected, unafraid, holding out a hand to me.

"Please, take my hand."

Something about his calm composure, his certainty, offers me some reassurance. Hesitation slows my movements as I reach for his outstretched hand. A moment before our skin makes contact, he vanishes.

Fear rips through me. I'm alone with this Power tearing me apart. The ground around me begins crumbling, falling away.

Then I'm jolted awake.

"Paige, wake up!" Easton snaps.

The station around us quakes. Easton stands beside me protectively where I'm stretched out on a train bench. Olivia hustles our new friends toward the exit. Outside the train car window, Gavin holds his arms out, stance firm, as if holding back some invisible force. What is he doing?

I jump to my feet. My entire body aches as if the terror of the dream were real.

The quaking ceases.

I rush out of the train car to Gavin, hand on my gun. "What's happening?"

"No idea," he says, gritting his teeth. Sweat beads on his brow. "But this rail station is coming apart. We need to leave."

I sprint to one of the stone archways and peer out. The road below must be at least twenty feet. I might make that leap. Easton, too. But the rest of our group certainly won't. And there's every chance we will suffer injury in the fall either way.

Emil nods toward one of the arching doorways. "This way. There's an exit nearby."

We quickly snatch up our belongings and race after Emil. He leads us into a dark, narrow tunnel. Some chunks of the ceiling have collapsed, making me wonder about the integrity of any of this structure. Flashbacks to the cave-in at the Greenhouse resurface. I fight them off. Now isn't the time for panic.

No one speaks as we run. None of us dare. I'm not even sure what I would say. Whatever happened, it's clear we can't stay underground any longer.

Easton clicks on his light at the head of the pack, racing beside Emil. A hunk of concrete and brick blocks our path. Emil emits a curse, spinning around to survey the stone around us.

We're trapped. The walls are literally closing in on us. My panic breaks down the barriers, overwhelming me. I draw in a deep breath to try and get control, but it doesn't help.

"We're trapped," I moan pitifully.

"Is there a place where the walls might be thinner?" Gavin asks. "I can try to mutate the stone into an opening for us to get out, but the wall needs to be super thin."

Olivia rubs at my back as I hunch over. An aftershock rattles dust from the ceiling. I cry out in alarm.

"Maybe..." Drake pivots. "Yes! The old doorways they bricked over centuries ago."

"Let's go, Paige," Olivia says gently.

I can't stop shaking, as if the tremble in the earth is also in my bones, quaking in rhythm. She pulls me along gently as we follow the group. Easton casts a scowl in my direction. I know what he is thinking. He's seen this before. In training. Just once. Tudor pulled me through it. Easton knows I'm worthless in this situation, even if he doesn't know why. All my training is pointless. But I can't help my fear. This reminds me too much of what happened all those years ago.

Drake and Gavin take the lead. I don't pay much attention to where we are going, as long as I can still see them moving ahead of me.

"Here!" Drake slaps a hand against a brick enclosed archway.

Gavin presses the tips of his fingers to the bricks. I hold my breath—or maybe I can no longer breathe—waiting for something to happen. Olivia supports my weight as best she can, but I know I am heavier than she expects. I close my eyes and try to focus on breathing.

Stone grinds against stone. The sound stiffens my spine. This is it. Everything will collapse on us.

I will die underground, buried in ancient rubble.

Easton's arm is around me, his free hand cupping my cheek, tilting it up to him. "Paige, breathe. We're fine. Your brother is creating a doorway for us to escape through."

I open eye eyes, but all I see is the stone around us. Stone and darkness. My legs won't work any longer, as if the bones are slowly melting, making it impossible for me to remain upright.

"Yes!" Drake pumps a fist in the air. Then he disappears.

I howl in alarm.

"There's an old staircase, Paige. Let's go." Easton slings my arm around his shoulder and practically drags me down with him. I hate myself for being so useless.

At the bottom of the steps, Gavin uses his Matter Mutation to create an opening in the brick wall that had sealed us in this tomb.

The first hints of daylight break through. I cry out in relief, gulping down air as Easton drags me out behind the others.

He lowers me to the broken pavement outside. I collapse on my back, pressing my arm to my eyes so he can't see my tears. Despite my best efforts to remain collected, my shoulders shake with relief. I am never, ever going underground again.

Easton rises beside me, surveying the landscape. "Any idea what happened?"

Emil shakes his head. "Earthquakes can happen, but they're rare. Extremely rare. And I've never heard of one that strong before. It was more likely something else."

Gavin crouches beside me, taking my hand and giving it a reassuring squeeze as he addresses the others. "It was a Power. I felt it."

Drake's face drains of color. His shoulders tense. "The Kingdom?"

Emil scoffs. "Even they can't have anyone *that* strong."

"That's all good, but I was talking to her." Easton glares down at me as I lower my arm. "You seized up in there, Paige. What the hell happened?"

Gavin rises in my defense. "She suffers from claustrophobia!"

"Gavin," I groan.

Easton's jaw slackens. "How did you pass the entrance exams to become a Specialist?" Then his expression shifts to anger. "Never mind. I already know the answer. Connected little princess like you would get past, regardless."

Anger flows through me, evaporating the anxiety in an instant. I surge to my feet and shove Easton back. "I'm sick of your crap! I don't have to explain myself to you, but you sure as hell will accept that I'm just as good at this as you."

He sneers. "Clearly not. I'm taking charge. I can't depend on you in a crisis." He turns his back to me to address the others. "Gavin, you have what we came for. We're returning to the truck. Time to go home."

My fists shake at my sides, and my body is rigid. I bare my teeth. The heat of anger rises in my face. An animalistic growl climbs up my throat, and I lunge at Easton. I barrel into him and the two of us tumble to the ground in a tangle of limbs. He grunts as his back slams into the street, but quickly recovers as I pin him down. Despite my reflexes, he is stronger. I throw my fist into his jaw. He responds by hugging me close and rolling, pinning me under him. His powerful legs trap mine down. Pebbles and weeds dig into my back.

His musky scent, so close to me, fuels my rage. I try another swing, but his massive hands grab my wrists, pinning them to the ground. I squirm and kick, but he is so much stronger. His Power engorges his muscles.

"Stop," he snaps. "I don't want to fight you."

I snarl at him, then slam my forehead into his.

"Stop, please!" Olivia calls. She tries pulling Easton off me, but it has no impact at all.

Easton's forehead reddens from where I rammed into him. His lip trickles blood from my punch, but he gives no other indication that I have harmed him.

Emil and one of the women join Olivia, pulling Easton back. The moment my leg is free from his, I kick out with all my might, just like Bianca taught me.

The three of them stumble backward. I roll to my feet, preparing for the next attack.

Gavin grabs me and pulls me back. Drake is on the other side of me.

"Paige, calm down," Gavin says. He sounds so patient, so clinical and collected that I relax slightly. "Maybe he's right. We can agree on a rendezvous point with the Haven, a neutral location, and return once we have shared this information with the Council of Representatives. You know Dad will want to know what's going on. And he's probably worried sick about us."

Easton shrugs the other three off, running his hand across his split lip and glowering at me.

"I'm sick of his attitude," I snap.

"You're only proving his point," Gavin says quietly, stepping between Easton and me. "Take a breather." He turns to Emil. "Do my terms sound agreeable? There is another city two hundred and fifty miles east of here. We can meet there in two weeks."

Emil eyes Easton and me with clear discontent. I stretch my back, trying to loosen the muscles Easton ground into the pavement. The outburst has obviously made Emil hesitant.

Did my loss of control, my anger toward Easton, hurt our chances of allying with the Haven? I hold my breath, waiting for Emil's response.

25

Zephyr

I N THE GROWING LIGHT of day, I can clearly see the remains of the arch my mother spoke of. The Tribute carriage plods along with a handful of men riding in the front and the rest walking along behind it. The Builders work on reinforcing the bridge as we cross the expanse of the river. Broken concrete mends back together. Steel posts reinforce the road for the carriage to safely pass. I dash ahead, riding one of the horses from another carriage.

Near the bridge, a paved path leads right into the park where the arch lies in ruins. Going around could take extra time we don't have. Nineteen men died in the collapse of our shelter. The remaining sixty-one soldiers are restless to return home. The earthquake and collapsed campsite have rattled all of us.

But I know what caused it. Or at least, I think I do. If she is close—as my magic tells me—then I need to find her. I need to see her with my own eyes. If she isn't real, I would rather know that now before I chase after a ghost.

I stop at the stone railing and point my Builders toward the park. "Create a shortcut for us through here," I order.

Immediately, the stone begins shifting before my eyes, floating apart by an invisible force before mending together again to form a passage wide enough for the carriage to cross. They pull concrete and stones from anywhere they can around us. Boulders whiz past me from somewhere at my back. Steel girders embed in the path. I marvel at how some people can create such things. Not that they do it alone. It takes a team of at least ten men to build structures like this. The larger it is, the more men it requires.

The girl isn't far. And she isn't alone. I felt another surge of intense magic as we crossed the bridge. I intend to find both and bring them back to the island.

Part of me hopes I will find them in what remains of the arch. It would make things much easier. If that is where the community lives, I would be killing two birds with one stone. And the men would be happy to head home before dark.

The moment the bridge is completed, I ride across ahead of the others. The horse seems happy to stretch his legs with only me on his back instead of the weight of a carriage. These horses are bred for pulling heavy loads, but that doesn't mean they, like the rest of us, don't appreciate reprieve.

It doesn't take long to reach the steel structure of the broken arch. It's much larger than I expected. I slip off the horse's back and tether it to a nearby post. The ground around the arch is littered with steel broken off from what must have once been the top. Girders, twisted metal, stone. Some of the materials appear to have been picked over. I wonder who would need these materials, and for what? How would they even move them? The rubble must weigh tons.

What remains of the lower spikes of the arch is pocked and twisted out of shape. Time, it seems, has been cruel to all remnants of life before the collapse.

I continue my journey around it as I hear the carriage approach.

Below the arch, a doorway is half sealed with collapsed debris. Some of the arch that fell embedded itself so deep in the earth I wonder if it comes out the other side of the tunnel below.

But this reminds me of a story Mom told me. I must be close to her people. Would they welcome me? Would they still be here?

I duck and weave through the debris, busted glass walls, and twisted support beams until I reach the interior.

As predicted, the impact of the top of the fallen arch collapsed whole sections of the underground space. But what I can see makes it clear this is the place Mom told me stories of. Right down to the seated pods the children slept inside. There are only seven of them. How many people lived here? Mom had made it sounds like a huge place.

Scorch marks mar the walls. I brush my fingertips over the marks. Dust and soot stick to my fingers.

Another surge of magic strikes me. I freeze, turning in circles. Is it in here?

"Captain?" Nat calls into the dim lobby.

I make my way toward the exit. The pull toward the magic growing stronger as I do. By the time I reach the outside, I can almost point directly at it. Several levels and types of magic. All clustered together.

"Did you see the dust cloud?" Nat asks, pointing west.

"One of the building probably gave out," I say. "That earth-quake likely did it in."

Nat shakes his head, smirking at me. "Tell me honestly. That wasn't a normal earthquake, was it? You felt something. That's why you wanted to come here so badly."

I grimace and start toward my horse.

Another wave of magic hits me and I stumble into the mount's side. Pressure against my head makes me dizzy and I press a hand to my temple. Nat is at my side in seconds.

"What is it?" he asks, already waving men to survey the surrounding area.

I groan. "I've never felt anything like this before, Nat." The words drive out through gritted teeth. "I'm not even sure I can hold this magic at bay."

His brows shoot up. He chews his lip, wringing his hands. "Well, we should go check it out, at least. If something that strong exists, it could be a danger to the Kingdom." He squints toward the dust cloud from the collapsed building as it spreads across the morning sky.

Just as quickly as the magic hit me, it disappears. I stumble upright, ignoring the building. The magic is so strong it leaves a residual effect, like a string of smoke leading directly to it. With a few quick commands, the men break off into smaller groups to close in on the location.

26

GAVIN

EMIL IGNORES MY QUESTION regarding potential terms for peace. After eyeing my sister and Easton, he moves toward the two women in his group and murmurs something to them. My stomach sinks. That can't be a good sign, can it?

I edge toward Drake, who appears torn by this situation. He's been reasonable so far. Perhaps I can make him see reason. If I can return to the Council with a proposal from another community, they will be more likely to send me out here again. Who would have thought I would want to return? To think just a week ago I was too scared to come out this far. Now I can't imagine not coming back. It would be amusing if I weren't so worried about not receiving Emil's agreement.

There's so much to see out here, and if Drake's community exists in peace, how many others are out there? I have to know.

"Is there any chance you can get him to agree to meeting with us again?" I ask Drake, keeping my voice low.

Drake bites his lip and eyes Emil sideways. "Honestly, I would like to say yes, but I'm not sure."

"We mean no harm," I say, closing the gap between us and leaning closer, pressing urgency.

"You say that, but you also said your own father led a revolt against his own government to create a different system to his liking." Drake smiles at me, but it wavers. The lack of enthusiasm in his tone makes me wonder if he means what he says. "Emil is only trying to protect the people of the Haven. What you propose is no small thing, and it's a hard decision to make." Once more, he glances toward Emil and the women. "What would your people want from us? We don't have much to offer."

"Don't have much to offer?" My shoulders sag. I glance over at Paige as she and Easton confer with the radio, likely talking to Harper and Doctor Adams. Olivia sits on the ground, hugging her knees to her chest and watching Emil in clear worry. I slid a hand through my hair and shake my head. "Look, I can't tell you what they would want. I guess that depends on what we can offer your people and what your people can offer ours."

Drake places a hand on my forearm, his dark eyes driving his words home with urgency. "I believe *you*. And so does Emil. But it's the unknown that he fears. If your government decided to force us to follow their rules, we don't have the power to stop you." He cuts off, biting his lip as if he has said too much. "You know...those are our families back at the Haven."

Numbly, I nod. They don't really think our government would just try to march into their territory and take over, do they?

That isn't the plan, is it? I can't imagine Dad being okay with something like that. Not after everything he went through.

"Drake, time to go!" Emil calls.

Drake's hand slides off my arm and he almost looks sorry. He takes a few steps to follow Emil and the two women—whose names I wish I had taken time to learn—but then he stops and turns back to me. "I'm sorry, Gavin. Truly."

I've never been great at reading people, but I can clearly see that Drake means it.

He jogs a few steps to catch up to the rest of his party.

Paige steps up beside me. "It's okay if they don't agree right now, Gavin. We can go home now and let the Council know what we discovered. They can figure out how to proceed."

But part of me is worried that if I let these people go—let Drake go—I won't ever see them again. Paige tries to coax me back toward the truck. Easton and Olivia are already marching the other way.

No. The future of not only Elpis, but the world, could hinge on my decision in this moment. What if, by walking away, I doom the world to this continued desolation? Dad's legacy was standing up for equality. Is this my legacy? To save the world or leave it to continue unchanged, a desolate wasteland? The burden of this moment presses down on my shoulders. It makes my feet itch.

Paige reaches for me to turn me away from the Haven citizens as they head toward the park. But my feet launch into action. I race after the Havenites. "Wait!"

Drake stops and spins toward me.

I square my shoulders as I stop in front of him. "Let me come with you."

He glances over at Emil, hope shining in his eyes.

Emil is less convinced. His lips thin.

Paige stops beside me, her back to them. "What are you doing? Dad will—"

"He would do the same thing in our place, and you know it." I glare at my sister, daring her to stop me.

She raises her chin. "Fine. Then I'm coming, too."

"Paige!" Easton waves us over as Olivia continues up the path away from us.

Emil opens his mouth to respond, but before he can say a word, everything around us explodes into chaos. The ground beneath our feet rolls out in a wave, throwing all of us off our feet. The walking bridge at our backs collapses.

27

PAIGE

I SEE THEM. AT least sixty men in similar uniforms closing in on our location, taking the women captive, shackling Gavin. Killing Easton and Drake. Then killing Emil as he rushes them in a fit of animalistic rage. The entire scenario plays out in a heartbeat, but as clear as if I am standing in the moment.

Before I can process what I've seen, the ground beneath our feet rolls in unnatural waves. The Havenites and Gavin are thrown off their feet, but my Muscle Memory keeps me on my feet. I run, pulling the gun from my belt as I leap from one wave to the next toward the source, thankful for the earthquake simulations where I taught my muscles to react like this to extreme ground movement. Clouds of dust and dirt create a haze the sunlight illuminates. It's impossible to see clearly.

Easton shouts commands I can't hear. Gavin calls my name.

"Run!" I shout back over my shoulder, firing at the first form that appears in the dust cloud in front of me. Fourteen more rounds.

The man grunts and falls.

I take out another. Thirteen rounds.

A hand clamps on my gun arm as the ground stops moving beneath my feet. Muscle Memory reacts for me, jerking him around as my other elbow pops up into his cheekbone. Then I stretch out the arm and push down on the back of his neck. In seconds, I've broken his grip and reversed my own to bring him down. His arm snaps. He screams.

The Kingdom is here. I can't think of another explanation for this sudden attack. Based on what the Havenites told us, they will capture the women. The vision I had a moment before the attack started sends my terror into overdrive. Are the visions a new Power?

The dust cloud shifts, gathering around Gavin and the Havenites like a tornado of earth. Who is doing that? Gavin? One of the Havenites? I will thank them for clearing my line of sight later.

Dozens of men in similar uniforms—the same uniforms from my vision—close in on us from three sides across the park hillsides. At our backs, the crumpled footbridge. They have us pinned and have the upper ground.

I fire a few more rounds with expert ease, taking out the man with the broken arm first. There aren't enough bullets for all these men. Not even with Easton rushing forward to join me and fire in equal measure. He reacts faster than I expect. In a matter of seconds after the dust clears, he is at my side. The two of us concentrate our fire, dividing the battlefield.

"Emil, get the women out of here!" I shout back, not daring to take my eyes off the force collapsing around us.

"Paige!" Gavin's shout sends a jolt of terror through me.

I risk a glance at my brother. His arms are raised high as he takes control of the cloud of dust. Despair darkens his marble eyes. I follow his gaze to the group of soldiers at the back of the line.

"Paige, run!" Gavin screams.

But I can't. Not now that I see what is happening as clear as day. A knot of twenty soldiers is clustered together, working together with their arms raised toward Gavin. It doesn't take me more than a second to realize he is holding *all* of them off. Naturalist

Power against Naturalist Power. The dust tornado struggles in the direction of the lines of soldiers who edge toward Easton and me.

"Almost out of rounds," Easton says.

"Me too." I've been keeping careful count. The second we stop firing to reload, the force will tighten around us.

"Alternate reloads," he says.

I nod. "I have three more."

"You first."

I squeeze the trigger. Another soldier falls. "Two."

Easton takes his time aiming before firing a round.

I fire again. "One."

He hits one square between the eyes. "Three," he says.

I let the last round loose into the neck of a man only a few steps to my left. "Reloading." Easton covers me with careful shots as I swiftly switch out the clips. It only takes a few seconds.

Easton curses as I resume my fire. His gun jams.

I glance back at Gavin and the Havenites as I fire. Where did Olivia go? "We need to retreat with them."

My gun jams.

"We have lower ground, and I can't get a clear line of sight," Easton says. "Gun won't work."

I don't need him to tell me. It's no coincidence that both of our guns jammed at the same time. This is the work of Powers.

The soldiers tighten around the two of us. There is no escape. I turn, my back against Easton's as we take in our surroundings. The rubble from the fallen footbridge has changed shape. Drake and Emil have hold of Gavin, dragging him away as he screams for me.

In seconds, Easton and I are surrounded. We attempt fighting our way free, but there is no point. We won't escape. A stream of soldiers flows past us toward the tunnel in the footbridge where the rest of our group has disappeared. Gavin continues screaming my name and I know he is fighting to get free.

Please get him out of here!

The ground around us opens. Nearly a dozen soldiers fall into the sudden pit. The scent of fresh earth wafts up. And just as suddenly as the pit appeared, it closes over the poor souls below. As Gavin's voice fades in the distance, screaming for me, begging to be let go, the world changes shape. The hills flatten out. The ground beneath Easton and I shifts us upward, away from the soldiers. A gentle slope guides the way to the gap the others disappeared into.

Easton launches to his feet, grabbing a soldier and throwing him like a limp doll into a crowd of men. He then snatches my arm and hauls me to my feet. The two of us turn to run after the others in a narrow gap in the lines of enemies created by the shifting landscape.

The tunnel collapses, crushing at least a dozen men and cutting off our chance at escape.

"Run, Paige." Easton pulls a smoke bomb from his belt and pulls the pin.

"Let's go together."

"You heard what Emil said. They want women. I won't let them take you." He lobs the smoke bomb to the right where fewer soldiers will block our path. "Run. I will hold them off as long as I can."

But it reminds me of leaving Tudor behind in the simulation. Of my hesitation. Of my vision of Easton's death. I won't leave him. "Together." I yank his arm, forcing him to run with me.

Easton grumbles but joins me. The two of us sprint through the smoke, only pausing long enough to take out anyone in our way. The smoke clears. I wonder again where Olivia is. Did she go back to the truck, or did these men capture her already?

Easton trips over a chunk of debris and pitches forward. "Run!"

I ignore him, doubling back to yank him to his feet.

It's just enough hesitation for the soldiers to overwhelm us. One catches the back of my jacket. I dip down, shoving Easton onward, and try to slip out of the jacket. But as I slip my head under the material, the soldier twists it around, jerking me back and trapping my arms like handcuffs. It's a clever move.

It takes three men to pin me down on my knees. One of them yanks my hair, forcing my head back at an uncomfortable angle. Pain shoots along my spine. I whimper, knowing I won't escape again.

Easton is at least twenty feet away, barreling onward toward escape. I can hear him shouting commands into the radio, but I can't make out what he says. Something about 'rendezvous' and 'return to Elpis'.

When I yelp at a jerk to my hair, Easton skids to a stop and spins around. His gaze falls on me. I pray for him to leave me for the sake of the mission, like he so often did in our training simulations. But something crosses his face. An anger I've never seen in him before. He throws his radio at the ground, stomping on it, and I know what he is planning. A foolish attempt at rescue.

"No!" I scream for him to stop, but Easton is already charging into the fray. He plows into the soldiers with enough force to knock two of them off me. Unfortunately, the third has a firm grip on my hair.

It takes six men to subdue him, forcing him face-first into the earth. His dark eyes bore into me. Is he blaming me? He could have escaped! The one time I wanted him to do what he always does...

"You should have left me," I whimper.

He opens his mouth to respond, but a knee in his back cuts him off with a grunt. Then his enhanced muscles give out. Terror crosses his face. Easton rocks, bucks, and struggles to break free, but he is as Powerless as Dad.

At the same moment, my body gives out.

Something is cutting us off from our Powers.

28

GAVIN

BEFORE I REGAIN MY footing, Paige runs into danger, gun drawn. I clasp my trembling hands over my stomach, scanning our surroundings for somewhere to go. Some place of safety. Huddling back to make myself as small as possible, I raise my hands and begin by clearing the air. First, we need to see what we are dealing with.

The dust cloud thrown toward us fights against my will. I've never pulled so much of my Mutation Power at once before. It takes every ounce of strength to use the dust cloud as a barrier, hoping it will help mask our escape.

"We can't get through," Emil snaps. "The footbridge is blocking our path. They have us pinned."

Sweat rolls down my temples. My spine straightens. My entire body trembles as pure Power pulses through me, consuming me, burning me from the inside out. All I can imagine is Paige fighting off all those soldiers. Her training doesn't matter against such odds. If I don't help her, they will capture her.

My stomach rolls as I recall what Emil told us last night. "Once every generation, they call for Tributes. Young women with strong gifts who might be worthy of marrying the King." What happens if they get a hold of Paige? "We never see any of them again." An ache swells in the back of my throat.

I shift my body, half turned toward the collapsed footbridge. With a grunt, I break one hand away from the battle with the dust cloud and grit my teeth as I split the Power in half. A tunnel slowly forms through the footbridge as concrete rolls aside and steel rises to reinforce the opening. I utter a cry. Blue sparks emit from my fingertips.

Drake and Emil each grab an arm, pulling me into the tunnel with them.

"No!" I kick, losing focus on my Power. I fight them off, scream for my sister, but they don't relent.

Nothing I do changes anything. Tears stream down my dirt-stained cheeks. "Paige!" I release another howl, horrified as a wall of soldiers surround her and Easton. An agonizing blast of Power shoots out of me. The ground around her opens and swallows the soldiers.

More soldiers race straight toward us. I can no longer hold myself up. My throat aches from screaming for my sister. Every part of me is about to give out as we disappear through the tunnel I created.

The earth itself begins shifting as I pray with every ounce of my soul for Paige to find a path to safety. And one opens up, a slope straight for our tunnel.

Then I can't control the Power, the pain, any longer. My vision darkens. The tunnel collapses.

Please, let Paige escape, is my last thought before I lose the fight to my Power.

29

Zephyr

So MUCH RAW, POWERFUL magic. The thrill overwhelms my senses. Almost intoxicating. The phenomenon slows my steps as I fumble to find my way through the battle. One of them is taking on all of my Builders. Alone. He can do what they are capable of with earth and stone—but so much greater. My hands shake, my steps leaden as I shuffle onward. It's too much strength for my magic to stop.

"Captain!" Nat has been shouting at me for a few minutes, but my mind cannot seem to pick up what he is saying.

All at once, ten of my men turn and... well, they don't flee—that would require them to run—but they are moving away from the fighting. My stomach clenches. Are they choosing this moment to turn against me? I have it coming. How many men have I lost already?

Intense pressure against my mind blurs my vision.

"Captain, we need to retreat!" Nat shouts.

How far away is he? I blink slowly, in a daze as I turn and seek out my First Mate.

"No." My voice slurs each word. "It's so much...so much power... We need—" But I cut off, unable to form any more words.

Then the ground swallows another group of my men whole, like some starving beast beneath the earth. A few of the men nearby stumble back and attempt fleeing until they see me. The earth beneath our feet shifts, flattening, as two distant figures fight against what remains of my men, then turn to flee toward a tunnel leading to the river.

Then the tunnel collapses. The shouts of at least a dozen of my men cut out with it.

During a battle, I hang back until my men gain control of the situation—as they always have in the past—because otherwise my proximity hinders their own magic. They have always taken control swiftly in the past.

But we are losing.

To a mere handful of people.

A muscular man and a slight woman sprint away. We can't let them escape. I have to capture as many of them as possible. I don't know how many men they have already killed, but I do know that the cost has been high. I need some of these magic users in my possession when I return to the Capital, or I face deadly consequences. I need something to show for it.

I must step in.

The battlefield is a disaster. A graveyard of bodies. A whole new landscape. It takes all my concentration to avoid lingering on the lifeless soldiers as I pick my way toward two captives. The two who tried to run.

Both are secured by the time I approach. The man fights hard to break free. A valiant effort. I can feel the intensity of his Strength probing for a hole to break free. But it's nothing compared to the extreme magic rolling off her. It fills me with headiness.

I stroll around to get a better look at them, then freeze. "You," I breathe.

The girl from my dreams. The one who has haunted me for the weeks. The one who invaded my sleep last night, cowering in fear, shaking the earth.

She meets my gaze as best she can with her head yanked back. But the way her eyes widen upon seeing me, I know without a doubt that she recognizes me.

If she is the same girl from my dreams, that means she has far more magic than she put on display here today. Why would she hold it back?

I clear my throat and quickly collect myself. "If I allow my men to release their hold on you, will you fight back?" There's no way I can hide the tremor in my voice. Hopefully, no one else has noticed.

She sneers. It's answer enough. There's a lot of fight left in her.

I crouch in front of her. "We don't mean you harm. There's no need for conflict." Some part of me worries she will hate me for this, but I'm as helpless as she is. If I let them free, I am as good as dead—especially considering how many of my men they killed. If I take her back to the Capital, I might be able to help her there. And redeem myself before Baron and Cypress for losing so many men.

Deep in my bones, I know I need to stay close to her no matter what. The magic inside of her is dangerous. So dangerous even she fears it—or at least she did in her dreams.

"Disarm them," I command.

Her umber eyes remain locked on mine, full of fury and hate—and curiosity—as my men search both. The pile of weapons is impressive. Guns. A couple of grenades—or something grenade-like. A hunting knife on her. Three of them on the boy. Nat hands me a small black box taken off the boy. I flip it open.

Inside, nestled in a cradle of black foam, are two syringes without the needle tip. I pluck one out and turn the flat end toward the tip of my finger, then glance at the boy.

He's grinning at me, daring me to touch it with his dark eyes. It's all the warning I need. Careful not to brush the tip against my skin, I place it back in the foam and close the metal box, then pass it back up to Nat.

"Don't let anyone touch that."

Nat slides it into the deep pockets of his pants. I notice the way the boy watches where it goes. What does it do?

"Let go of the poor girl's hair," I command.

As the soldier holding her obeys, another yanks the boy to his knees beside her.

"As I said, we don't mean harm," I say, addressing her and ignoring him. "If you come peacefully, you will be safe."

She snorts and rolls her eyes. "*Safe.* If that were the case, you wouldn't have attacked us in the first place. I know what your kind do." She leans closer, magnificent fury heating her tawny skin. I want to touch her. "Take me to your leader. I dare you."

For a moment, the two of us stare at one another. The threat to Cypress is clear in her sharp tone. Perhaps my mother or sister will be able to cure her of some of this resentment.

Or maybe I can.

Fool. That won't happen. Not only will she hate me, but she is without a doubt the strongest woman we have ever found. Cypress will want her for certain. It makes the next words even harder to utter.

I avert my gaze, unable to witness the anger in her a moment longer. It undoes me. "Load her in the carriage." The words leave a sour taste in my mouth.

The guards yank her to her feet. She kicks back, slamming her head into the face of one while ramming her foot on the instep of another. Free of their grasp, she lunges at me.

I grab her arm and spin her around, pinning the arm behind her back and holding her back tight against my body. It sends a shock of warmth through me. Suddenly, my limbs are too heavy to move.

The momentary rebellion sends the boy into another fit of fighting. But his magic is useless against my men. His efforts are futile.

With a hand wrapped around her upper body to hold her tightly in position—for security and *not* because of how it feels to have her so close—I touch my free hand to her temple. My magic pushes into her, but something resists. Some barrier on her mind makes it hard for me to lock her magic away.

Knowing none of the men will be able to handle her—that her magic is right there on the surface waiting to break free—I escort her toward the approaching carriage.

"Wait!" the boy calls out, his voice cracking. "I volunteer for recruitment!"

"Easton, no!" she calls out.

I pause, half turning with her still in my arms, fingers still pressed to her temple.

Easton raises his chin high and meets my gaze fearlessly.

"You're too old," Nat says. "We only train boys."

Where are these two from that they don't know this already?

"I'm already combat trained, so it should be easy to catch me up," Easton says. He isn't speaking to Nat though. He has already deduced that I'm the one in charge. Those hard eyes are fixed firmly on me. "I will come quietly."

The odds of him being allowed to enlist even if we take him back are slim, considering the damage to our force he has already caused. However, he has information we might need. Valuable information about their origins.

"Easton, what are you doing?" the girl hisses.

The moment he looks at her, the hardness shifts to something softer. It gives me pause. If the two of them are a couple, and I bring *both* back, Cypress will not thank me. Yet I can't let this chance to question him slip away. It will have to wait until we get back to the island and in an isolated place though. Away from her.

"Trust me, Powers. I can't go back. There's nothing for me there."

Her body tenses in my arms. For a moment, I wonder if she will try to break free again. But it passes. She relaxes against me, shoulders sagging. Were his words a code?

The carriage stops beside me. Nat opens the back door.

Easton stares into the carriage, his expression unreadable.

"Prove you will come peacefully," I say, nodding toward the open doors. "Like they all did. Let him go."

The challenge is clear. Easton nods once. The men holding him down ease a few steps back as if expecting him to attack. He rises fluidly and struts toward the back of the carriage. Just before climbing in, he pauses, glaring at me.

"But if you hurt her..."

"She's safer than you," I say. My fingers slide off her temple and I nudge her toward the open carriage doors. She stumbles into him. He quickly catches her in his arms, glaring at me.

Without another protest, the two of them climb in. The door slams shut. Nat bolts the lock. Once it's secure, he spins toward me, arms across his chest.

"We shouldn't have been here, Zephyr," he says under his breath. I'm not sure if he is worried our new recruits will overhear, or the men. "Now we have to explain why we lost more than half our men."

I wince. "So many?"

"Captain!" One of the Builders rushes toward the two of us from the riverside hill. He's out of breath. "There's a boat...heading north...along the river."

The boy who had more power than all of my Builders combined! He must be on that boat, escaping. I'm about to tell the Builder to stop the boat when Nat edges closer.

"Thirty men, Zephyr. We can't chase them down. We need to return to the Capital."

We left *Wave Slicer* with eighty. In less than a day, our force was shredded to ribbons.

I nod. We can't chase down this mystery boat. Perhaps, if we had our own here, it would be doable.

Coming this way had been my way of seeking out my mother's old community. But we found nothing more than remains and lost fifty men in the process.

Were it not for the girl, this side-trip would have been a complete disaster.

But hopefully, she can abate some of Cypress's anger when we return.

We've never had such a powerful Tribute before.

30

PAIGE

THE CARRIAGE DOESN'T ROCK nearly as much as I expected. I can only assume it's been upgraded with some sort of
shock absorbers or equalizers. Part of me is thankful, part of me
is convinced it doesn't matter. We won't be in this carriage for
long. There is no way my brother won't try to rescue me. Gavin
wouldn't want to return to Mom and Dad with the news that I've
been taken captive. What would Dad do?

Easton leans against the carriage wall beside me, arms crossed
and eyes burning into the closed door. Neither of us speaks. The
silence is preferred. Something tells me that the moment we speak
to one another a fight will break out.

The other occupants of the carriage eye the two of us curiously.
Our clothing is vastly different from their own. While the styles
they wear are slightly different, the general quality remains the
same. Where our clothing is created with Powers back in Elpis,
reinforced so we are safer from radiation and the elements, fitting
to our forms, theirs is clearly stitched together from old pieces of
clothing to create something new.

The younger boy—Finrik, he says his name is—and a
black-haired girl who doesn't utter a word, have no shoes. Finrik's
eyes drift to our boots longingly. The other two have footwear,
but it appears more hobbled together from abandoned remnants
of the old days. What must we look like to them?

The other boy, Ian, stares at me for so long it makes me uncomfortable. Something about his stare gives me déjà vu.

After the first hour, I worry that maybe Gavin hasn't been able to find Olivia, Harper, or Doctor Adams. Where did they go, anyway?

After four hours, I worry that Gavin is dead. But I can't allow myself to believe it. Last I saw him, Drake and Emil were dragging him away to what I can only hope is safety. The tunnel collapsed, but I know Gavin's strength. He wouldn't have been crushed under that rubble. Maybe they were just cutting off the soldiers who approached the tunnel.

By the time the carriage stops for the night, I know that no one is coming for us. We are at the mercy of the Kingdom now.

The carriage door opens, and Ian is the first to slip out. He leans close to the man who captured us and whispers something. Ian is a spy. Thankfully, neither Easton nor I said anything at all.

The leader frowns, his gaze falling on me. He nods and points Ian over to one of his men. The boy dips his head and hustles away.

Easton stands, trying to use his size to intimidate our captor. But the ceiling of the carriage is low, forcing him to bow. "We haven't eaten in a day," he says.

Our captor nods. Easton's little display didn't intimidate him in the least. "You are welcome to stretch your legs and join us, as long as you stick close to me and don't cause trouble. My men are angry about how many of their friends you killed. Wander too far or make a wrong move and I won't be able to stop them."

I rise and make my way toward the exit.

Our captor points at me. "You last. And you stay right beside me."

I gape. What does he think I will do surrounded and in unfamiliar territory? I certainly can't fight my way out and flee.

The other two girls give me a sympathetic smile before shuffling out and stepping to the side. Finrik follows them, then Easton. When his feet hit the ground, he stretches languidly.

I sink back down on the bench. If this man thinks he can force his company on me, he has another thing coming.

He heaves a dramatic sigh and nods a couple of his men into the carriage. "Tie her wrists."

The two men climb in and inch back toward me, clearly scared. It amuses me that they are afraid of me. But even more so that they think tying me up will prevent me from fighting back. I smirk and raise my wrists toward them.

When the first one reaches for my wrist, I react quickly, snatching his own wrist and twisting it back. But my reaction time is slower than I'm used to.

"Paige, stop it!" Easton hisses.

The second man is faster than I am, twisting my arm around behind my back and forcing me to the floor. The impact knocks the breath from my lungs. Am I Powerless? My Muscle Memory should have kicked in.

Once my hands are bound tightly behind my back, they drag me out of the carriage and drop me at our captor's feet. *He* has nice boots.

He crouches beside me, helping me to my knees. "Paige, is it?"

I glare at him. It seems the only thing I have going for me at the moment is my defiance.

"You can call me Lord Zephyr," he says. The tone in his voice suggests I'm not being held prisoner and we are about to become fast friends.

I snort. "Lord. Right. And I'm a princess."

The corner of his mouth tilts up in amusement. It makes my cheeks heat.

At his back, Easton is glaring at me, giving a subtle head shake. He wants me to stand down, to accept this fate? Unlikely. Though maybe this isn't the best time for me to pick a fight, hog tied and at Zephyr's mercy. Who is he anyway? Why was he in my dreams?

"You could call me Zephyr, if we were friends," he says. Once more, his patient tone fans the flames of my anger. Is that alcohol on his breath? "Are we friends, Paige?"

I laugh in his face. I can't help it. The question is beyond ridiculous. Tears well in my eyes as I continue laughing.

Zephyr cocks his head. "I take that as a no. I will admit, that makes me a little sad, Paige."

"You can call me Princess Powers," I retort, spitting the words in his face. "Only friends call me Paige."

A cloud of curiosity passes over his face. Then he laughs. Not in a mocking way, like I was laughing at him a moment ago. It's sincere, full-bellied amusement. I clench my jaw so hard it hurts.

"Very well, Princess Powers." He stands, gazing to the right.

I follow his line of sight to the boy Ian. He stands a long distance away from us, at least fifty yards, surrounded by six muscular soldiers. But his path to me is unhindered. His face has paled since leaving the carriage—or maybe the carriage lighting was just too poor to see him as well. His hands tremble as he murmurs something to one of the men beside him.

The man's lips thin and he shakes his head slightly at Zephyr.

With a sigh, Zephyr reaches down and hauls me to my feet. *What just happened?*

All eyes follow our small group to the fire. Easton sticks close to me, and I know he is evaluating the situation just like I am. Probably calculating our chances of escape.

Zephyr's hold on my arm isn't tight. Instead, he seems to only be there to help me balance. Not that I would need his help if he would untie me. When we reach the fire, the other captives settle in a cluster on one side. All but Ian, who refuses to come to our side of the fire until one of the soldiers shoves him toward us. Ian trips over his feet, nearly falling into the fire, drops on his side at Easton's feet.

In an uncharacteristic show of compassion, Easton helps the boy up and checks him over for injuries. Easton emits a calm patience that reminds me of his openness to criticism from our team leader in training. How is he not angrier about this situation? Did he really not want to return to Elpis? What if he thinks this life will suit him better?

He turns to settle on the ground, and his gaze meets mine. I shoot daggers at him. How could he? Easton grimaces and ducks his head.

Zephyr helps me to the ground. The tenderness of his touch once more confuses me.

Once I'm settled, he motions Ian over. The boy glances at me, giving me wide berth as he approaches Zephyr's other side, kneeling at his shoulder. He leans close and whispers into Zephyr's ear. I wish I could hear anything Ian said. Especially after Zephyr gives me a sideways glance. His focus is so intent it makes me squirm.

Ian shuffles farther away from me and digs into his meal.

As the food is passed out to the captives, the soldier delivering it stops in front of Easton and drops the dried strip of meat and apple in the dirt. Easton remains outwardly cool, picking it up and brushing the food off before tearing into the meat without comment.

Warmth at my side makes me flinch away.

Zephyr leans around me, shaking his head as he loosens the knots binding my wrists. He leans close. The scent of sea water washes over me.

Zephyr keeps his voice low as he speaks. "These men are terrified of you. One wrong move and they will kill you without hesitation." The warmth of his breath against my neck rises gooseflesh and sends a shiver down my spine. Sea water and alcohol, for certain.

Once my hands are free, I bring them around slowly and rub at my wrists. "Thanks," I mutter. "I don't suppose you would tell me what that boy said to you about me."

He scratches the scruff on his cheek, then gives a small shrug. "Nothing important." He holds an apple out to me. "Just that you will bring the end of the world."

I freeze, my fingers brushing over the skin of the apple. My gaze shoots up to him, then narrows. "Whatever. Keep your secrets."

He smirks, then bites into his own apple.

I turn the fruit over in my hand. Where did it come from? How safe is it to eat? All my life I was taught to be wary of eating anything not grown and cleansed in Elpis. But our rations are gone.

"It isn't poisoned or drugged," Zephyr says around a mouthful of his own meal.

Everyone else is eating the food, so I assume it must be at least safe enough to consume.

As we eat in relative silence, my mind races. The very idea that I could bring desolation to the world is laughable. How would I even accomplish such a feat? Some superstition must fuel this belief, which is why Zephyr's men fear me. It makes no logical sense. Despite my dreams, none of my Powers even hint at anything which could have such devastating results. In fact, the jury is still out on whether or not I have retro or precognitive dreaming skills.

From the corner of my eye, I watch Zephyr as he keeps a keen eye on the rest of the men. There isn't a doubt in my mind that he is the same guy from my dreams, but it doesn't make sense. If I do have some sort of Dreamer Power, why did it never manifest before. Only in the last month have I had dreams that even seemed remotely like a Dreamer. The Specialist Promotion is the first. And that one was spot on, word for word and action for action. If my dreams about the red Power and Zephyr are the same as that promotion dream...

I'm too old to have newly developed Powers.

But I'm also different.

Suddenly, my appetite is gone. I can't stomach another bite while worried that I might have some latent, consuming Naturalist Power. It can't be real. And I have to find some way to prove it.

It isn't long before we are escorted back to the carriage. Apparently, we won't be allowed to sleep under the stars like the rest of the men. As we are locked back in our carriage together, I watch Ian.

Ian and his premonition about me ending the world.

He takes the furthest bench from me, pressing into the opposite corner. If people with Powers are valuable to the Kingdom, Ian must have some sort of Power. Perhaps he can read minds...or is he a Precog?

I try reaching out to him in the softest, most reassuring manner I can, but it produces no noticeable results.

Easton stretches out on the carriage floor near me. I settle on the bench above him, then nudge him with the toe of my boot.

"Hey, what's your deal?" I ask, keeping my voice down in case anyone outside is listening.

"Just trying to get some rest," he mutters.

"Why did you volunteer? Are you really so eager to escape Elpis? It's certainly better than the world out here."

Easton shifts upright, facing me. He rests a hand on his knee as he eyes me. "Don't talk about home." His gaze flicks to the others in the carriage. They have all settled down for rest, but it's a small space. I get his meaning. At least, I think I do. He wants to be sure we don't divulge too much about home to strangers. "CapT."

I nod in understanding. Part of our Specialist training was extensive lessons in how to protect the city if we were taken captive on a mission. CapT is Captive Training.

"But you are accepting all of this," I say, leaning forward. "And you said you had nothing to go back to."

"Paige, remember what Emil told us. The Kingdom wants recruits with Powers, and women with Powers. They aren't ever seen again once they are taken. Do you really think I would leave you alone in this? We stand a better chance together."

He volunteered to help me? I shake my head slowly. It doesn't make sense. "You hate me."

He grimaces. "I don't hate you."

My jaw slackens as I search for words. Impossible. "All the scathing words, belittling, arrogance." I must have heard him wrong then.

Easton's hand inches toward mine. My breath catches. He bites his lip. Then he retreats, settling back down on the floor.

"What do you think happened to the others?" I whisper.

"Harper and Doctor Adams are headed back home," he mumbles. "Olivia is dead."

I didn't hear that right. "*Dead?* How do you know?"

"I saw her go down just before they took you. The other two had orders to return home immediately if we missed the rendezvous. These guys didn't go after them, so it's safe to assume they made it back."

In the midst of the fight, just before he broke his radio, I heard him say something about the rendezvous and returning home. He ordered them to abandon us. Just like our training taught. If it's a no-win scenario, always ensure that someone gets back alive if possible. Harper and Doctor Adams had the data and the means to escape.

Olivia is dead. I liked her. Smart. Kind. She would have fit in well at a Powers family game night. Now she's dead. Will they send someone to retrieve her body?

It occurs to me that he failed to mention one person. "What about Gavin?"

Easton eyes me, his lips drawing in a tight line. "I don't know. He was with the Havenites. Maybe they escaped. But the tunnel collapsed with him inside."

My heart lurches at the same time as the carriage. I can't believe Gavin is dead. I can't. The very idea of him crushed under that rubble makes my gut churn and my heartbeat quicken. Tears burn my eyes and I blink furiously to fight them back.

Easton reaches up and takes my hand, giving it a small squeeze. His eyes are closed, so he can't see me cry. But he must know. "Get some sleep. We need to keep our strength up."

Did Easton think he would die if he tried to run? Or did he really turn back to help me? Either he is a genius or an idiot. I can't decide which.

31

ZEPHYR

I AN PRACTICALLY JUMPS OUT of the carriage when we stop for the night. The fear in his eyes isn't toward me, but Paige. He grabs my arm and almost appears mad as he leans close.

"I can't see it, but I feel it." His hiss borders on lunacy. "Let me see it. Please. I can't take it anymore. I won't run. Promise."

The twist of his lips and his jetty eyes makes me relent. I nod and motion toward some of the men in the distance. Ian dips his head down and murmurs thanks as he rushes over to them.

But it's what he says afterward that sends chills down my spine.

"She comes from a legacy of creation. She is part of a legacy of balance. She carries within her a legacy of desolation." Ian's warning plagues me. "Keep her close. I don't know how, but your fates are connected."

What does that even mean? And just how accurate are Ian's Aurological foretellings?

The spark of fire burning within Paige draws me toward her throughout the meal. The way she mocked my title amuses me even now. Could she truly be a princess? From where? Her companion, Easton, has answers, but until we get home, I won't dare to ask.

The two of them need to be separated. I noticed the way he looked at her when he volunteered to join us. It's there again at the campfire. His interest in her will be dangerous to their survival in the Capital.

Her magic is chaos. I can usually get a sense of what people are capable of. Easton has muscle control. Finrik can persuade people. Holly has visions of the near future. Alice, elemental control.

But Paige is everywhere. Natural instincts, for certain, but more. And not just one more. Dozens. They are constantly shifting, probing at my own magic to break free. I've never met anyone like her before.

The fact that I can't seem to separate myself from Paige only makes me more curious about just how our fates are connected. Does that mean Cypress will choose her? If she can tone down her attitude, she will be a natural choice for him. Yet something tells me she will only dig in her heels more stubbornly and resist every step of the way. And how does a marriage to my brother connect her to me, aside from the obvious.

Those dreams must mean something. It can't be a coincidence.

The first night headed back to the Capital, I sit awake on the bench of the Tribute carriage, not daring to remain far from Paige even with magic-dampening walls around her. I'm not sure those walls alone can contain her if she tries to break free. The others couldn't use their magic no matter how hard they tried, but Paige...

The pull toward her is overwhelming. It's the power inside her that draws me like a siren's call. It must be the power of her magic.

It *has* to be.

We need to keep moving. Instead of resting in one place for the night, I order shifts for the men so we can get home faster. The sooner I can get her to the Capital, the better.

For both of us.

32

GAVIN

MY STOMACH CHURNS, AND I'm certain I'm about to vomit. The abrupt onset of sickness wakes me quite suddenly. My eyes shoot open, only distantly registering the bed. It was all a bad dream. I'm back home. But as I sit up, my head smacks against the ceiling. When I open my mouth to groan, vomit climbs my throat. I slap a hand over my mouth and scoot to the edge of the bed for somewhere to release the contents of my stomach.

Everything is spinning as I step on the wooden floor. The world seems to sway and tilt, increasing the nausea. After only a couple steps, I spot a small bathroom. I make it to the toilet and lift the lid just in time.

By the time I finish, I'm certain nothing remains in my stomach. The taste is abhorrent, lingering relentlessly.

Where am I? What happened? Where are the others?

"Paige?" I moan pitifully on the bathroom floor, leaning against the cool toilet bowl.

The world heaves and rocks again. My stomach lurches.

"Paige?" I call again, only slightly louder.

A door clicks open nearby. For a moment, I swear I hear water.

Someone approaches. Paige. It must be her. I reach toward the door by my feet.

Drake ducks in, a look of absolute sympathy in his eyes. "Motion sickness? It passes."

I blink to try and steady my vision. Will this nausea ever stop? I've only had motion sickness once in my life. In the back of a self-driving tram when I was thirteen. "Where's my sister?"

He disappears. Hopefully, to retrieve Paige. Something clicks twice, then he reappears, holding out a canteen toward me. "Water. Drink it slowly or you'll end up sick again."

I offer him a weak, thankful smile. I need the fluids after emptying my stomach. The water coats my insides like ice over a fire. I sit upright as the nausea fades—though it doesn't go away.

"My sister," I repeat more insistently.

Drake dips his chin to his chest as he averts his gaze to the wall panel beside me. He gnaws on his lip like it's a chew toy. If he doesn't stop, he's going to draw blood. Then he stills. The reaction accompanied by his lack of response does nothing to help my already churning stomach. Thickness swells in my throat. He doesn't have to tell me she isn't with us. For once, I can read the emotions clearly.

Sorrow. Pity. Regret. They slam into me just as surely as the motion sickness.

Using the wall and adjacent sink for leverage, I pull myself to my feet. My limbs resist, shaking and weak.

"Is she dead?" The words are thick with terror. I don't want to hear the answer, but I need to know.

His eyes shoot back to mine, suddenly wide. "No! They...wouldn't kill her."

"They..." I'm about to ask him who, but I already know.

The Kingdom.

They captured her.

The battle plays out in my mind in perfect detail as I probe for answers, weakness, mistakes, any clues that might help me put all the pieces together.

Olivia had already left to return to the truck. Did she make it there?

Easton took a stand beside Paige so the Havenites could escape. "Is Easton here?" I push past Drake in the narrow doorway, practically colliding with him as the floor pitches beneath me.

"No. We don't know what happened to him." Drake is on my heels. He rushes around me, blocking the only other doorway in this tiny bedroom. Where are we? "Gavin, I'm so sorry. They might have taken him as well, but it's just as likely they would have killed him. He's too old to be a recruit."

Sweat beads on my forehead. My bones tremble. Then I can no longer hold myself upright. My knees give out and I sink back on the edge of the bed.

Drake shifts and sits beside me. He attempts comfort, sliding his arm around me and rubbing my back. For a moment, I lean into him, welcoming his warmth as my entire body goes cold.

I take another careful sip of water, hand trembling violently. My throat refuses to open at first and I choke. What happened to Harper and Doctor Adams? Are they still waiting for us to return? Do they know about the attack? Easton sent them a couple of messages over the radio. Did he tell them to turn back if we didn't return?

"Olivia?" I mumble, hardly able to speak.

"We don't know that either. Maybe the Kingdom got her, too."

They didn't seem to know much.

I close my eyes as everything sways again. If Harper and Doctor Adams are returning to Elpis, they have the equipment with them, and the data. The council will get what they need. Dad might even send out a search party. I know Easton told the two of them as much as we knew about the Haven and the Kingdom the night before the attack. I heard him relaying the information through the radio. Probably a good thing, too. It's the only information Dad will have to find us.

The image of Paige and Easton fighting back-to-back in rhythm, surrounded by soldiers, floods my mind. And I remember the hands on me, pulling me away as I fought to free myself from their grasp. As I screamed for my sister.

Anger chases away the cold that seized me moments ago. Drake did that. He pulled me away. He left my sister. He separated us.

All the nausea lingering within me washes away as I shove Drake away and surge to my feet. My hands clench and unclench at my sides, nostrils flaring.

"You did this." I tower over him as he shrinks away.

"Gavin, no—"

"You and Emil dragged me away kicking and screaming!" I stab a finger in his face. He flinches away. "My sister is gone because of you!" Rage narrows my vision as I spin around toward the door. "But I will find her. I won't leave her in their hands."

I jerk the door open and lurch through the kitchenette, startling the two women whose names I no longer care about. At the other end of the narrow space, another door is closed. I yank it open only to find another room. Backtracking a few steps, I spin around, seeking an exit. Where are we?

"Gavin, you can't leave," Drake insists as he rushes out of my room.

Stairs! I march toward them. "Watch me."

My steps are determined as I open the hatch and climb out.

It only takes a second to understand Drake's assertion. I freeze in place, holding a nearby rail, and gaze out at the deck of a small sailboat. It takes a moment to shake off my stupor. Fumbling along, I stumble toward the rear of the boat and sink down on a cushioned bench, watching the water thread around the hull and wake outward.

The coastline is alight with fall colors. The skyline of the city is nowhere to be seen.

Drake settles on a bench across from me. "I'm sorry. They are well on their way to the Capital by now."

Tears blur my vision. My own voice is thick and foreign to my ears. "How long was I out?"

"A day." Drake shifts to the edge of his bench, leaning closer. His hand falls on my knee. "You wanted to come back to the Haven with us. We can introduce you to the elders and continue with your original plan."

My original plan. It seems feeble and pointless now. Not when all I can think of is my family, and how I am nowhere near as strong as Dad. I can't talk to people and read people like he can. How could I ever facilitate peaceful talks? I'm not sure I have much choice right now. I don't have the supplies to travel all the way back to Elpis on foot.

Overwhelmed, helpless, trapped, the dam breaks. I buckle over, bury my head in my hands, and cry. The harder I cry, the harder it is to draw air into my lungs. A dull ache seizes my chest. If only I could go back and change things. We never would have been in that park. Those soldiers never would have found us. Paige would be beside me, safe and sound.

"Oh, Gavin." Drake's weight shifts the cushion as he settles beside me. As he draws me into his arms, hugging me close to his chest, I lean my head into his body, trying to siphon some comfort from his presence.

Instead, it only reminds me of the void where my sister should be. I gulp air between sobs. Drake says nothing. He simply rubs my back, leans his cheek against the top of my head, and makes soothing sounds.

33

PAIGE

THE CARRIAGE IS TOO small. The walls are too close. There are too many people inside. Being trapped in the confining space makes it hard to breathe, to think. Now that my secret claustrophobia is out of the bag with Easton, he recognizes the signs and does his best to keep me calm and distracted.

Easton and I exchange few words. He distracts me with exercise. Floor stretches. Sit-ups. Push-ups. Ab twists. The others watch us. The competitive streak in us kicks in quickly each time as we work until we collapse, determined to be the one who can do more.

Despite there being only six of us in the carriage, my legs cramp up as if I just can't stretch them far enough. It only takes us a day and a half to figure out that we will only be allowed out once a day to eat or use the facilities—if going to the bathroom in the woods under Zephyr's guard could be called "facilities." The meals aren't terrible. Dried meat. Apples. The rations are reasonable. Apparently, we need to keep our strength up to be presentable for the king.

I have a few choice words I'm looking forward to sharing with their king. Who kidnaps girls then expects them to agree to marriage? What kind of danger will I be walking into?

The smell in the carriage gets overwhelming. None of us have showered in days. Easton and I had cleansing wipes in our packs, but Zephyr has those now. Has he gone through our possessions?

The thought of him poking through my stuff irritates me. I can't help wondering what he would think of some of it. The packaged food and cleansing wipes. The water purifying tablets. Does the Kingdom have anything like it?

Ian won't look at me. The boy is petrified of me, which makes Zephyr's amused proclamation that I will bring about the end of the world even more ominous.

Holly remains mostly quiet throughout the ride. She offers me smiles, but not much more. It isn't until the fourth day of our trek that she finally lets slip that she left behind the love of her life to save him from certain death. When I gently prod for more, she clams up.

Alice is a little more talkative, but she keeps her own life guarded. Sometimes, I think she has already convinced herself that she doesn't stand a chance in whatever comes next. If all the king wants is a woman with strong Power that's nice to look at, Alice is certainly a contender. Those long lashes and mysterious eyes even draw *me* in.

Alice asks endless questions. What will happen once we reach the Capital? Will we be imprisoned until the Choosing—which is apparently some bizarre series of events where the king chooses his wife based on our Powers and a few dates—or will we be given rooms in his palace? What does the palace look like? What does the *king* look like? I grow bored and keep my responses short so I don't seem rude, but I don't care about any of this. It isn't like I have any more answers than she does. If anything, I have less.

When we are released on the third night to relieve ourselves and eat at the fire, Zephyr informs us that we should reach the ship in two days. Then it's just a day to the Capital. I don't know how he can tell. Every time I catch a glimpse of the landscape, either through the narrow carriage window or when we emerge from our cocoon each night, it looks so much like our last camp that I can't tell how far we have come.

On the fifth day, Easton sits beside me on the bench like a lump, his hands folded anxiously in his lap.

"Paige," he says softly, not looking up from his hands. He scratches at the beard growing on his chiseled face. "When we get there, remember why we left home. Don't do anything to get yourself into trouble."

I cross my arms and lean against the wall. "Don't tell me how to conduct myself. If they plan on parading me in front of this king like some prize, I intend to tell him exactly what I think of their little show."

His shoulders sag. "That's exactly what I'm afraid of. But you will have his ear. I won't. Which means, whether I like it or not, our fates are dependent on your performance."

"I will *not* perform for him," I snap, irritated that he would even suggest it.

"Do you think I like leaving the fate of our people in your hands alone?" He glares at me. "Just be careful and protect yourself."

I snort, rolling my eyes to show him just what I think of his recommendation. "Don't start acting like you like me now."

"I told you I don't hate you." He straightens a little. "Anyway, I would like to think they will send me to recruitment with those two." He waves toward the boys. "But I'm not an idiot. They can't hurt you. They need you. I fully expect to be interrogated...and I'm not sure it will be a pleasant experience."

Deep down, I knew this was a possibility. Hearing him confess it out loud only makes it more real. Will they torture him for information about Elpis?

"Easton..." I place a hand on his arm. "You can't tell them anything."

He nods stiffly. "I can't tell them nothing either. I'm prepared for whatever comes, and I won't tell them anything we can't afford for them to know. I need to be valuable to them to stay alive." He glances at me. Lines of worry stretch around the corners of his eyes. "But I need to know you are safe. It will make the interrogation easier to bear if I know you are safe. Promise me you will be careful."

The two of us stare at one another. I know what he wants me to say. That I'll be on my best behavior. That I won't mouth off to this king or his people. That I will do everything I can for the security of the mission. But I'm not sure I'm capable of keeping the promise.

I chew my lip as my mouth dries. My hands begin sweating and I pray he can't feel it through the sleeves of his jacket. Am I really worried about him? Easton is a jerk, always sharp with his words, haughty, insufferable.

"I have to ask again," I say. My voice is tight, surprising me. "Why did you volunteer? Why did you come back for me?"

The laugh that rolls out of him is tense and brief. "This job is all I have, Paige. Do you really think that, if I were to return to the community without *both* the Minister's kids, I would be allowed to keep my job?" He sinks back against the wall, studying his hands as he rubs them together. I note how he calls Elpis a community, probably to play down the size of it for anyone listening. "No. Our best chance is together."

"But the mission—"

"This isn't a training simulation. I won't abandon you to death or worse."

What could be worse than death? Easton's entire demeanor is a stark contrast to what I'm used to. All his confidence is smothered beneath thick layers of worry.

"You've done it before," I whisper.

He rolls his head along the wall until our eyes meet. I can't decipher that look in his dark eyes though. "You really believe I hate you." Hurt. That's what the look is. But why? "Paige, listen to me. This is important. I need you to understand, to believe me." He takes my hand. If he notices how sweaty it is, he gives no indication. "You are the strongest, smartest woman I have ever met. But you constantly doubt yourself. You see yourself as inferior. Probably because of who your father is and what your brother is capable of. But you are capable of so much more than you give yourself credit for."

My breath catches. His grip on my hand tightens as he shifts his body around and leans closer. *What is going on?*

"I didn't push you because I hate you," he continues, lowering his voice. "I did it because you were incapable of doing it yourself. Admit it. If I hadn't pushed you, would you have fought as hard to prove me wrong?"

The way he stares at me as he waits for my answer makes my insides twist. He's right. I hate it. I wanted the job but constantly doubted whether I was good enough. I had something to prove but didn't believe I could ever prove it. Not until he started poking at me. Then I dug in my heels just to rub it in his face.

He made me hate him to make me better at my job. And it worked.

All I can do is shake my head slightly. He already knows the answer.

"I knew how my prodding would make you feel about me, but I also know that you are capable of being better than all of us." His thumb brushes my clammy skin. "If making you hate me is the price I have to pay to see you reach your real potential, then I'll pay it."

I can't look at him any longer. It makes me uncomfortable. But I don't pull my hand away from his either.

34

Zephyr

THE RETURN TO THE *Wave Slicer* moves along smoother than I expected. The men don't complain. They go about their business and hardly spare me a glance. The recruits and Tributes in the carriage have all settled into the routine well enough that I'm no longer worried.

I have tried several times to engage Paige in conversation over dinner. Her retorts are sharp and sarcastic. Always with extra emphasis on the "Lord" title whenever she dips her head in mock subservience. I've given up attempting to be friendly with her. My job is to get her back home. After that, she can be Cypress's problem.

On the fifth night, I step away from the carriage to relieve myself before I need to release the people inside. A group of men nod respectfully as I pass them and step around a cluster of trees. Mid-stream, commotion interrupts me. I grumble under my breath. Can't a guy have just a second of peace to himself?

The moment I emerge from the trees, an arm wraps around my neck. Out of instinct, I reach up to pull the arm away as it tightens against my throat. Something cold presses against the soft flesh of my chin. Not a blade. I can fight my way out of this easily enough.

"Don't put up a fight, Captain," the man hisses behind me. "I don't know what this thing does, but I imagine it isn't pleasant."

That effectively freezes me. What is he holding to my chin?

A quick scan of our surroundings reveals several my men unconscious. Nat among them. A handful are holding weapons ready.

One man steps forward, and I recognize him immediately. The same one who was giving Alice funny looks a week ago. The same one Nat has been warning me about.

"This is treason," I rasp, surprised by the strain in my own voice.

"No, what you did is treason," the leader says. "Because of you, we lost our friends. We never should have been in that city."

I wish he weren't right, but the deaths of all those men have plagued me for days. They are dead because of me. And I didn't even catch the man responsible. He escaped. Just thinking about how overwhelming his magic was gives me chills.

"What's the plan, then?" I ask, hoping to sound calm despite fighting for breath. The arm around my neck is too tight. "Kill us and tell the king we died in that fight, too?"

He laughs. "If I told you, the fun would be over." His gaze flicks past me to the man holding me in a firm grip. "See what that thing does."

"No wai—"

A cold shock blasts through me. Then nothing.

35

PAIGE

TEARS PRICK THE CORNERS of my eyes. I can't decide whether I'm angry with Easton for mistreating me for the last year, or I'm happy that he did it. The hair on my arms stands at attention as he continues stroking my hand with his thumb. My head is swimming in all of this.

"You and Tudor insisted that kiss in the club meant nothing," Easton says.

Just thinking about Tudor makes me clench my jaw. That jerk. He turned on me so quickly.

"That's not the truth though, is it?" he asks.

Sink or swim on you own. My grip on his hand tightens. Easton knows. There's no point denying it.

"It wasn't at the time." Anger burns in my voice. "It is now."

"I noticed the looks you two shared when you thought no one was looking." He sighs. "It made me jealous, if I'm honest. Jealous and angry. I tried so hard to follow the rules, and the two of you were breaking them."

Jealous? "Nothing to worry about anymore. He made himself perfectly clear the day I was selected. I'm pretty sure he was using me."

Easton slides his free hand to cradle the side of my face, forcing me to look at him. "When those men surrounded us, I told you there was nothing for me back home." He is so close this musky scent fills my senses. His touch sends a jolt through me. As he whispers his final words, his warm breath rolls across my face. His dark eyes draw me in. "It's right here."

His lips brush mine softly. My brain is telling me to push him away, but the rest of me yearns to pull him closer. I don't have feelings for him, do I?

Breathless, craving more, I press my own lips decisively against his. Warmth floods through me as he pulls me closer, crushing my body against his as if afraid letting go will tear us apart forever. I still can't explain why I need this so much, why I need him. The boy who has always mocked me. The closeness of him dancing with me in the club makes so much more sense. All the fights, deaths, sparring matches, take on a whole new light as heat builds between our bodies. My lips hurt from the intensity of our kiss, but in such a wonderful way.

Then a dozen hands grab me at once, yanking me out of Easton's grasp. I hardly have time to realize I'm being dragged out of the carriage before Easton is shouting my name, barreling toward doors. One of the men punches him hard in the temple. He crumbles in a heap on the carriage floor.

I kick and scream, reaching for the Power just out of my grasp. The other two girls scream for help. Alice bucks in wild-eyed terror as she is pulled away. Holly kicks madly, dread shining in her eyes as the men take her across the clearing.

The carriage door is open, but the men bar the exit as two of them tow a body toward the open doors.

It only takes a second to scan my surroundings. Several soldiers are unconscious nearby. The three of us girls are bound and dragged away from the clearing.

The body loaded into the carriage is Zephyr's.

It's a mutiny.

36

ZEPHYR

COLD DEEP IN MY bones makes me shiver violently as I wake. A moan of agony slips past my lips. I press my palms against the ground. Mutiny. The men did exactly what Nat feared. Is Nat alive? His body was on the ground, but I can't seem to remember if he was breathing.

The texture beneath my palms is strange. Familiar, but not earth. Terror rushes through me as I brush the tips of my fingers over the recognizable metal pattern.

A thunderous bang makes my ears ring.

"No," I mumble, pushing myself to my feet in a panic. The men didn't just knock me out. They locked me in the carriage with the Tributes and recruits. *What do they want?*

Another bang, followed by a feral growl of rage.

I blink rapidly, forcing my eyes to adjust to the dim light inside the carriage. My magic is there, just out of reach.

Another bang, then a grunt, a screech of metal.

"They took the girls," a small male voice says from behind me.

I spin around to find Finrik cowering in the far corner of the carriage. Ian is near him, back pressed to the wall. *Took the girls...* My stomach twists in sickening knots. What do they want with the girls? The way they looked at Alice worries me. If they harm those girls...

Another screech of metal forces me to cover my ears. I turn, squinting toward Easton deeply engaged in battle with the door.

"It won't open," I shout at him. "Stop trying." We're trapped in this cage while my men are doing who knows what to the girls.

Easton rounds on me, his shoulders hunched and nostrils flaring like an enraged bull. The pure fury makes me shuffle a few steps back. But he's surprisingly fast, crossing the carriage in just two long strides. He grabs a fistful of my jacket and jerks me close. It seems he doesn't need his magic to be strong. His hot breath washes over me.

"This is all your fault!" Spittle flies from his mouth, hitting my face. He's in a mad fury.

I swipe the spittle away with a grimace. "I know."

The admission makes him flinch in shock. Clearly, he didn't expect me to agree. But it is my fault. Those men blamed me for what happened to their friends. We weren't supposed to be in old St. Louis. What happened there, and what happened here, are most certainly a mess of my own making.

Nat tried to warn me. I was too determined to listen. Too arrogant to think the men would actually turn against me.

"Give me my Power back and I will make short work of that bloody door," Easton snaps.

I raise a hand slowly between us and gently ease him back. "It doesn't work like that. It's more of a proximity thing. I don't take it and give it back. Just being near me..." The thought trails off as another one hits me.

Paige is no longer shielded.

Easton scowls. His grip eases. "What?"

"We are all in serious danger," I tell him. How much does he already know about what she is capable of?

"No shit." He shoves me away as he lets go and turns his attention back on the door.

"No—I mean, the girls are no longer shielded." I rush toward Easton, glancing at Ian.

The poor boy is white as a ghost.

"Good. That means Paige can fight back." Easton runs his fingers along the edges of the carriage door, searching for something. Does he think he will find a weakness he can exploit? I almost laugh. These things were built to withstand all kinds of magical powers. There aren't any weak points.

"She can do more than that," I say, edging closer to him. "If I don't find her soon, it can be much worse than her getting hurt."

He snorts. "Don't pretend to know her because you had a couple conversations with her. I've been with her a year. I know what she can do."

A year? "Wait, what do you mean been with?"

Easton pauses, eyeing me up and down. "Why? Jealous?" He resumes his search of the door. "Relax. It isn't like that. We were in training together. She can handle herself."

Finrik sniggers. "Looked like *that* before they dragged her out of here."

Easton pivots to glare at the boy, shoulders tightening even more than normal. His face heats. For a moment, I'm worried he will lash out at the boy. But he isn't angry with Finrik. He's embarrassed that he was caught in a lie.

"That wasn't... It's complicated."

"Forget it," I step between them, forcing Easton to meet my gaze. "I can also sense the strength of magic in a person, and hers is off the charts. There's class one." I hold my hand close to the floor. "Class four and five." I raise it to my waist, then motion to each of us. "Class seven." I hold my hand above my head. "Then there's her." I stab a finger through the roof.

Easton's brows knit together, and he cocks his head to the side. "What are you saying?"

I lick my lips. "There's a religious cult somewhere in the north that believes we will one day encounter two different Idols. A Bringer of Creation and one of Desolation."

He snorts, crossing his arms over his massive chest. "And you think she is creation."

I shake my head. "No, Easton."

His lip twitches.

"She carries the power of Desolation," Ian says in a small voice from his wall on the far side of the carriage.

Easton's jaw slackens. He turns toward the door, spins back toward us, then rubs at his eyebrow. "Are you being serious right now?" He shakes his head. "We have no idea what those men are doing to those girls, to Paige, and you are worried about some dumb prophecy?" He waves us off and turns his attention back to the door. "Believe whatever you want, but I'm getting out of here to help the girls."

A bolt slides across metal from outside. I edge closer to the door, ready for a fight.

The door to the carriage creaks open. Nat's pale face is illuminated in the moonlight. I've never been so relieved to see his face.

"You're alive." Nat's shoulders sag in relief.

Easton shoves his way past Nat, jumping out of the carriage. A couple of men—those still loyal to me—rush forward to stop him.

"Don't. He's fine." I jump out and survey the area. Three of the men are dead. A few appear to be still breathing. The rest stagger to their feet. Twenty. Only twenty of my men are still here and alive. Seven of them turned against me. I make a quick mental note of who is gone. If I ever catch them, I will gut them slowly.

We need to find the girls and take back control of this situation before they reach the Wave Slicer. "Did anyone see which way they went?"

Nat shakes his head.

"I can track them," Easton says, marching away from the camp.

I follow on his heels. "Gather the dead and unconscious men on the carriage. Bring them and the boys."

I can't allow Easton to get too far away. Whatever is happening between him and Paige, he is a raging bull right now. I can't let him loose so close to the ship.

We only make it about twenty yards from the camp when the ground beneath our feet trembles. Rock and earth ripple like a serpent underground.

Easton takes off in a sprint along the spine of the ripple. His movements are graceful, like a wild cat. I can't help admiring the skill it takes to move like that. Or the training.

37

Paige

THE MOMENT THAT CARRIAGE door closes Zephyr inside, my Power pulses to live inside of me once more. I drink it in, holding it like a filling cup, waiting for the moment to allow it to spill out.

I can't just attack. If it were only me, I could escape. But I can't leave Holly or Alice with these men. No good can come from those greedy looks in their eyes. Their intentions toward the three of us can only be evil.

Holly openly weeps, stumbling along without giving any further struggle. Alice tried tugging away from the men holding her arms until she realized there was no point. Now she just marches along with a hollow look in her eyes. She knows as well as I do what is likely coming for us. I can't let these men get away with it.

The farther from the camp and the carriage we travel, the harder it will be for them to reach us if they do wake up or break out of the carriage. No doubt Easton is raging in that metal box. If he gets out, he will come. I just need to buy us time. If I plan my moves carefully, use my training to my advantage, I can take the men by surprise and save all three of us.

Seven against three. Not terrible odds.

If nothing else, I will fight to give the other two girls a chance to flee.

The men make lewd comments, and sometimes get a little too handsy for my taste, but I grit my teeth and bide my time.

"Here." One of the men stops in the middle of a ring of trees. He glances at the sky, then nods. "We should have a little time before they wake. As long as we get to the ship before they do, we are safe."

"We should have killed the Captain and his first mate," another man says, shoving me to my knees. "They will find a way back to the island."

"Doesn't matter." The first man, clearly the ringleader, is unbothered. "By the time they find another ship and reach the Capital, it will be too late." He spins slowly, eyeing the three of us in a way that makes my skin crawl. "Her." He stabs a finger at Alice.

She whimpers, attempting to scramble backward away from the men approaching her. I close my eyes, drawing on my Power and preparing my muscles to launch into action.

Alice screams as they drag her away, kicking her feet helplessly against the leaves and tree roots.

Breath in the cool air. Plan the next step. Act.

The hand on my shoulder slackens as the man on my left shuffles half a step toward those dragging Alice around a set of shrubs. As if being unable to see anything will prevent the two of us from hearing any of it.

I move quickly, ramming my elbow into the man on my left. He stumbles back, breaking his grip. The man on my right reaches for my hair, but I ram the back of my head into his crotch. In seconds, he is on the ground. I jump to my feet.

The left man rushes toward me once more. I duck under his arm as he reaches out for me, then sidestep and sweep my leg out to catch his. He stumbles over into his companion.

But the other three quickly descend on me. I allow my Muscle Memory to take over, relieved that it has returned to me. Each breath is careful as I grab, punch, kick, and dodge. One of them wraps an arm around my neck, hoping for a chokehold. Instead, I surprise him by flipping him over my side and slamming him down into the ground.

"What is going on?" the leader shouts as he rounds the corner, holding Alice by the hair. She claws at his wrist.

I snatch a heavy stone from the ground and whip it at the eye of the man holding Holly, throwing everything I have into the strength of the pitch. The rock punches through the socket. Holly screams as blood splatters on her face and shoulder. But her captor is dead.

"Run!" I shout at her.

But the poor girl is too stunned to move. She whimpers, staring at the fresh blood she just smeared over her hands.

The leader marches over to Holly, grabbing her hair at the scalp just like Alice. The two girls stumble as they cry for him to let go.

A punch hits my kidney. I buckle over, gasping for breath. A boot rams into my knees, knocking me to the ground. Another hammers into my spine. I cry out as something pops. My mouth cracks against a root. The metallic tang of blood coats my tongue.

I roll over, moaning, reaching for the source of pain in my back. Another kick to my ribs. I manage to get hold of his leg and yank him off balance, but he is only replaced by another man.

I hear the first man growl, knowing the command is meant for the other two girls. "Stay."

A moment later, he looms over me as four of the men pin me to the ground. "Someone has trained you to fight." He drops to a knee at my side, smirking. Then his hand moves along the fabric over my stomach. "This is fine clothing, too. Maybe it's time you tell me where you are from."

I sneer. "Your nightmares."

His hand continues moving up my torso, but he winces as if he suffers the worst headache known to man. The two girls cry in a huddle a few feet away. I wish they would run.

His hand snaps tight around my throat as he leans so close I can almost smell the testosterone on his skin. I open my mouth to tell him just what I think of his disgusting breath, but I cannot draw in my own.

"Smart mouth," he says, breathing the words directly into my open mouth. It tastes like death. "Perhaps if I break you, it will be lesson enough for those two. Fighting will get you nothing."

I pull in every ounce of breath I can muster to utter just a few words. "What...about...the...king?"

The men laugh. Their leader reaches up with his free hand, brushing hair away from my temples. "He will never know. And you will never remember."

Terror rips through me. Can he do what was done to Aunt Bianca? Can he erase my memories? The fear warms my veins, then becomes a burning ember. I fan it until the ember bursts into a blazing inferno. Despite his grip on my throat, I scream. His Power pushes against my mind, but something resists.

He frowns. "What?" The confusion on his face is worth the effort. He releases my throat and presses his other hand against my temple.

My body relaxes, but the fire raging inside ripples outward. I close my eyes. The earth beneath us trembles. The men holding me lose their grip, but I don't have the ability to move a single muscle in my body. The trees rain ash, as if slowly burning away from top to bottom, inside-out. Screams of terror, of agony, fill the air. From the men around me. From the two girls cowering ten feet away. *From me.*

Sweat beads on my forehead, rolls across my skin. My hands involuntarily clench into fists. The muscles twitch. My jaw clenches so tight I'm afraid I will crack teeth. My brain is on fire. Then the only scream I hear is my own, shattering the sky.

38

ZEPHYR

EASTON MOVES QUICKER THAN I expected for a man of his size. Each step is sure, despite the unknown terrain. He hops from one stone to the next along the small ridge deftly. I don't know how he is so certain he is even going the right way, but I follow. A few of my men trail along behind us. The rest will catch up with the carriage once they load up the bodies.

A scream shatters the night sky, followed moments later by what sounds like a raging bonfire.

"Paige." Easton breaths her name in desperation. Somehow, he picks up his pace.

His attachment to her will be a problem once we reach the Capital. No one is allowed to fraternize with the girls until the king dismisses them. If Easton fights against the rules, or if Paige does, it's considered treason. Their relationship, whatever it is, could be the death of them both.

"Easton slow down," I call. "We don't know what's happening."

"That's what I'm worried about."

Then the screaming cuts out, plunging us into silence suddenly. Have I gone deaf?

"Paige!" Easton screams.

Nope. Not deaf.

"Way to warn them," Nat snaps. He is trying so hard to keep up, but I can hear his labored breathing.

Panic has me by the heart as well. I join in Easton's call. "Paige! Holly! Alice!"

Easton skids to a halt so quickly I nearly run into his back.

Ahead of us, the forest is gone. A ring of ash surrounds Paige. My heart jumps into my throat when I see her unconscious on the ground.

Nat edges forward, emitting a low whistle. "Where is every-one?" he whispers, as if afraid they might hear him.

Alice and Holly huddle together, sobbing into one another's shoulders. We won't get answers from them until they've calmed down.

But Nat is right. Aside from the three women, no one else is around. Ian's warning rings in my mind. Did Paige do this? Did she kill the men? If she is responsible for whatever happened here, Paige is far more dangerous than I anticipated.

Easton picks his way through the ash, approaching Paige with an eye on his surroundings. He wasn't kidding about being well-trained. Ash swirls around his ankles with each step. I join him, watching the ash with intense curiosity. The trees, grass, green. It's all burned away.

Nat eases toward Holly and Alice, speaking in a soothing voice to calm the girls down.

I kneel on one side of Paige as Easton kneels on the other. He strokes hair from her face and uses his sleeve to dab away the blood on her lip. I check for her pulse. Alive, but unconscious.

We need to keep moving. I don't know what happened to the men who mutinied against me, but I have no desire to wait around and find out if they abandoned the girls to get a hold of my ship. My instincts tell me that Paige somehow killed them all. I fight off the nausea that thought brings on and lock the treacherous sensation away.

Tenderly, wary of any potential injuries she might have, I slide my arms under Paige and hoist her up.

"What are you doing?" Easton snaps, surging to his feet. "Let me carry her."

"I think, until we know more about what happened, it's best if I make direct contact," I say, keeping my tone as reasonable as possible. She's heavier than she looks.

The resentment rolling off Easton is palpable. "You don't think she did this. She's not capable."

Nat coaxes the other two girls to their feet. Both whimper when they look at Paige in my arms.

"She will be fine," I reassure them.

"It was her." Alice's voice trembles over each word. "Sh-she killed them. B-burned them alive."

Easton pales, but remains close to my shoulder, hovering over Paige like a hawk. He doesn't protest as we march back to the carriage. All his attention is on the girl in my arms. While we walk, his gaze continuously flits back to her, and his brows draw tighter together each time.

I glance at Paige's pale face, the pain twisting her features even in sleep. My fingers twitch. I want to smooth out the lines, help her find peace. After only a few steps, those lines melt away on their own.

Once we reach the carriage, we will ride to the dock, board the ship, and go home.

What if bringing her back to the Capital brings about its destruction? Maybe that's what Ian tried to warn me about.

Even in sleep, her magic pulses, fighting to break free. I'm not sure I have the strength to keep her at bay.

39

GAVIN

THE CLOSE QUARTERS ON the sailboat give me little to do but think. About my loss. My failure. My sister and parents. The rest of the team. The depression threatens to swallow me whole.

At first, the Havenites give me space. I move into the smaller of the two rooms so I can be alone. Drake and Emil take turns sleeping on the dining room bench. The two women—Dani and April—share the larger bedroom. I was content with the distance for the first day, but the dangerous thoughts and deep shame of my failure are all-consuming. Being alone hurts my logical brain, like a festering disease eating away at it.

This realization brings me out of my room. Crying, sleeping, and wallowing in turn will solve nothing.

I get to know Dani and April a little better after emerging. April is Naturalist—though she calls herself a Wind Dancer. The truth is, she can essentially do the same thing as Mom. Dani is also a Naturalist, but her Power relates to Transmutation Conversion, allowing her to take the materials they find and convert them into something smaller and easier to transport home. Their understanding of Power is extremely limited. On a level with barbarism compared to the advancements in Elpis.

When I launch into an excited debate about the various classifications of Powers, their eyes quickly glaze over. They have zero interest in benefiting from my knowledge. Hopefully, their elders will have more interest. At this point, my knowledge of Powers is all I have to offer to broker peace—and maybe a way home.

The motion sickness doesn't fade until Dani offers me an herb she says helps her. I'm hesitant to try anything I don't know much about, but as another bout of nausea leaves me bedridden for an entire afternoon, I cave in.

It's impossible to sleep. The battle loops in my dreams, but each time the details become more gruesome. Torture. Dismemberment. In the last one, the soldiers burn Paige and me for witchcraft. I startle awake, dripping sweat, and make my way to the upper deck for fresh air.

It's so cold. The breeze knocks the breath from my lungs. Sweat freezes against my skin. I hunker down against the wind, gazing into the dark distance.

There are so many stars out here. I've never seen so many before. It's comforting, reminding me of a story Dad told us several times.

Drake steps up beside me, wrapped in a blanket. "You shouldn't be out here in the cold." He holds the blanket open.

"D-did I wake you?" I ask, teeth chattering. Clearly, he's right. I slide into the blanket with him.

The warmth of his body instantly heats my cold skin. Each of us holds a side tight around us, huddled close together.

"It's okay," he says. "We reach port tomorrow, then it's a hike to the Haven."

Only the lapping water and occasional moans of the wind make any noise for a while. The air has a distinctly clean smell out on the water. Were I not so homesick, I might actually enjoy it.

"How are you doing, Gavin?" Drake's voice is soft, as if the air around us is sacred space.

I give a small shrug, adjusting the blanket when it slips. "I miss home. I'm worried about my sister. About the rest of my team."

He says nothing. His silence is companionable, like he knows I prefer not talking in moments as deep as this.

"I was just remembering a story my dad once told me about the stars," I say, reverent of the quiet. I glance at Drake. He is watching me with interest. It's hard to meet that gaze for long. "When he was about my age, he had this friend, Celeste. She was like a little sister to him. Her Power was up there." I nod toward the sky.

"The stars?" Drake asks.

I chew my lip a moment. "She once showed him the true color of the cosmos. It isn't as dark and dismal as what you and I see now. It's a swirling hue of deep shades of blues, purples, reds, yellows. Always ebbing and flowing, but never really changing. He says it's a gas in space that does it." Tightness in my chest gives me pause. "His friend disappeared in a cosmic ray of her own creation. No one ever figured out what happened to her. But one night when Dad was in danger, he thought of her and looked to the stars." A small smile tilts the corners of my mouth. "And the stars steered him to safety. He believes it was her, in the cosmos, guiding his way."

Silence settles between us as I watch the stars shine in the sky. Drake watches me. I can feel his eyes peering into my soul. But I can't tear my gaze from the stars, willing them to guide me like they guided Dad all those years ago.

"Your family is important to you, isn't it?" His question is so gentle I almost don't hear him as the breeze rips past, fluttering the blanket.

"No." I close my eyes, picturing our dining room. Everyone sits around the table. Mom and Dad tease one another playfully, as always. Paige rolls her eyes and acts disgusted, but I know she enjoys the show of affection just as much as me. It gives us hope that the world isn't such a dismal place. "Food and water are important to me. My family is far more. They are the colors of the cosmos, ebbing and flowing, but always there."

Except Paige is lost to us. The Kingdom has her. Emil insists that no one who goes to the Kingdom is ever seen again. I can't handle losing her, like losing some of that light that shines over me. How much will that loss change my universe?

I imagine the grief and disappointment on Dad's face when I return without my sister. Did the others return to Elpis to report what happened?

The entire reason I came on this trip was to protect Paige. I failed. And Mom... Will she resent me for allowing this to happen? I had the Power to stop it. I *felt* it. Raw, burning, intense, limitless. Yet it was not enough to save Paige.

Dad's voice consumes me. I squeeze my eyes shut to fight off the tears. *You are just as powerful without Powers as you are with. Just remember they aren't the answer to everything.*

Except, in this desolate and dangerous world, they are the answer. If anyone can use knowledge about this world to make the most of their Powers, it's me. And if I truly have so much Power at my fingertips, I need to learn how to harness it properly. Brains can only get you so far. I won't be weak any longer.

The greatest journey in your life is not where you stand as much as in what direction you move. And it begins with a single step.

I *am* my father's son.

I will show the Capital the pure strength of the Powers family.

I will take that first step.

40

PAIGE

NIGHTMARES STRUCK THE MOMENT I fell asleep, but as the monster under the earth opened its mouth to consume me whole, everything in the nightmare vanished.

"How's she doing?" Zephyr's whisper stirs me awake.

"Fine, I guess." I don't recognize the second voice. It's a man. That's all I know for certain.

I blink, but by the time I've opened my eyes fully, Zephyr is gone.

My gaze sweeps the cramped room around me. Dozens of bunk beds in even rows. Some occupied by snoring men. No one I recognize.

As I sit up, I hear the hum of an engine. A bay of windows half covered by bunk beds shows the water beyond. Are we on a boat?

"You're awake. That's a relief. The captain will want to see you." A young man with a kind face sits on the bed across from me.

I press the heel of my palm to my head. Something is hammering at my skull. "Wh-where are we?"

"Aboard the *Wave Slicer*," he says. "We should reach the island shortly." He motions toward the door. "You're free to move around at your leisure. No one will harm you here."

I snort, then wince as the throbbing intensifies. "I've heard that before."

His kind smile falters. "Sorry you got caught up in all of that. It was nothing personal and those men are…" He swallows and dips his head away. "…they're gone."

I slide my feet to the floor where my boots await. Once they are laced, I stand slowly, using the beds for balance. "Where's Easton?"

"Uh, well, he's in the brig."

"What?"

The man rises quickly, holding out his hands as if to calm a startled animal. "It's nothing personal. But it's best if the two of you are kept apart. All things considered."

I close my eyes and count to ten. All things considered. Someone must have told them about our very brief kiss. I can still feel the intensity of his lips crushing my own.

"I'm Nat," he says, placing a hand to his chest. "Zephyr's First Mate."

"First name basis," I note. "Must mean you're friends." I march toward the door, not waiting for a response. Not caring, really.

In the next room, Alice and Holly sit together at a table playing with a deck of cards. They seem calmer, almost happy. The moment I step into the room, they freeze and stare at me in dread. Why? I offer them a kind smile but can tell they want nothing to do with me. I would have thought they would be more grateful that I took on all those men to save them the pain. Some girls can be petty.

It takes me a minute to find the stairs. First, I head down, but a soldier posted at the door stops me.

"Lower deck is only for disembarking," he says. His Adam's apple bobs. Sweat beads on his forehead. Why is he nervous?

I let it go for now. At the moment, I don't care.

Instead, I turn and head up until I find the steps leading up to an observation deck. The ship is much larger than I expected. Clearly, it's a relic from before the collapse. It was either well cared for or restored with Powers. How the engine is running, I'm unsure. Gasoline is a relic of a long-lost world. They would need something else to give it power. Wind, maybe. Sun, though there isn't much of that today. Hydropower, maybe? Gavin would be fascinated.

Thinking of my brother sends a pang of sorrow through my heart. Easton insisted that he must be alive—and I cling to that hope—but how will he handle my capture? Where is he now? I'm worried for him, wherever he is. Did he go with the Havenites, with the rest of the team back to Elpis, or is he alone? Gavin won't survive out here alone.

I reach the edge of the observation deck, wrapping my fingers around the railing and peering out over the water. So much of it! This lake is huge. I can hardly see land. The wind is bitterly cold, and the water is choppy. But the ship still slices its way across the water with relative ease.

Somehow, I have to find a way out of this situation. I need to escape the Kingdom and find my brother. I must get home. Maybe Easton was right. Maybe the best way to handle this situation is to lean into it. I have the ear of Zephyr. If I play my cards right, I will also have the ear of the king. That gives me something to work with. Some route to find my way home again.

"Glad to see you on your feet." Zephyr steps up beside me. Something about him is different. Like he is at home here on this ship. His body is much more relaxed. "You had us all quite worried."

"Doubtful."

He glances at me and smirks. "Especially Easton."

My cheeks heat and I avert my gaze back out at the water. "Why is he in the brig? Did he try to kill you? That would be his style. He's done it to me."

Zephyr's brows shoot up at that, but I give him no further explanation. "It was voluntary."

He rests his forearms against the railing, hands folded together, watching me. The collar of his gray overcoat flaps in the breeze. His dark hair swirls and he swipes it back with practiced ease that tells me he has spent a lot of time on the water. Despite the lack of sunshine, his skin takes on a golden glow. It's almost as if he is completely in his element here at sea.

"The connection between the two of you will be a danger to you both when we reach the palace."

"Can't I at least see him? I'm sure he's worried about me."

"Oh, he is. I will let him know you are better." He inhales the lake air, then exhales slowly. "But I can't let you see one another. He says there's nothing going on between you, but everyone else in that carriage disagrees. If it's still new, it's best to let it go now."

I snort and roll my eyes, hugging my arms against my chest both to ward off the chill, and to ward off what is headed my way. The air is so cold and crisp out here. "You really think I'm going to play your king's games?"

His mouth curls up in the corner, dark eyes sweeping over me. "No. But my brother does like a challenge, so if you don't want to catch his interest, you might want to tone it down."

My chest tightens. I should have put the pieces together. Lord. King. Of course, they are brothers. I lick my lips, then regret it immediately as the cold air stings them. "Noted. Thanks for the warning. What happens to the girls he doesn't choose?"

"They are given comfortable accommodations on the island to build their new lives, usually in a profession of their choosing. Or they find themselves happy with one of the more influential men on the island."

I balk. "They don't go home?"

He frowns, eyeing the water as if unable to look at me. "No."

Silence settles over us as we stand at the rail and stare out ahead. If the girls don't go home, is it by choice or force? I need to learn as much as I can about these people and this Kingdom. There must be some way I can get home.

My throat scratches, the inside raw from the chokehold that horrible man had on me. I don't want to ask Zephyr what happened to the men who captured us, but I need to know how we ended up back with this group. The last thing I remember is being pinned down, the leader taunting me, then unimaginable pain.

"Zephyr?"

"Paige?" He raises a brow at me.

My cheeks warm as I realize I've just used his name instead of mocking his lordship like usual. I swallow the lump in my throat. "What happened to those men?"

"Dead."

"Okay, but how did they die?"

He shakes his head. "Sometimes it's better to leave the past behind us or it stirs up unwanted memories." There's a pain, an understanding in his voice. Like he really does know what it's like to be haunted by the past. I wish I had gotten to know him a little better instead of mocking him all the time. Something tells me once we reach the island, everything will change. And I will need him, somehow.

I only nod. Whether he is protecting himself from those memories, or protecting me from them, I appreciate the intention.

Land begins taking shape on the horizon. At first, I can't tell what I'm seeing, until the trees and shoreline, then buildings and the docks, all come into view. It's a stunning vista of fall-colored civilization. Were I not so anxious about what comes next, I would marvel at the beauty of this island.

On a hill near the coast, a massive white building with impressive pillars overlooks everything. Zephyr leans closer, pointing at the building, the palace, talking about the grandeur of the rooms, views, and food.

Instead of looking at the palace, I watch him, mesmerized by the way his dark eyes shine as he takes in the sight before us.

"You should see it in the summer," he says, turning his gaze to me.

Silence swallows us. His face is so close. Too close. I need to pull away.

Zephyr edges back, clearing his throat and turning his gaze back out at the island. "Everything is green in the summer. Flowers are abundant. The pool is open for swimming. The palace guards open the doors to let in the cool summer breezes that come off the lake."

He sounds impressed by the grandeur of the palace. And it is grand.

But it is likely also my prison.

For better or worse, I am entering a dangerous game. One that will determine not only my fate, but that of Elpis as well.

I only wish Gavin were with me now.

———❖———

Curious what Ugene uncovered to make this mission possible? Wondering about the barrier?
Download the prequel, Revelation, only available at Starr ZDavies.com.

Ready to find out what happens next? Get your copy of
Infiltration **and let the adventure continue!**

I hope you enjoyed Paige, Gavin, and Zephyr's story. If you did, please consider leaving me a review. I love hearing what people liked about the book.

ACKNOWLEDGMENTS

First and foremost, I have to thank Paige. She sprang to life in my imagination while I was writing a whole different series, and she refused to be silenced. Her tenacity helped bring this story to life.

I am thankful for my husband and his patience, even if he doesn't fully understand how hard it can be to meet self-inflicted deadlines. Tazz, you give me the ability to spend my days slaving away at a computer writing what I love. And of course, my family for the endless support and encouragement (even if you aren't really readers). My daughter, Ty, is partly to blame for this series. She loved Ugene's story so much I had to write another.

To my amazing friends, your boundless patience while I shut myself away in my office never ceases to amaze me. Amanda, thanks for understanding when I was probably a little distracted by my books while we were talking on the phone. Melinda, who sends me text messages gushing about my books as she reads them.

This book wouldn't be where it is without the dedication of my beta readers: Kevin Mackie, TaniaRina Perry, Asher Jones, Jared Goldman, Kris Shotts, and Jennifer Garcia. Nor would it have been fit for print without the steady hand of my editor, Maddy, who always has the best suggestions, advice, and praise alike. The support from my fellow dystopian authors in the Dystopian Author League were critical to title selection, cover artist suggestions, blurb advice, and so much more. Thank you!!!

And of course, I want to give a big thanks to you, my dear reader. Because without your support, my books would go unloved and unnoticed.

POWERS LEGACY SERIES

A POWERS UNIVERSE SERIES

A ROYAL ROMANTIC DYSTOPIAN FANTASY SERIES
FEATURING DIVERSE CHARACTERS,
POWERFUL FAMILY BONDS, DYNAMIC
RELATIONSHIPS, AND FORBIDDEN ROMANCE

WWW.STARRZDAVIES.COM/POWERS-UNIVERSE

POWERS TRILOGY SERIES

A POWERS UNIVERSE SERIES

A SUPERPOWER DYSTOPIAN SCI-FI SERIES
FEATURING DIVERSE CHARACTERS,
FOUND FAMILY, DYNAMIC FRIENDSHIPS,
AND POLITICAL CORRUPTION

WWW.STARRZDAVIES.COM/POWERS-UNIVERSE

About Starr Z. Davies

STARR Z. DAVIES is an award-winning author of over 20 tales that span dystopian realms, epic fantasies, and echoes of forgotten histories. Dubbed the "Character Assassin," she weaves stories where heroes are tested by fire—both emotional and physical.

From her woodland home in northern Wisconsin, she crafts worlds while surrounded by her greatest allies: a supportive husband, two imaginative children, and a curious menagerie of robotic pets. When not conjuring new adventures, she dabbles in home enchantments, swims like a siren, battles through video game quests, and devours books like ancient tomes of power.

If you want to become friends with Starr, dark chocolate, Doctor Who, Parks & Rec, The Office, and the MCU are all fantastic ways into her heart. That or a love for fantasy books by indie authors.

Learn more about Starr and her books.

Keep up with Starr by signing up for her newsletter.

Want to be part of her community? Follow Starr on social media.
facebook.com/szdavies□
instagram.com/s.z.davies□
threads.com/s.z.davies□
tiktok.com/starrzdavies